*To Broo Doherty – thank you for having faith in Goodhew,
the series and my writing.*

PROLOGUE

30 March 1991

'Thank you, Nadine,' the guitarist shouted and the crowd cheered for more but she handed the microphone back to the band. She knelt down to unclip her guitar case, taking her time to remove the strap from her Gibson before placing it in the velour-lined case. Her slowness was deliberate; she loved the singing but hated the fuss. Hated the drunks nearest the stage – not them perhaps but their cigarette-permeated breath and their insistence. And lack of inhibition when it came to pulling at her, or grabbing her into a hug and giving advice and compliments with alcohol-spittled words. She turned her back on them to pack away. It was usually enough for them to disperse.

The Boat Race pub had its music-loving regulars but tonight, hours after the actual boat race, it seemed it had become the place to go to commiserate over the latest Oxford win, and new faces outnumbered the familiar. She glanced up a couple of times and, on the second, caught sight of Theo near the jukebox. He leant back against the wall, typically unhurried. 'OK?' he mouthed.

She rolled up her strap and tucked it away in the space left by the guitar's cutaway body, slipping her capo and picks into the space alongside it. She could sense Theo watching and, inside her head at least, she smiled. Securing the case was another not-to-be-rushed ritual and, by the time she'd clipped the last latch and turned back to face the room, the majority of the punters had moved on.

Carrying a guitar before a gig would always illicit '*go on love, give us a song*' type comments. Afterwards, it seemed to get a little respect; she didn't need to push through the stragglers to reach Theo; people, even the drunk ones, stepped aside or shook her hand and said she'd done well.

Theo took the case from her and she followed him out onto East Road where it was almost as noisy but less congested. 'How was it?' he asked.

'You were there, weren't you?'

'Hiding at the back. I mean how was it for you? It's hard to tell when you're so wrapped up in what you're playing.'

They were walking side by side now and she grabbed his arm and squeezed her face against it. Apart from that, she didn't reply. She couldn't imagine how she looked when she sang; she felt as though it was all written across her face, a transparency – it was never acting and her emotions were so on show that it had to be obvious to anyone watching that they were real. Singing to herself and practising new songs never had the same effect. It was only from the moment that the audience started watching that she had no choice but to commit to the performance. She could sing and play and be barely in the room then, free to touch the thoughts that were too hard the rest of the time. She doubted whether she wanted to know what expressions might flash onto her face. She preferred the idea that there were none.

She didn't ask where they were heading. The evening had become cool but she was content with the idea that they'd take a slow walk and eventually find their way back to Theo's flat.

She wondered whether it always took an unhealthy relationship to make a good one seem valid. Maybe only screwed-up people felt the need to put themselves through that. She slipped her hand into his. 'I can stay over, you know.'

He grinned, 'I was hoping you would but I've still only got a mattress on the floor. It's still pretty squalid.'

'It's not squalid. Just basic. And it's the rest of it that needs to catch up.'

'You're not wrong there. I'll move my furniture in the next couple of weeks.'

'Don't rush because of me.'

Eventually the house would be divided into six letting rooms but, at the moment, his was the only finished floor. 'When Dad offered it for free I imagined it might be unsophisticated . . .'

'You have electric and running water.'

'And I'm just like the live-in guard on a building site.'

'It's not so romantic when you put it like that.'

'Still coming?'

'Of course.' He wrapped his arm around her shoulder and she curled hers around his waist. Neither of them seemed to set the pace but they meandered, each in step with the other until they reached the rise of the Mill Road railway bridge. They stopped and watched a packed train rattle towards the station

Passengers crowded the aisles, waiting to disembark, to swap a day in London for a night in Cambridge. She rubbed her thumbs against the guitar-string hardened skin at the tips of her fingers. How many train songs were there? Was there a better metaphor for life than a train song?

'What are you thinking about, Nadine?'

'About train songs and wondering which one fits me.'

'I wasn't expecting you to say that.'

She looked up at Theo. 'I'm pretty sure mine's about coming home.'

'I hope so.'

Instead of moving away again, he leant against the metal panel, his back to the tracks now. It was an exposed spot and she shivered. 'Can we go?'

'Of course,' he said, but still didn't move. He seemed to be waiting for something, but she didn't know what.

'Is something wrong?'

'Nothing.' He shook his head slowly; 'I was trying to find the words to tell you how much it means to be here with you.'

'Watching trains?' She always found it easier to deflect serious comments but this time she wished she hadn't. 'Actually, there's nowhere I'd rather be.'

He kissed her gently, then his cheek brushed hers as he spoke softly in her ear, 'I love you, Nadine.'

She closed her eyes and let her senses fill with the smell of his skin and the warmth of him. She had been scared that her feelings had jumped too far ahead but now she knew that they both felt the same way.

And, as though he'd read her thoughts, he pulled her closer. 'You don't ever need to worry, Nadine, I've felt like this for a long time.'

'Really?'

'Absolutely,' he grinned and Nadine smiled too. He kissed her again, their lips lingering and the last of the tension melting away. The air no longer felt cold and her earlier unease vanished. Maybe this would be OK. It felt right in the kind of way that she'd never experienced before. And that's what people always said, *you just know.* They took their time walking back to the house in Romsey Terrace. She'd spent the last night there too but now she was more aware of the short street with one terraced house wider than the rest: the only one with a window on either side of the front door, the only one with loft windows and brand new frames.

'It will be lovely when it's finished.'

Theo's gaze followed hers towards the roof, 'I'll have to share it then, won't I? I like this endless building work; it means there's just the two of us.' He slipped the key into the lock and Nadine spoke quietly before he opened the door; all this would be forgotten once they were inside. 'I felt uneasy earlier, kind of restless. Nervous for no reason. Like I shouldn't come.'

'And now?'

'It's gone and I'm glad I'm here. Glad I'm with you. I just wanted to say it before we went in.'

'Speak your fears and chase them away?'

'Something like that.'

He opened the door, set her guitar down in the hallway and reached back to her, 'Don't worry, we're good. Everything's good.'

The stair carpet hadn't been laid yet and their footsteps clattered on the stairs with enough noise for more than two people. The second set of stairs sounded like a distant echo of the first. A few noises made it down after that, the running of a tap, a squeal of laughter, the bang of a door, then silence.

Another hour passed. The other houses stood with curtains drawn and lights extinguished. The bare windows let the sodium orange street light slip into the ground-floor rooms, the open doors letting it trickle into the hallway, picking out the outline of paper and paint and a guitar case standing on the bare boards.

At 3 a.m. the light died and the letterbox creaked open. The fluid trickled, softly splashing onto the coir mat, too quiet for upstairs to hear. A ball of paper was wedged in the letterbox, resting there just long enough to be lit then poked through. It hit the mat glowing then disappeared in the bloom of flame that rose from it. The hall and stairs flushed orange, then black as the smoke thickened. It crept up the stairs as the guitar case slowly melted.

CHAPTER 1

Amy wouldn't recall much about that morning. She remembered ordering a cappuccino and weaving between tables to her favourite at the furthest corner. Her dad was running late so she studied the faces of the jesters, hobos and harlequins on the walls and shelves, trying to pick out any new additions. Many had been here since her childhood when clowns had scared her and she'd stared at the straw bobbing in her milkshake to avoid meeting their gaze.

She saw them differently now, of course, and today it was the clown blanc that caught her eye. He stared sorrowfully, a black painted tear resting on the top of his cheek, his head tilted as though he was ready to listen. Had she felt melancholy he might have seemed sympathetic; instead, she looked towards the door and sipped her coffee as she waited.

It was less than a minute later when the door was opened by a woman wrestling with a pushchair. The sounds of outside burst through for several seconds, with the hum of the city cut through by the siren of an ambulance. Amy moved towards the entrance, curious but not yet concerned. She must have spoken because she could remember the woman looking at her then gesticulating in the direction of the city centre. Then the wave of apprehension. And Amy dashing onto the pavement with silence rushing in her ears and the only thing in focus was the patchwork of paving stones as she ran across them.

He lay on the pavement beside the kerb.

There was no crowd, just a couple of bystanders and two paramedics.

And her dad. He was already on a stretcher, his shirt pulled open with wires and an IV line hanging from him. He lay still, his face bloodied, pavement dust and grit smeared across grey skin and she shouted even though she was close enough to touch the ambulance men.

'Did someone hit him?' When no one replied she added, 'That's my dad,' and repeated it before anyone had the chance to respond. A stocky paramedic knelt close to her father, another, a lanky guy who looked about thirty, had opened the ambulance doors and was now bringing out the gurney.

'What's his name?' he asked.

'Robert Buckingham. I was meeting him for lunch.'

Perhaps they already knew his name because there was no demand for any proof of identity. 'Does he have any existing health issues you're aware of?'

'No, I don't think so.'

The other paramedic looked up, 'Can you travel with us to Addenbrooke's?'

'Of course.' She hadn't taken her eyes off her dad. 'What's wrong with him?'

'We're running checks at the moment. I'm Grant. What's your name?' The paramedic spoke to her father next, 'Mr Buckingham, your daughter Amy's here. Mr Buckingham?'

She saw his mouth move, an attempt to form a word.

'Dad?'

Recognition flickered on his face. Her world slowed and steadied again, she clasped his hand until they loaded him onto the ambulance then strapped herself into the spare seat. Would they let her travel with him if he was about to die? The younger of the two paramedics was driving now while his partner continued to work on her dad. They kept the sliding window open between them and passed comments back and forth. She felt the ambulance take a turn and, glancing forward, could see the traffic on East Road parting to let them pass.

'Amy?' Grant the paramedic prompted. He had a large notepad on his lap now, pre-printed with questions, boxes and the outline of a human body. 'Are you his next of kin?'

'I suppose so, I mean, there's his mum and my mum but my grand-mother's in a care home with dementia and my mum . . .' She stopped mid-sentence.

'Are they married?'

'Not any more. They don't maintain contact.' She studied her dad for a second, then added, 'Unless they have to.'

Grant shot her a wry look. 'Parents, eh?' He reached across to check her dad again. 'Mr Buckingham?'

Amy leant forward. 'What's happening?'

'He's gaining consciousness. Has he had any alcohol?'

'I doubt it.'

He would have had a glass at lunch if he'd made it that far but he wasn't an excessive drinker. At least as far as she knew. 'Did someone hit him?'

'The person who called us said he'd fallen and banged his head. People often say just that, though, it doesn't always mean much.'

'So it's just a head injury?'

Grant pointed to a small square monitor. 'We collect information on the way in, to give the maximum information. Your dad's suffered a head injury but there's ECG activity . . .'

'His heart?'

And all she remembered of the rest of the journey was watching her father's expression, silently trying to communicate, to let him know he wasn't allowed to die young like his own father had. Beneath his tan, his skin had paled to the colour of alabaster and she remembered the clown with the tear on his cheek.

The weight of the day descended in early evening. Amy had spent the afternoon in a bubble; her dad had been wheeled into A & E and throughout the afternoon he had been seen by a succession of staff. Each had done something and asked something else before taking notes and moving on. And she had watched them move between beds, do the same with other patients then, in so-quiet tones, share their details with their colleagues. There was no panic here, no sense of shock or desper-ation. No windows either and the clock on the opposite wall ticked on calmly. They wheeled him away and left her to wait.

Finally, a doctor appeared, a Chinese lady with rectangular framed glasses and a clipboard pressed to her chest.

'You are Mr Buckingham's daughter?'

Amy nodded.

'It seems your father suffered a cardiac incident and a head trauma as he fell.' She stopped speaking long enough to see that Amy had listened and understood. 'He is expected to make a full recovery. He has regained consciousness and you will be able to see him, but briefly. He will be drowsy.'

Amy didn't absorb the rest of the details – she guessed there had been an operation – but she shook her head when the doctor asked if she had any questions. She sat beside her dad's bed and his expression changed just enough for her to know his mind was clearing. The gash on his temple had been patched, the wound itself looked tame but the skin around it was swollen and turning purple. 'You scared me,' she told him quietly.

His right eyebrow twitched but he made no attempt to speak. She took out her mobile. 'I'll phone the agency. I won't go in tomorrow.'

'You don't need to miss work because of me.' His words were monotone and slow, but clear. 'You need that job.'

She shook her head, 'It's just holiday cover, Dad, and it finishes tomorrow. I'll explain and it will be fine.'

'I worry about you.'

'Well, you shouldn't, temporary work suits me.' She sat back in the chair and the PVC upholstery squeaked, 'The doctor said I shouldn't stay too long but I'll come back up in the morning. Obviously.'

'Thanks.' He managed an indistinct nod.

She wanted to ask how he was feeling but it seemed as though it was a question for the start of a visit, an opening question. Instead she asked, 'Can I get you anything?'

He turned his hand over and gently squeezed hers. 'Would you ask your mum to come and see me?'

'Really?'

'I ought to give her the pleasure of seeing me like this.' His brief smile vanished. 'Seriously, Amy, some thoughts are very clear when you are lying in a pool of blood. You should get a regular job. I shouldn't

9

smoke. And, as much as we've never been amicable, your mother and I have unfinished business.'

She caught a bus back to the city centre, the artificial colours and sounds of Addenbrooke's were gone and she was returned to the other end of the same day. It had grown dark outside and the face of the clown blanc seemed to be a memory from another day entirely. Her phone was still cupped in her hand and her hand cupped in her lap. The bus was empty apart from two ladies near the front. Amy sat at the back. She could have called her mum right then but instead she closed her eyes in weariness and chose to speak to no one.

CHAPTER 2

'Mum?' Amy still had the key to her mum's house. She used it whenever she visited but never went beyond the threshold without making sure her mum knew she was there.

'I'm out the back.'

Amy walked through the kitchen and out to the conservatory on the other side. Her mum sat with her back to the window and an open book on her lap. Outside, the sun was strong enough to backlight the clouds and fill the space with a hard grey light.

'Mum?' Amy repeated, quietly this time.

Geraldine smiled as she looked up but that faded as she saw Amy's expression. She set the book aside, her fingers finding the bookmark and the side table in a single, fluid move. 'What's wrong?'

'It's Dad. He's in hospital.' Even after all the years they'd been divorced the mention of either parent to the other caused tension; usually a barely perceptible hesitation. They both tried to show nothing but Amy always picked up on it. This time, though, all she saw in her mum's expression was the need for answers. 'He's had a heart attack. He's conscious.' She started to tremble. 'It looks like he'll be OK.'

'When did this happen?'

'I went to meet him for lunch. He was late but it turned out he'd collapsed.'

'Why didn't you call me?'

'I don't know. I didn't want to call anyone. It didn't feel real and I

11

decided I just wanted it to be me and him if . . .' She didn't finish the sentence; either she'd said enough for her mum to understand or else she'd already think that was as selfish as it had just sounded to her.

'I understand why you didn't phone immediately, Ames, but half a day later?'

'You're not married any more,' she pointed out, then apologised. 'They asked me for his next of kin and I didn't know whether that was me, you or Nan.'

'You as much as anyone, I suppose. Not me in any case.'

Amy took a breath. 'He's asked you to go.'

'To the hospital?'

'Dad said you and he had unfinished business.'

Her mum turned from Amy and stared into her small walled garden but not before Amy had seen the quick widening of her eyes. 'Did he?'

'What did he mean by that, Mum?' Her mum had a strong profile, high cheekbones and features that were neat and in proportion. She was elegant and polished, the sort of woman that Amy thought would find it easy to attract a new man. Amy didn't think she'd ever tried.

'One of your dad's jokes, I expect.' Geraldine laughed lightly as if to prove the point. 'Apart from that, I really don't know.'

'Will you go?'

'Maybe.' Geraldine swung her gaze back to meet Amy's. 'Do you want me to?'

'I think you should.' She almost added *just in case*. 'See him tonight, Mum.'

'I'll go now.'

'I'll come with you.'

Geraldine squeezed her hand. 'I can manage, Ames.'

'I'll see him first, Mum; I feel I should say goodnight.' Amy smiled suddenly. 'And warn him that you've actually turned up. I can get a taxi home afterwards.' She squeezed her mum's hand in reply. 'I won't be a fly on the wall, Mum. I mean, when was the last time you actually spoke to him?'

Geraldine shrugged, 'I don't know; I've blanked it out.'

* * *

Visiting hours had long since passed but Geraldine Buckingham hoped that compassion would win over red tape. She spoke quietly when she asked permission for them both to visit and the duty nurse seemed to run a critical eye over them before agreeing. 'As long as he's happy to see you,' she replied, and then called Amy through as soon as she'd checked. Ten minutes later and it was Geraldine's turn.

Robert lay propped up at a forty-five-degree angle. He didn't look as frail as she'd feared but the drip beside his bed and the charts above it were enough to remind her how complicated their lives had become.

'We're not teenagers any more, are we, Gerri?'

She gave a wry smile and shook her head, 'Too much water . . .'

'And too many bridges?' he said, ending a familiar sentence.

'Exactly that.' She pulled a visitors' chair closer to the head of his bed. 'Amy just told me what happened.'

He shook his head as if to say that it didn't matter.

'She said you wanted to talk to me.'

'I said we had unfinished business.' He pushed himself onto one elbow then up into a more upright position. 'I remember feeling faint for just a second or two before I fell. I didn't get sudden pain and didn't know I'd hit my head even though there was blood.'

'Did you know you had a heart condition?'

'Does it matter? I've got one now.'

'So you did?'

'Blood pressure, that's all.' He brushed it away with his cannula-free hand. 'Not enough to make me think morbid thoughts.'

'But now you have?'

'Exactly.'

Gerri could already see where this conversation would be heading. She clasped her hands together – it appeared casual but the fingers on one hand were gripping the others so hard that her knuckles had started to throb.

'What are you planning?'

'To tell Amy.'

'Tell her what?'

'Let me explain something to you first.' He leant towards her further but she didn't reach across to him. She felt her expression set and knew

13

she was glaring. He refocused on the wall behind her and continued to speak. 'What if I'd died? I never felt as though I was going to but I was drifting in and out and Amy was there. It's not right that I could die without telling her the truth.'

'But you're not dying, Rob.'

'But if I did . . . this is my wake-up call, Gerri. It's what I meant by unfinished business.'

Geraldine's anger rose swiftly. She stayed silent for several seconds as she tried to bite back the rage. 'And you're going to tell her what exactly?' she hissed. She was trying to be quiet but her voice had risen to a loud whisper that stabbed the words at him.

'Gerri, shush. You'll get kicked out.'

She had no desire to do as she was told but didn't want to be asked to leave either. 'Amy doesn't need this.'

'Why not? She has nothing to occupy her apart from one dead-end job after the next. It's 2014, Gerri. We've all been living with this for far too long. It's got to stop now. Amy needs to know I never started that fire.'

'You've told her enough times.'

'She needs to know for certain. What have you told her?'

'Nothing. It's between the two of you.'

'Does she ask you about it?'

Gerri pressed her lips firmly shut and shook her head.

He glared back at her. 'Is that nothing or no comment? Because she has lived with this for over twenty years and she asks me questions all the time. Wants to know why we divorced. How can she believe that I'm innocent when she thinks the reason you left was because I was guilty? It's illogical and she knows it.'

'You were guilty.' The words slipped out before Geraldine had a chance to check herself. 'You wrecked our marriage and, if Amy knows the truth about that, how much respect do you think she'll have left for you?'

'I had a fling, I'm not saying "so what" but that isn't the same as killing people, for God's sake.'

'An *affair*, which isn't the same thing, Robert.'

'You could have given me an alibi for the fire.'

'It would have been a lie.'

'Yes, but it would have led to the truth. You know I didn't start it.'

'It doesn't matter. They had evidence, they made the case.'

Robert sighed and let his head drop back against the pillow. He stared up at the ceiling. 'When I was first arrested you told me so often that you knew I was innocent. Do you even believe that any more?' He turned to look at her. There was no frustration or anger now. He was serious and tired. 'We've done each other some serious damage, Gerri. The worst betrayals.'

'I know,' she felt the tiredness too. 'Of course I know you never killed them. I couldn't prove it, though, and part of me . . .' She hesitated and chewed at the top of her thumb. She guessed that she would regret, in the cold light of day, what she was about to say but he was asking for unadorned honesty and it felt like the wrong time and place for any more half-truths 'I decided to let the justice system carry on. I could have lied for you or gone out of my way to persuade people of your innocence but I would have looked like the disillusioned wife blindly believing her cheating husband, wouldn't I?'

'Maybe,' he conceded.

'So I told myself that whatever you'd got would be karma for what you'd done to me.'

'And if I'd been found not guilty? What would have happened to us then?'

'Same outcome, I guess. There were too many barriers between us by then. You can't run around with other women then complain that your wife wants a divorce, Rob.' Geraldine's gaze met his and they both seemed to be waiting for the other to speak. He'd never been reliable as a husband but perhaps he was still a decent man. A man who loved his daughter and had missed out on years of her childhood. She pushed the thought aside; she knew better than that.

He broke the silence first, 'I'm going to speak to Amy and I'd like you there.'

'And tell her that I always knew you were innocent? It wasn't my job to salvage you from the mess you made. Why try to hurt me now?'

'It's about her knowing the truth.'

'Talk to her on your own. I don't want to be there to see the look on her face.'

'I'll tell her everything, Gerri. Everything that led up to it. She'll understand.'

Geraldine shook her head. 'She won't, Rob.' But as she said it he looked away in surprise. She turned her head too and saw Amy half-way between the doorway and the foot of the bed. She stared from her mother to her father and back again.

'I heard most of that,' she said quietly. 'Whispers carry well in an empty room. The bit I didn't catch is how you're not cruel, Mum.'

'Cruel? Because I wouldn't perjure myself?'

Amy's expression turned stony. 'You let me believe that two people are dead because of him. Did you really hate him that much?'

As Amy had stood at the foot of her father's hospital bed she'd been aware that her view of her childhood had begun to warp and blur. She was the same but they'd revealed a different version of themselves and the ground beneath her had felt as though it was beginning to crumble. She'd been too young to understand anything when her dad had gone to prison. But when she'd started school it had caught up with her; she doubted that she'd ever forget the taunts in the playground and waking in the small hours, her pillow wet with tears. And her mum holding her gently and telling her, 'Your dad did a very bad thing but we'll start again. It will be all right.' Then years later her father asked her to trust him, 'I did nothing wrong, Amy. I need you to believe me.'

The bus travelled back towards the centre of Cambridge. She sat on the front row of the upper deck and closed her eyes against the car lights and street lamps that poked at her through the panoramic front window.

At first, she couldn't remember what she'd just said to them, or what they'd tried to tell her. It seemed as though she'd stood on the one spot for many minutes with the world moving around her and a muffled underwater sound filling her ears. She hadn't decided to walk away; her instincts had decided that on their own. She'd turned and then hurried towards the exit, just short of a run. She'd grabbed the first bus into town. Now, finally, she could feel her breathing settle and her thoughts slowing enough for her to catch hold of them. If everything she'd just heard was the truth . . . she broke off mid-thought to argue that it might not be.

The bus was in Perne Road now; she stared down at the houses. The street was lined with 1930s semis, almost all of which had been altered in some way or another: new windows, replacement doors, paved driveways. All unique, she supposed, but somehow all the same. Her family would never belong there and neither did she, but the idea of a life unblotted by extreme events appealed. If her parents had made up any part of their story she was sure they would have painted themselves in a better light, pretended they had once been the kind of family that had lived a fictitiously contented life in their suburban home.

There was, she concluded, no reason for any of it to be a lie. And, more than that, this new version of events made sense in a way that the version she'd grown up with never had. It felt like the truth.

She ignored the queasy feeling that had stayed within her since the hospital. Suddenly, she had no desire to rush home. She rang the bell for the next stop. She had no one to answer to but she didn't want to bring this back home with her. Right now, she needed space to sift and sort her thoughts and to make sure they remained her own.

Alighting at the Brook pub wasn't a random decision, just a spontaneous one. In secondary school her bus had passed the same way and this bus stop had been part of a regular pilgrimage. It hadn't been the closest stop to the site of the fire but the walk had given her a few extra minutes to shake off whatever the day had held. At each visit, she'd spoken silently to her dad and then visited the remnants of the house she'd thought he'd destroyed. She'd stayed loyal despite the people he'd killed.

It was easy to remember everything about the short street; each detail, from the terrace of houses with front steps overlapping the pavement to the camber of the road and the angle that lamplight shafted into Romsey Terrace, was familiar. She'd been four at the time of the fire, too young to visit, the subject too taboo for her to ask. By the time she'd first come the house had gone, leaving nothing but a layer of its brickwork pinned to the property next door. That's what she'd always stared at, looking for answers in the silent remains.

But this time when she came to the corner she stopped at the head of the street. Her reasons for visiting felt different now. She frowned. The idea that the situation was impossible had been replaced by opportunity.

Once again she stood with the rest of the world drifting past her, but now the shock had faded and it had been replaced by clarity.

Her parents had given her a single, sharp shard of information and the rest had to be up to her. She walked towards home, following the route her bus would have taken; she could have waited at the stop for the next one but her lethargy had vanished and her only instinct was not to stand still any more.

CHAPTER 3

Amy had been halfway home when she'd decided to call Neil Frampton. She'd waited for him outside the Earl of Beaconsfield, thinking that they would be able to go inside and find a discreet corner. He pulled his F-Type up to the kerb, lowered his window. He'd always been a big man but he'd put on weight since she'd last seen him and he seemed too bulky to belong with the car.

'Did your mum give you my number?'

'No, I took it off her phone a while ago. I'd like to speak to you.'

'So you said.' Then he waited as if he expected her to have the conversation out here in the street.

She tilted her head in the direction of the pub. 'I thought we could go in there.'

'I'm not in the habit of slipping out of the house to meet women. What do you actually want, Amy?' His tone had turned impatient, or perhaps he'd been impatient all along. His heavy hands squeezed at the steering wheel. She realised then that the engine was still running and wondered whether he was about to pull away.

'I'll tell you what,' she began, then hurried around the back of the vehicle, pulled open the passenger side door and dropped into the seat next to him, 'we can talk wherever suits you.'

He glared straight ahead then pulled into the traffic without any further discussion. The interior smelt of leather upholstery mingled with musky aftershave. They'd driven the length of Mill Road before the silence became too much. 'I remember you visiting us when I was a kid. But not once I'd started secondary school.'

'I knew you well back then.' He glanced at her, then back at the road. 'But it was time to call it a day.'

'Why?'

'I think you know.'

'Because my dad was being released. What I didn't understand was your relationship with my mum. I knew you weren't having an affair with her . . .'

Amy had guessed where he was taking them and Neil Frampton only responded once he'd pulled up in King Street close to the flight of sloping steps that led to her flat. 'You're correct, I wasn't.'

They were within sight of Clowns and the spot where her father had collapsed just a few hours earlier. 'So why did you help us for all those years?'

'Your mother and I were friends.'

'No, it's not that either, is it? Friendship would have continued, and you like one another but you weren't ever that close.'

Neil shifted in his seat, turning his upper body to face her. 'Amy? You're twisting things round to point in a certain direction. What exactly do you want to prove?'

'I want to understand it.'

'Perhaps it's none of your business. And you didn't get me out here to ask all of this. You said you needed my help.'

Neil was overweight; there was no sign of any great physical strength in him but he still seemed intimidating; a man with high blood pressure and low reserves of patience.

She raised her palms in surrender, 'I'm sorry, this is coming out all wrong. The last thing I meant was to sound critical.' She was messing this up and the fear of the door closing before it had opened made her voice wobble. 'I really need a job,' she stumbled over the words and then bit down on her bottom lip, hoping that her awkward half-truth would be taken as embarrassment at having to ask for help.

'Why ask me now?'

'Because I don't know who else I can turn to.'

'But why today?'

'I've been temping and the contract ends this week . . .'

'And your father has been rushed to hospital this afternoon.' Neil ran his tongue across his teeth. 'Amy, I'm always going to know what's going on with him.'

'That has nothing to do with why I'm asking.'

'You're lying.' Neil's eyes flashed wider. 'Did he put you up to this?'

'No! And he doesn't know I'm here. Do you really think he's in hospital thinking about you? And do you know how hard it is for me to ask you for work?' she reached for the door handle. 'I'm totally at the end of my options.'

He reached for her arm. 'Amy . . .'

But she pulled away and scrambled out of the car and onto the pavement, 'Just tell me one thing. Were you helping us out of guilt?'

'Guilt for what?' She slammed the door and started to walk away. She heard his door open and he shouted after her. 'I said, guilt for what?'

She turned and took a couple of steps towards him. 'You tell me. Seems like a man who helps the family of his son's killer has to be motivated by something. I've thought about it and if it's not sex and not money then guilt seems like the answer.'

'And asking me this on the day he's rushed to hospital?'

'Coincidence. I need a job, that's all.'

He didn't move for what felt like a considerable length of time. Amy waited. 'Go to our yard in Argyle Street tomorrow morning. I'll tell Moira to expect you.'

Amy nodded. 'Thank you,' she breathed.

'Nine a.m.,' he told her and she could feel his eyes on her as she walked towards home.

CHAPTER 4

The flatbed truck drove into the yard, its wing mirrors passing within a couple of inches of the narrow brick entrance. The driver immediately spotted the two figures in the Portakabin as the strip lights drenched the interior in an unforgiving starkness. The window stood out like a huge flat-screen TV in the dull enclosure. He swung left into the gap between scaffold poles and a compact trailer carrying a generator, and then adjusted his rear-view mirror to take another look at the two women. Moira was the finance manager, but the other . . . It was rare to have visitors although, occasionally, a car might pull in. But this woman was younger, not the middle-aged dominant type who'd arrive by Mercedes or Audi and use it to block the entrance and attempt to demand obedience from him or his men. Moira held a sheaf of papers in her hand and the pages flapped like a semaphore flag. She moved towards the spare desk and put her hand on the back of the chair. He couldn't see the newcomer too clearly but she seemed familiar.

He slid down from the cab. He was a big man, a couple of inches short of six foot but solid. The heavy tread of his boots ground mud stains onto the concrete.

When he opened the door their conversation trickled dry. Moira smiled uneasily, 'Stan, this is Amy Laurence, our new temp.'

He wiped his palm on the thigh of his overall and stepped forward to shake her hand. She looked in her early twenties although he knew she wasn't that young. He muttered 'hello' and her grip attempted to be firm but he was aware of overpowering it with his own. 'I didn't know we were employing anyone.'

Moira glanced at Amy then back to him, flat-eyed, 'Neither did I.'

'I see.' Stan stared at Amy but continued to address Moira. 'So who sent for extra help? Neil?'

'Who else?'

Stan grunted and Amy made a point of pretending that she was unaware of his attention but her shoulders were tense and her hands had balled into small fists. Stan went to his own desk and pulled paperwork towards him as he sat. 'Let's see what other shit the day has to offer then.'

Moira slapped her own papers onto her desk, loud enough for him to glance up. She shook her head at him. 'We don't need a bad atmosphere in here, Stan.'

He leant back in his chair and forced the tension away. 'It's a bit of a hangover,' he told her.

She raised an eyebrow. 'Well, don't make us all suffer.'

'I'm happy to make coffee,' Amy offered. 'Would you like coffee?' She had regained her composure very quickly and smiled as though she found the idea of making his coffee amusing for some reason. Perhaps she was about to spit in it.

'Yeah, white with two.'

She seemed to know where to find the kettle. Her eyes were brown and her smile made them sparkle, made her cheeks dimple. Her curly brown hair bounced when she moved. She disappeared towards the kitchenette, her straight skirt doing nothing to hide her figure. He registered all those things but doubted he would ever see beyond the only fact that mattered; this was Robert Buckingham's daughter.

Moira gave her desktop an urgent tap. 'Don't glare at her like that.'

'I wasn't.'

When his coffee arrived he left it untouched. By then he had sent an email across the office and told Moira to meet him at the end of the street. He had almost reached the corner when she drove alongside him. She lowered the driver's window of her Audi A4. 'Get in then,' she told him.

She drove away before he had the chance to put on his seatbelt.

They sped through several back streets until she found an unoccupied residents-only parking space in Vinery Road. He was the first to speak. 'Did you think I wouldn't know her, Moira? What's the idea?'

'I don't know why she's here either. Neil just rang this morning and told me that he'd offered her a job. He said it might be a six-month contract no less.'

'Just out of the blue?'

'She contacted him apparently. She was desperate for work,' Moira raised her hands in despair, 'and he's jumped in to rescue her.'

'Of course he has,' Stan replied. He and Moira had been working together throughout; they'd seen Neil Frampton and the company come back from near bankruptcy. He was a smart man over most things. But not this. 'Where does he think this will end? And how are we supposed to work with her? *Hey Amy, I used to be your dad's mate until he killed those people.*'

'Stan . . .'

'Does she know that payments go to suppliers, not to her own bank account? Sorry, Amy, can't let you loose with a lighter or matches, a cheque book or even a pen.'

'Stan, stop it.' Moira was far better at holding everything in than he'd ever been and watching her restraint now was just aggravating him.

'I want you to admit to being as angry as I am, Moira. Or you can coach me and we can all sit around drinking coffee, sharing stories about the old days.'

'She's not her father.'

'We don't know what she's not. And we don't get a choice either. Thanks, Neil, thanks very much.'

Moira restarted the engine. 'We'll go back, talk to her and clear the air. That's the best way forward.'

Stan exhaled a heavy breath and let his head loll back against the headrest. 'Fucking hell, Moira.'

CHAPTER 5

Three months later.

Sue Gully had curled up on Goodhew's sofa, too exhausted by recent events to worry about politeness or her usual self-consciousness around his home. They'd returned from a funeral and it had marked the end of the previous case in a way that the arrest of the killer hadn't and the conviction wouldn't. This, for her at least, had been the sign-off. She guessed it was the same for Goodhew too; the restless expression that haunted his features during an investigation had gone for now. He'd been sitting on the floor next to her, leaning against his jukebox and telling her about his family, memories of his childhood, even about how he had felt as a young boy when his grandfather had died. It had happened in this very room, the only part of the rest of the house below his flat that Goodhew occupied.

'I may have moved some of my things in here, but I still feel this is his study,' Goodhew now said to her. 'And even though I now know how he died, I still feel that this is a peaceful place.'

It felt right to move onto the floor beside him, but she didn't. Maybe he thought the same because, now, he'd come to sit beside her. It wasn't the first time she'd imagined being close to him. But this was real and she had one inescapable reason why she should not let it happen.

He studied her expression for a single still moment and she felt as though he could read her every thought; she was used to his intensity, but not when she was the absolute focus like this. She held her breath and didn't turn away from his gaze. His fingers touched her cheek, then, as their lips met, he wrapped his arms around her. She pulled him closer. She pressed her fingers against his back, felt the tautness beneath his shirt; the strength she'd watched him regain after his accident. It was the way she'd imagined. Stealing her breath. Making her float. Making anything seem possible. Except she knew it wasn't.

She waited until the moment when there was stillness. She lay in the crook of his arm, her cheek against his chest. They still held each other even though she knew it had to be time to let go. She scoured her thoughts, trying to find the right words, the ones that would explain enough but not hurt, or raise questions or, worse still, leave the door ajar. Her hand rested on his arm and she could feel his warmth through the thin cotton of his shirt.

'Will you stay?' he asked.

She drew a breath. She still didn't have the words but needed to trust that they would come. 'Why now, Gary?'

'Too soon or not soon enough? And does it really matter?'

She shook her head. 'I don't know,' she replied. But she did know and the truth was that there might never be a right time. 'It would be a mistake for us. We work together.'

'Is that the only reason?'

He rolled onto his side and their faces were close. Almost touching. She wanted to kiss him again but instead she pressed her palm against his shoulder. 'We've been to a funeral and then there's . . .' She trailed off, not wanting to raise the subject of exactly what had happened to his grandfather. 'Two shocks, Gary. I get it.'

'This isn't about needing company or not thinking straight . . .'

She knew that. She felt the edge of a void beckoning. If she stayed longer it would only grow more difficult. Her answer had been wrong. She slipped out of his arms. 'I need to go. I have nothing against one-night stands, Gary, just not with colleagues.' She turned away to take her jacket from the armchair. She felt her cheeks flush and was relieved that the half-light hid that at least.

'You know that's not what this is.'

'It always makes things complicated.' It was easier to leave it like that; he didn't know much about her private life; she might have a different bloke every night for all he knew.

She slipped her arms into her jacket but didn't button it. She pushed her hands into her pockets and waited for him to stand. His expression was back to its most unfathomable.

He walked her down both flights of stairs and by then she found the silence too much. 'The thing is, Gary, you don't know me. Not really. I don't want it to get weird between us or to ruin our friendship.'

'I think I know you, Sue. And you know me better than anyone else does.' Without warning he hugged her, kissing her softly on the cheek before opening the door and letting her go.

She hurried down the steps and crossed onto Parker's Piece, walking quickly without glancing back. She concentrated on keeping her speed constant and her step determined until she knew that she was out of sight. She slowed then and took twice as long as usual to reach home and the entire time she could still feel his lips on hers. If her brain worked differently she would have stayed, and damn the consequences, but she'd never understood the throwaway intimacy of a one-night stand. And that was never what she'd wanted with Gary. She doubted there was the possibility of more than that, though, and the thought of him pushing her away later hurt more than ending it before it had the chance to begin.

CHAPTER 6

Goodhew sat on the top step of the short stone flight that led from street level up to his front door. He leant back against the darkly painted wood the weak sunlight had warmed, and he watched Parker's Piece through half-closed eyes. When he was younger he'd believed that the paths crossing the green had marked the centre of Cambridge, like a giant X-marks-the-spot. Unless it was the dead of the night, there were always people crossing it on foot or bicycle; easy to believe that everyone who lived in the city passed through here at one time or another.

His relationship with the city was as complicated as his relationship with this house. He'd grown up with both. The house had belonged to his grandparents but he'd visited most days and had grown up thinking of it as his true childhood home. He'd jumped at the chance to take the rooftop flat when his grandmother had decided to move out. Ownership of the whole building had been passed over to him, but he had continued to live in the flat, leaving the other three floors almost entirely empty.

The ground floor stood half a storey above street level. He had walked down the front steps with Sue, and watched her until she'd disappeared from view. That had been an hour ago and he was still there, trying to re-anchor his thoughts after the shifts and reverberations of the previous few days.

My grandfather was murdered.

That simple sentence had been on repeat since he'd found out. It punctuated every other thought he'd tried to corral. Yes, it had been a shock but not in the same way as if a sudden or violent death had just happened. That shock would be sharper, louder even, the epicentre tangible and the rewritten picture of the future would lie ahead with its debris there to step over and around. This shock was different; it had taken place in July 1992 and the twenty-two years since now looked altered. He had yet to know how far or how deep the rewriting needed to go. His parents and his grandmother had both known the truth and so had DI Marks and potentially any officer old enough to have been part of the investigation at the time.

For the first time in almost six months he'd phoned his sister Debbie. She hadn't known either and they'd spent several long phone calls since dredging up fragments of memory, trying to piece together clues they'd missed. But she'd been nine and he'd been eleven, and he'd been the only one of them who'd seen or heard anything of consequence. He told Debbie how he'd hidden in their grandfather's study when the two men had visited. How he'd done exactly what he'd promised their grandfather he would do and had sneaked back into school and said absolutely nothing.

He'd heard Debbie draw a sharp breath and he could guess the words she'd wanted to say, 'You should have told someone, Gary.'

She'd been right, too, he might have been able to give some kind of description. He'd heard their voices, one sounded much younger, he talked less. The older man had a hard-edged voice, he sounded angry but his tone was thin as though it belonged to a short and wiry body. Goodhew had seen the man's shoes from his hiding place too. Brown leather, the soles newer than the rest. If Goodhew had told the police any part of that description it might have tipped the investigation in a better direction. They were small details but sometimes that was all it took. He'd felt the nausea of guilt.

'If I'd spoken up they might have been caught,' he told her.

'You didn't know there was any investigation and he'd asked you to keep a secret. You just did what he asked, but I'll tell you something, Gary,' she sighed, 'it explains why you joined the police.'

He didn't comment even though the same thought had occurred to him. Being a detective had been a childhood ambition but he couldn't remember having any interest before his grandfather's death. He wasn't ready to admit that, though. 'I'm sure I was younger than that when I first mentioned it.'

'No. You were at boarding school,' she said firmly. 'I clearly remember. I wanted to travel the world and you wanted to stay in Cambridge. It makes sense now, doesn't it?'

It made sense if it really had been bothering him all those years; if, subconsciously at least, he'd always known about his grandfather's murder. He hated it that his grandmother and DI Marks – people he knew and loved – had kept it secret from him. He hated it more that he might have kept it from himself.

His mobile lay on the step beside him and he glanced down at it a moment before it began to ring. His grandmother's mobile number flashed onto the screen. His phone was on silent but the light on the screen pulsed at the same rate as a ringtone. He watched it until the call was diverted to voicemail and the screen faded back to black.

It wasn't that he didn't want to talk to her; just that he didn't know what to say. And, for different reasons, that had been the same with Sue. He could still feel their kiss and the moment he'd realised that she was gently pulling away from him. He picked up his phone and scrolled down to her number before changing his mind and returning the phone to the step.

'Are you avoiding me, Gary?'

His grandmother stood on his garden path. She wore a deep maroon suit and looked like she'd come straight from a wedding; elegant even by her own standards. He saw that she held a leather document wallet; not a wedding then. She'd been to see Mason, her solicitor. Their solicitor actually. 'Not entirely. I didn't know what to say.'

'Isn't that the same thing?' She didn't wait for a reply. 'There's something I'd like to show you, assuming, that is, you're not about to dash off to work?'

Goodhew shook his head. 'I'm in tomorrow. Right now I'm not going anywhere.'

'Can we talk then?'

'I think we should,' he replied, but reluctance swept over him. He felt no rush to go inside the house and didn't move at first. 'Not here though.'

'I thought not. Hobbs Pavilion?' She glanced over her left shoulder at the former cricket pavilion that had housed the Mai Thai restaurant since the summer he'd moved into the flat.

He didn't feel hungry but suddenly realised he hadn't eaten for hours. They crossed the road in silence, glad that the walk wasn't long enough for either of them to feel the need to talk.

They sat at a table laid for four, choosing facing seats and a window view of Parker's Piece. She placed the document wallet on the seat beside her.

He ordered noodles without paying much attention to the menu. The food arrived quickly but he barely noticed; he was more interested in hearing what his grandmother had to say.

'I suppose knowing that I planned to tell you isn't much help?'

He shook his head. 'Debbie and I should have grown up knowing what had happened to him. You and I have always been close and it's a shock to discover that you've lied to me since I was a kid.'

His grandmother watched him for some time. 'How much do you know?' she asked finally.

'That he was beaten to death. He collapsed with a head injury and was rushed to hospital but there was nothing . . .'

She raised a hand to stop him, 'Your grandfather had an old head injury and it was that which ruptured. He may have died if they hadn't hit him, he might have fallen or been in any minor accident and the result could have been the same.'

'He died because they hit him.' Goodhew leant back in his chair and studied her carefully. 'How can you be so calm about it?'

'I'm not.' She pressed her lips into a tight smile, her focus drifted beyond him for a moment and her eyes began to mist. 'Your grandfather and I had an agreement; we accepted whatever time we had together and certain parts of our life, our career if you can call it that, were to be kept secret from almost everyone, including you. No matter what,' she whispered. She blinked quickly and looked at Goodhew again. 'But that was a long time ago and I'm going to let it go now. After all, you made him a promise too and that didn't help. This isn't the time for any more secrets. When I just asked how much you know, I meant about his life, not his death.'

Goodhew shook his head. She reached for the folder beside her. 'What's in there?' he asked.

She moved it on to the table in front of her, one neat hand pressed flat on its tooled cover. Now he could see it more clearly and it was far older than it had first appeared, with little vein-like cracks along the spine where the leather had aged. She lifted her hand very slightly as though prepared to let him take the file but then changed her mind. He could tell that she was hunting for words – precise words. He said nothing, just waited.

He knew that she and his grandfather had loved each other deeply. She'd been in her late forties when she'd been widowed. Forty-nine by his calculations, although her exact age had always been vague. Young enough to have considered marriage again perhaps, but she never had; she enjoyed romance but remained robustly independent. There had never been any sign of frailty or uncertainty about her, not even now as he watched her consider sharing details of her husband's death.

He had no idea what he was likely to hear.

'Mount Kilauea has been erupting every day since 1983, you know that?'

'Yes, but that's not exactly what I thought you would say.'

'I'd hate to be predictable, Gary.' She looked amused for a moment. 'The point is the lava destroys everything in its path, trees, buildings, people if they don't get out of the way, and then you speak to the locals, the ones at the heart of it, they don't see it that way at all. The volcanoes created the land and Mount Kilauea is adding to it. The eruption is about the birth of the island. Your grandfather and I shook things up and we knew it might end badly. But we were happy with the risks.'

She released her hold on the folder and he took it, pushing his half-eaten meal to one side so that he could give it his complete attention. The pages it held formed an inch-thick sheaf, their edges still sharp even though it had clearly been many years since they'd been written and the ink on them had faded. He recognised his grandfather's hand-writing at once. The top page was filled with names and comments. Some were ringed and connected by lines. Others were enclosed in boxes and several had been scrubbed through. Goodhew was startled by the similarity to his own way of working. 'What is this?'

'We called those pages firsts because each is the first page of notes he would make on each new job.'

'What kind of job?'

She smiled softly and as she spoke he knew that she was watching to see what his reaction would be. 'We searched for missing people. At the very first meeting with a potential client your grandfather would make those notes. They were like word doodles, they contained key pieces of information but also any thoughts or feelings that came into his head.'

Goodhew shook his head in disbelief. 'And each of these pages is one case? One missing person?'

She nodded.

'How did I never know this?'

'We didn't want you to.'

He turned the first page and then separated the pile at random points. He spotted place names he didn't recognise, scribbled last-known addresses in unfamiliar towns in Bulgaria, Italy, Hong Kong, Thailand, American states and remote Australian towns. 'How many years . . .' he began.

'Always,' she replied. 'We loved it and we were good at it. And, as you can see, we travelled the world. We found runaways, absconders, people who were trying to hide and some that were desperate to be found.' She ran one fingertip down the side of the pile. 'There are more folders than this one, and I want you to see everything now.' There was nothing wrong with the food but neither of them finished eating. She left cash on the table. 'Come with me, there's something I must show you.'

Goodhew followed her outside to find her waving down a taxi. He held the door open for her. 'Where are we going?'

'Hope Street Yard.'

He didn't ask why, he wanted to work it out for himself. He began turning over the pages one by one, trying to spot any clue that would explain why they were about to visit a cluster of units selling antiques and vintage collectibles. The journey would be ten minutes at most so after the first few pages he began to flick through more quickly. He stopped at a sketch of a lion; it was drawn in the style of a heraldic symbol, rearing up on its hind legs with flames dancing at his feet. 'I recognise that. It was on a pen in one of the drawers in the study.'

'Very good. Do you remember what he told you about it?'

Goodhew's grandfather had repeated stories about many of the objects but he couldn't remember anything specifically belonging to this. 'I don't think so . . . he had hundreds of items and he seemed to have stories to go with each of them.'

'All true.'

'Really?'

'Perhaps the odd embellishment,' she conceded. 'He had a sense of drama.' She touched her hand on his. 'We're here.' She let the taxi go and he followed her into the yard. Most of the units stood with their doors open, many with items standing outside. Reclaimed doors and a radiator at one, a rail of second-hand clothes at the next. She passed all of these and headed towards a locked unit in the corner. With her own sense of drama, she reached into her pocket and produced a small key on a large leather fob. She handed it to Goodhew. 'All yours.'

He'd already guessed, or hoped he had. He swung the door open and light fell onto its contents. He had been correct but seeing all the furniture from his grandfather's study still took his breath away. Every item was instantly familiar although not quite as he remembered. The desk looked smaller and the bookshelves less grand; he'd changed, not them. He pushed the folder into his grandmother's hands and reached for the nearest drawer.

'It's all there,' she assured him. 'I didn't know what to do with everything so I took it, lock, stock and barrel, and stored it here.'

'You could have left it in the house.'

'And it would have turned into a museum instead of your home.'

Gently he picked through the contents and among them found a single playing card, a cufflink and the head from a decapitated figurine. 'I remember all of these.'

'One souvenir per case.' She picked up a wooden pawn, long since separated from the rest of the chess set. 'I thought it an annoying habit at first, but I look at these things now and I'm reminded of so many details I might have forgotten.'

In this drawer alone there were more items than he could count. 'That's a huge number of cases.'

'We certainly were busy. People do go missing for very many reasons. And sometimes clients wanted us to find relatives or former colleagues when they'd just lost touch over the years. It didn't all involve anything illegal or underhand.'

'But it sometimes did?'

'Frequently.'

Goodhew opened every drawer and cupboard, taking out items he recognised, remembering fragments of stories that his grandfather had told him. 'What else do you know about his death?' he asked.

'We'll walk back.' She waited for him to finish looking through the drawers and cupboards. He locked up and they walked through the passage to Mill Road. He didn't look at her directly but in the corner of his vision he could see that her gaze was fixed on the street ahead. 'I have another set of keys so you can keep those,' she said.

He wondered whether she hadn't heard his question or had decided to leave it unanswered but either way, he wouldn't ask again until they were back at his flat.

They'd walked for another five minutes before she spoke. 'The skills needed to find a person aren't too different from the ones needed to help them disappear. We knew how to search data trails – different back then, of course, but we made those impossible to follow.'

It took Goodhew a few seconds to grasp what she was saying. 'You helped someone vanish?'

'Once or twice.' She glanced at him. 'Sorry, I was in a train of thought and just started in the middle. You asked what else I knew about Joe's death and there's not much. But about two years before, we'd been contacted by a young history student named Melanie Franks. She was pregnant and already estranged from her family, in debt and desperate to continue her studies. She'd become involved in something illegal, but wouldn't tell us what it was.'

'But you still helped her?'

'I didn't want to unless we knew more, but Joe felt strongly, probably because she was expecting a baby, I don't know. It was very rare that we disagreed about helping anyone; we had rules for which cases we took on and which we didn't. Anyhow, we set it up and she disappeared.'

'Where?'

'To Hereford; the major routes from here are north–south so we liked the idea of the west of England and she took the name Jane Williams. Clichéd as it is, the most common names work best. And that was all we heard from her as far as I ever knew.'

She stepped to the side of the footpath and stopped outside a computer repair shop, her back to the window. 'If Joe was talking on the phone he'd make notes, like the ones in that file. After he died, I found this.' She pulled a folded sheet of A4 paper from her pocket and passed it to Goodhew. He opened it out. There were few words on the page, just a mundane to-do list: renew car insurance, check smoke alarms, *Batman Returns*.

'He took me to see that.'

'June '92. And look.'

She was pointing to the corner of the page but Goodhew was already looking. The name Melanie was written and circled and the ink was several layers deep as if his grandfather had kept tracing the letters as he'd thought about her.

'It doesn't mean she contacted him,' Goodhew said. 'Perhaps someone else was asking or she was on his mind.'

'Maybe,' she replied but shook her head as she said it. 'When the police had gone I checked and every document mentioning her had also gone. There wasn't much, mind you, and nothing that would have given away her new location, but it had all been taken.' She touched the sheet of paper. 'They missed this. And this too.' She removed a bangle from her wrist and handed it to Goodhew. 'I'd never seen it before he died but it was in the drawer with the other souvenirs. I'm sure I knew every item almost as well as he did and he must have acquired it very recently.'

Goodhew took the bangle and turned it over in his fingers. It was some kind of plastic, acrylic perhaps and was transparent with tiny straight fibres, like minute rods of dry spaghetti, suspended in the resin. 'You've had this for twenty-two years?'

'I have. I can't imagine it will tell us much, but who knows.'

'Could he have been working on something without your knowledge?'

'He must have been. And it seems it was connected to Melanie, perhaps proving she was in danger all along. If you can find her without putting her at risk, and if she'll talk to you, you might get your answers.'

'And I have your blessing?'

'Always, Gary.' Without either of them suggesting it, they started to walk again. She waited until they'd finished threading through the traffic on Gonville Place before she spoke again. 'When you mention him, you don't call him granddad any more.'

Goodhew had been very aware of this. He hadn't meant any disrespect but saying *my grandfather* to his grandmother seemed awkward and he found *granddad's murder* impossible to say to anyone. 'I'm sorry,' he replied. 'Would it be wrong to call him Joe?'

'Not at all.' She tucked her gloved hand in the crook of his arm. 'But you'll have to call me Ellie instead of gran.'

'You've never let me call you gran.'

'You say it sometimes and it makes me feel old. Ellie and Joe, please.'

'That will take a lot of getting used to.'

'You'll manage.'

And he had no doubt that he would. He glanced across to Parkside Police Station. There were answers there too and he intended to find them next.

CHAPTER 7

DI Marks wasn't at his desk when Goodhew reached his office. Two orange plastic packing crates stood on the floor and seemed to dominate the room. One was already filled and held the larger objects: several books, a couple of framed photographs and Marks's anglepoise lamp. Each item looked as though it had been packed carefully. The second crate contained fewer items and those seemed to have been tipped straight from a drawer. Marks had left his mug on the desktop, a foot away from the souvenir coaster from Malta. Goodhew wasn't about to check the drawers to see if they were empty but, if this was the sum total of all his boss's years in this room, it wasn't much. He turned to find DS Michael Kincaide standing in the doorway behind him.

'I wondered when you'd appear, Gary.'

'Is Marks around?'

'Do you want to see him or have time to go through his desk?'

Goodhew pretended to weigh it up. 'Both, I suppose. The same as you.'

Kincaide's dark eyes flickered with irritation, '*I* don't need to scavenge for information behind people's backs . . .'

Goodhew grinned. 'So he's on his way up then?'

Kincaide pulled a chair alongside Marks's desk and took a seat. 'Can you wait outside? I need to see him first.'

'No problem.'

Goodhew closed the door behind him and stayed in the hallway until Marks appeared several minutes later. 'I was hoping to ask you a few questions, sir.' Marks nodded towards his office but Goodhew shook his head. 'Kincaide's in there.'

'So you're in the corridor? Five minutes of small talk wouldn't kill either of you.' Goodhew wasn't convinced but didn't comment. He followed Marks back inside. Kincaide wasn't seated now but standing at the window and looking down on Parker's Piece. The mug had been returned to its coaster and Marks's own chair had been replaced neatly into the foot-well of the desk. Would small talk include asking whether Kincaide had really been swivelling in their DI's chair and pretending to be in charge? Goodhew stayed quiet.

Kincaide took a few minutes to run through some paperwork, fussing so much over the small details that Goodhew wondered whether his sole purpose was to hinder everyone else's day.

As soon as Kincaide had gone Marks opened one of his desk drawers and handed Goodhew a thick file. 'Most of this is what I held onto from your grandfather's case.'

'Sue told me about it. Can I have it, or take copies?'

'Take it, and I've also ordered all the documentation up from the archives. It will be here tomorrow or Wednesday.'

'And you finish on Friday?'

'Next Friday, not this. There will be time; you won't be able to take it from the building, though.'

'I understand.'

Marks gave a sceptical grunt. 'Just don't lose it. I might have been more junior back then, but I now know Joe's case well and I'd like to discuss it with you when you're ready.'

Goodhew was ready, but the information his grandmother had given him pressed harder. 'Where would you start if you were me?'

'If I were you?' Marks studied him intently for almost a minute, his gaze impenetrable. 'Somewhere along the line we missed the leads we needed. You might think that you saw nothing of significance but you are the only witness. So, if I were you, I'd sift through everything and see what jumps out.'

'It's not information I should have.'

'My behaviour is beyond improper.' Marks looked unconcerned.

'But I retire next week and this case won't be at the top of anyone else's caseload. You understand that you can't be involved in an official capacity?'

'Thank you, sir. There's one other thing – does the name Melanie Franks mean anything to you?'

Marks shook his head slightly. 'It doesn't ring a bell. Who is she?'

'That's all I have at the moment. She has no criminal record and her name doesn't cross-reference with any other cases.'

'And I'm guessing that this woman's name came from your grand-mother?'

'Possibly.'

Marks closed his eyes for a second. Goodhew guessed it was the equivalent of a slow count to ten. 'Have you asked Sheen?'

'He's not in today, I've left him a note.' Sheen was the oracle of all things local; he could often dredge up rumours and connections that had never made it into official documentation.

'He'll also ask who she is . . .'

'Like I said, she's just a name.'

Marks pursed his lips and tapped on the desktop with the tips of his fingers. 'It is still an open case, Gary.'

'And I won't hold back anything that I think is relevant.'

'It's not down to you to decide what counts as relevant, you know. A case is different when it's personal. It really is important that you keep me, or my replacement, informed of anything new.'

'I understand.'

'And Melanie Franks?'

Goodhew tried to look apologetic. 'I'm sorry, sir, as far as I know there's no connection.' He picked up the file and rose to his feet.

Marks stood too and walked Goodhew to the door, 'I always sus-pected that your grandmother was holding something back. Talking of which,' he nodded at the file Goodhew held, 'I kept a few files, each relating to an unsolved case. All were personal to me in some way or another, mostly because I was close to the investigation and hoped, one day, to have the satisfaction of seeing it resolved. This one was different, I knew Joe before he died; he and your grandmother were remarkable, they helped me several times on local cases.'

Goodhew was startled. 'I had no idea.' Until two weeks ago he hadn't known that Marks and his grandmother even knew one another.

'Not everything in there relates to Joe. I followed your early days and, when I started receiving your anonymous tip-offs for other cases, I filed those in there too. They do need to disappear from Parkside.'

'Was it that obvious?'

'That it was you? It wasn't my greatest feat of detection, Gary. You have Joe's doggedness and a similar mind. And you don't always know when to keep yourself out of trouble.'

Goodhew left Parkside Station and was halfway across Parker's Piece towards his house when he saw his friend Bryn's turquoise and white Zodiac pull up outside. Bryn waited in the driver's seat with his arm out of the window. It wasn't a sign of spring, it was just the way Bryn liked to pose.

Usually when Bryn turned up unannounced it was no surprise but today was different. 'What happened to Prague?'

Bryn reached across and opened the door for Goodhew. 'How about a curry, a few drinks and pool?' Bryn pulled into the traffic the moment that Goodhew closed the door. 'Maya and I have called it quits,' he told him.

Bryn looked and sounded casual but Goodhew doubted that he was. In the years that Goodhew and Bryn had been friends, the relationship with Maya had been the only that had lasted beyond a few weeks.

'When?'

'Yesterday, at the airport.'

'So you never went?'

'We went, but then we caught the next plane home.'

Goodhew waited for Bryn to add more but the conversation stalled until they were at the Earl of Beaconsfield and had taken their drinks to the pool table.

'We were taxiing down the runway and she hates take-off and landing so she's there with her eyes closed and her hands bunched into fists and she says, "It's not working." I thought she meant the seatbelt or something so I asked, "What's not?" And she opened one eye and said, "If we crash right now what hasn't been fulfilled in your life?"

Goodhew broke into the pack and potted a yellow. 'That's deep.'

'That's Maya,' Bryn agreed. 'But if we had crashed I wouldn't have got to hear her list. And if we'd crashed without her saying anything then I would have died happier than I am right now . . .' Bryn potted a couple of reds in silence. He wasn't great at playing and talking simultaneously. 'Apart from being dead, of course.'

'So she just finished with you on the plane?'

Bryn shook his head. 'We talked on the flight and at the airport, and then waited for the next one home.' He leant against the table and suddenly became pensive. 'The funny thing was that I understood what she meant. I thought we were fine but, when she explained, I got it. She doesn't want to spend the rest of her life in Cambridge any more than I want to live mine anywhere else. She wants to travel, to study politics, to become a journalist. I don't even know what I want but it's not all that stuff.' He potted a third ball, then ran the cue ball behind another red to leave Goodhew snookered.

Goodhew aimed the cue ball around the table and managed to pot another yellow. 'I can't believe you sound so philosophical about it all.'

'Yeah, well I wasn't when I went over to my parent's house last night. Last time I cried like that was when I crashed the Zodiac.' The joke didn't sound convincing. 'I was awake most of the night thinking about her and, when I went back to the flat this morning, she'd gone. I'm going to move out too, I don't want to stay there without her.' Bryn paused before taking his next shot, 'How can so much change in a single day?'

Goodhew considered his last twenty-four hours and decided to order more drinks.

CHAPTER 8

Ian Kincaide turned the key in the lock and opened the door an inch or two. She paused long enough to hear the muted sounds of the television in the front room, long enough to face the monotony that hung in the air, to take a breath and nudge herself inside. She dragged her case over the threshold, careful not to scuff it against her suit trousers. It was later than she'd planned by, she guessed, at least two bottles of beer. She dropped her keys on the hall table, leaving her case at the bottom of the stairs and walking towards the kitchen. Her husband Michael was in an armchair, staring at the screen but not watching, a pair of empty bottles on the coffee table beside him. She stopped in the doorway – extending her disapproval from the bottles back to the man.

'Welcome home?'

Michael turned his head a little, dragging his gaze away from the screen, 'Give me a chance. I didn't hear you come in.'

'I don't suppose you saved me any dinner? Or did you eat at work?'

'I didn't bother.'

She knew which he meant and that piqued her interest; her husband was slim but always looked after his appetite. She carried on to the kitchen and returned with coffees, leaving his on the coffee table next to him and still making no physical contact with him. She flicked off the TV and waited until she had his full attention before speaking. 'So, what's eating at you?'

'If you'd been here you would have known.'

'It was a seminar and you could have phoned any evening. And, if you had, I also would have known what was bothering you, so let's skip that self-pity crap, Michael. Unless, of course, you want to piss me off before you've even begun?'

'It was the funeral of that murdered homeless guy today . . .'

'Aaron Rizzo?'

'Yeah, Ratty,' he replied.

She was surprised. 'And you went?'

She saw the tell-tale flexing of his jaw muscles as he clenched and unclenched his teeth, 'Too right I fucking did. Since the last day of that last case I knew there was something going on, some private club that everyone was suddenly a member of.'

'Everyone, like who?'

'Goodhew and Marks, Sheen and Sue.'

'Oh, that everyone.'

Kincaide cocked his head. 'Meaning what? Here I go again? No wonder I don't confide in you when you just dismiss every fucking thing that bothers me.'

She sighed. 'Then say something I haven't heard before, Michael. It always comes back to Goodhew being treated differently, Goodhew getting all the breaks. Who got the promotion? You did. If there was that much nepotism you'd still be a DC and he'd be the DS.'

Kincaide gave a cold laugh. 'There's plenty you haven't heard before and it turns out it was all fucking nepotism, even when they promoted me I bet it was some twisted fucking way of getting me off of Gary's case.'

Jan blinked slowly, an attempt to keep herself calm. She shot an angry glance at the bottles. 'Have you been drinking more than that?'

'I'm not drunk.'

'But you've been at it for a while?'

'I'm a grown man. It's not a fucking crime to unwind with a drink.'

'You're swearing *and* ranting.' She said it as an observation, her tone matter-of-fact.

'Because I finally found out, and I bet I was the last to know.'

Jan dropped into the other armchair with a sigh. 'OK, what did you find out?'

'That Goodhew's grandfather was beaten to death back in 1992 and it's unsolved. Goodhew found out a couple of weeks ago and Marks knew about it all along.'

'You never told me.'

'Because *I* didn't know until a couple of days ago when it was officially reopened and suddenly it made sense. Marks knew the grandfather, he worked on his case; no wonder he's been pandering to Goodhew all this time.'

'Goodhew must have known.'

'Didn't know as a kid and no one filled him in until now.'

'And why's all this your problem?'

'He's like a thorn in my fucking side, Jan. Turns out he's been sitting on a huge inheritance all this time. We struggle for whatever we get and he doesn't even need to work; he's there playing a game while everything I work towards just drops in his fucking lap.'

He'd left his coffee untouched. She reached for hers and sipped it as she studied him. He wasn't hard to measure, for one thing too much alcohol made him swear and it had obviously taken him a while to work himself up to his current state. The bitterness wasn't drink related though, that rippled under his skin 24/7; it seemed to her that her husband enjoyed the role of being hard done by. But this level of anger was new. The question was whether he actually wanted to do something with it or just make her listen ad infinitum.

'There's no point telling me these things unless you're prepared to act on them,' she said quietly. 'I can't fix them for you.'

'I don't want you to.' He stared at her expectantly, though, as if she held all the answers or he was waiting for her permission to act. 'I want to deal with it but I don't know where to start.'

Or perhaps he really did need her to think for him.

She sighed. 'What would actually make you happy, Michael?'

'Goodhew gone . . .' He shook his head slowly as he thought about it. 'No, more than that. I want him to have to leave as a result of his own failure. He needs to be discredited, or isolated.'

Things were changing; she didn't see how that helped but ran through them aloud in any case. 'Marks is retiring, so is Sheen. You and Goodhew will both have a fresh start then.' Her thoughts began to gather momentum. 'He won't have his feet under the table with who-ever takes over from Marks and, apart from him, who else has he got?'

'Sue Gully for one. She was with him today at the funeral. They're always dancing round each other, covering each other's backs.'

Kincaide's lips curled as if there was a bitter taste in his mouth.

'Are they together?'

'Obviously, what else would be going on? He wouldn't bother if there weren't benefits, would he?'

Jan threw him a filthy glare.

'Why the dirty look?'

'I thought it would be obvious.' She fought the urge to clench her teeth.

He looked blank. 'How does Goodhew shagging Sue help me at all?'

'How does your apparently decent IQ leave you so clueless about the way the rest of the population thinks and feels?' Tiredness would not help her patience. 'Sex is not the common denominator in the way all men think towards all women.'

'That's because you don't *know* men, Jan.'

'But you do know the world's not flat, right?'

'Of course I do, and what the fuck's that supposed to mean? The world's not flat, how stupid am I? How clever are you?'

As he redirected his frustrations at her she could see the remainder of her evening being sucked down a drain of accusations and incrim-inations, ending with the expectation of sex, the avoidance of it and the good bits of the day going down the pan with the rest.

She took a deep breath, exhaled slowly and gave up. 'I meant, look at the obvious; Sue helps him, covers for him, he confides in her. She is Gary's Achilles heel. If you can't get to him, get to her. Drive a wedge between her and Gary or her and her job – it will amount to the same.'

He took a few moments to digest what she'd said but she saw him straighten in his chair and a smile begin to form.

'He won't be so cocky once it's just me and him. And I know exactly how to tackle Sue.'

CHAPTER 9

Amy had taken a longer lunch and walked across town to visit her mum. The day of her father's heart attack had been the last time she'd been to her mother's house. Geraldine lived in the narrowest house in Fair Street. The strip of front garden had been replanted with box hedging and there were new curtains at the downstairs windows; they'd all appeared since Amy's last visit. Her mum let her in, saying nothing but managing a watered-down smile as she led her through to the conservatory. The rooms smelt of detergent layered over dampness, as though the carpets had been shampooed but the dirty water was still in there, sinking into the pile and drying out in the vain hope of becoming undetectable. Nothing had changed in the conservatory but it was not as she remembered it; what had been a romantic mix of new and old furniture just seemed muddled now. Or like a storeroom. Ornaments and plants and photos that had been comfortably familiar looked dusty and brittle. It had been weeks since the last time she'd been here and those weeks had been difficult; right now she was seeing her childhood home with fresh eyes.

Amy watched her mum reposition pens and a remote control, moving them to one side of the coffee table from the other. A small thing perhaps, but the way her mum expended energy wasn't directionless like this. Ever. She had always been the pragmatist, the capable parent who'd guided her through. And now her mum was feeling vulnerable. Amy wondered whether she should have been feeling sympathy; she didn't, even when her mum spoke and her voice sounded hoarse.

'It's good to see you.'

'Avoiding you wasn't helping.' Amy looked away.

'Do you know what will?'

On the window sill in front of Amy stood a spider plant in a pot that was sun-bleached down one side. New growth sprung out at the ends of the tendrils trailing down to touch the floor. If it had been her plant, she would have binned the entire mess. When Amy replied her voice was clear: 'To discover that there was a genuine reason why you abandoned Dad and lied to me.'

Geraldine stiffened immediately. 'I never thought you would appreciate my reasons. I doubt you will now.'

Amy glared. 'Are you even going to try to explain?'

'We should just move on, Amy. There's no point in going over it, not now, not after so long.'

Amy didn't rush to reply. She forced her breathing to steady. 'Are you about to tell me it's just water under the bridge?' she asked.

She'd always hated the expression but her mum used it regularly.

'I think so, don't you?' Her mum had missed the sarcasm and, very briefly, her voice brightened.

'No, Mum, I really don't. I can't make you talk about it but if you want us to move forward then you need to tell me everything you can.'

'To stir up more trouble?'

'I'm not sure it can, really. And if there's worse then you can't leave it hanging over me. How would that be right?'

'There isn't worse.'

'Well then . . .'

Her mum began to speak but cut herself off before the first word was complete, stopped, then told her 'I just don't want to . . .'

Amy stood. 'Fine, but our relationship won't get over it.'

'Amy, it can.'

'Only from your point of view, Mum. For me, it's a deal breaker.'

'A deal breaker?' she echoed.

Amy wanted to apologise for the choice of words but not the sentiment. 'Yes, it is.'

She hadn't said it for effect or brinkmanship. She expected to leave and to be followed by nothing but silence. Her mum stopped her before she'd made it through the first door.

'OK, Amy. Wait. I'll explain.'

Amy returned to her seat, still expecting her mum to add some caveat to what she was about to share but, instead, her mother's guard dropped and Amy hoped she was about to be told everything she needed.

'I loved your dad, that's the first thing to say, and we had years together when I thought we were complete . . .'

Geraldine meshed her fingers together and squeezed to lock them tightly.

'He and Neil had started the business a few years earlier, your dad put everything into it and cash flow was always an issue.'

Amy shifted in her seat, biting back the urge to ask, 'So what?'

'We stuck together when there was no money, long hours, difficult contracts and tension between Neil and Robert. I was totally committed to him and our family. I thought he felt the same but he'd been having an affair . . .'

'With Nadine?'

'I didn't know it was her at the time. A fling, he said. He broke down when he told me. I hadn't suspected anything, he just came to me and confessed. I was stunned. And the fact that I hadn't seen it coming made it worse.'

She paused again and considered what she'd just said.

'It made it more difficult later when we tried to put it behind us; how would I ever see the signs when I hadn't spotted them the first time around?'

'So this wasn't when you and Dad divorced?'

'No, earlier.'

Her mum sat back in her chair and her thoughts seemed to drift off. 'Years ago, I was in a traffic queue on the M11 when a car behind didn't slow in time. It smashed into a Volvo next to me, throwing it forward and into the crash barrier.' Amy said nothing. 'The first driver was stunned, the driver of the Volvo stood on the hard shoulder telling everyone he was fine, that he just needed to get home. He actually asked who had his keys. His car was a foot too short, one wheel buck-led and going nowhere, but he couldn't see that. I found out later that his kneecap was shattered too but he'd still stood there, wanting his life to carry on just as it had before. That was me. I didn't want to deal with what had really happened, to acknowledge the damage or see that it couldn't ever be the same again. All I wanted was to get back to where I thought we'd been.'

'I'm guessing it didn't work out like that?'

'I suppose it did for a while. Our marriage had beaten the odds, come back from the brink, was stronger for what we'd been through – any cliché you'd like to throw at it. In reality, I think I became pretty bitter.'

'Even though you chose to stay?'

'Yes, and if appearances count for anything, I made a good job of it too, but I knew how I felt inside and I should have ended it.'

Amy's summary was pointed. 'So you had an unhappy marriage and decided to let Dad get locked up for it?'

'You make it sound as though I framed him.'

Amy pressed her lips together and waited for her mum to fill the silence.

'I heard he was messing around again and when the house in Romsey Terrace burnt down his excuse was that he'd been working late. I don't know what kind of *working late* that might have been but no one came forward to offer him an alibi. He asked me for one and I could see the fear in him. And I wondered why an innocent man would think he'd be arrested. I made him tell me the truth and I swore that I wouldn't help him if he didn't, so the full story came out. And then, finally, I saw how much I'd given up, and that it was all for nothing. You know, I thought we'd have another child eventually and in the middle of his *confession* all I could think about was how I'd lost that chance.'

She blinked slowly, carefully, as though steering herself through a painful memory. It was the first time Amy had felt anything beyond anger and if they had been closer she might have reached for her mum's hand. She'd never wanted to be an only child and hadn't known until now that her mum hadn't wanted it either.

'Robert was terrified. That's when I discovered it was because

Nadine had been in that house and that's who he was having an affair with. Affair, not fling, not an impersonal one-night stand. He broke down and everything spilled out, how it hadn't been a brief lapse but a full-on relationship, that she'd ended it, not him, that she . . .' Geraldine pulled herself up short. 'And it turned out that the meaningless fling he'd told me about was with another woman, and it wasn't the only one; he'd been persistently unfaithful.'

Her tone suddenly became monotone.

'There was no way that our marriage would bounce back from that, of course, but all I felt was rage; everything I'd suppressed through the previous months crashed in on me. He asked me for an alibi . . .'

She shook her head and leant closer to Amy, and her voice regained its vigour. 'After everything, he was asking me for more. I didn't act out of rage or hatred but I cut him from my life at that moment. I detached myself completely and decided that the police would take the action he deserved.'

'Mum, he was convicted of killing them.'

'And who was I to argue? He'd deceived me time and again.'

'I thought you believed he was innocent?'

'Your father wouldn't have deliberately killed anyone; that much I never doubted. I could believe he might burn a building, but if he'd set that fire and been responsible for those deaths then I think I would have known; he couldn't have handled it.'

'Then you should have spoken out.'

'And been discredited immediately? How could I have given him a character reference when I'd been taken in by his other lies; I had no intention of even trying. He was on his own.'

'And what about the real killer?

Amy stared at her mum in bewilderment; her mum met her gaze, her pupils dilated and her glare became dark and hard.

'That was for the police – you need to remember that my responsibility was to you and to us – I decided right then that the official verdict would be the only one that mattered in our home. It wasn't to spite you, but to protect us both.'

'Someone else murdered Theo and Nadine and by keeping quiet you've helped them get away with it.'

'There's no proof that I could have made any difference.'

'That's a weak excuse. Neil and Stan and Moira all hate Dad and why wouldn't they? But I'm going in there every day and hoping that eventually I'll be able to prove them wrong.'

'You're wasting your time.'

'In your opinion. Perhaps you couldn't have changed the verdict but you should have tried.'

She shook her head slowly and stared at Amy through unrepentant eyes. It seemed as though she couldn't comprehend what she'd done or maybe that she had no intention of trying to see it in any other way but her own.

Her mum's expression didn't change even as Amy gathered her bag and coat and hurried to her feet. When Amy had first arrived she'd thought she'd seen remorse, or at least hope of reconciliation, but now she saw that her mum was too far along her path to turn around. 'You're wrong,' Amy told her firmly.

'And you have a lot to learn about people.' Her mum's voice was cold but it wasn't hard to see the pain in her eyes.

Part of Amy wanted to reach out then but instead she swung her bag onto her shoulder and turned away. It caught the edge of a flowerpot, sending the spider plant crashing onto the quarry-tiled floor. The pot split open and the dry soil scattered. She felt the leaves break underfoot as she stumbled towards the door. She was sorry, but not sorry enough that she was prepared to stop and clear it up.

The plant had been several generations on from the one she'd originally bought with her pocket money. Her mum had kept it going, transferring it from pot to pot, from elder plant to younger plant to retain the link back to the one she'd been given. Amy doubted whether her mum even liked it much and that had made Amy love what it had represented.

But not any more.

CHAPTER 10

Amy returned to her desk at 1.25 p.m. Both Stan and Moira's desks faced hers but neither of them made any comment at her curtailing her extended lunch.

Stan left a few minutes later. 'Do you still want the overtime?' Moira asked once he was out of earshot.

'Yes, please.'

She watched Stan haul himself into the cab of the pickup. She often studied them both when they were unaware of it. She had slight and shadowy memories of them from her childhood. Stan on the local news, outside the court shouting at the camera. She mostly remembered the horrified gasp from her mum when she'd accidentally seen it. She guessed that the way she'd been scooped up and away from the TV had lodged it permanently in her brain.

Stan was only in his forties now but could have been ten years older; his broad frame was still formidable but the years of working outside had left his arms and face crazed with fine lines, his knuckles dark and gnarled like tortoise skin. He seemed the easier one of them to gauge. He was comfortable with being able to use his bulk and gruff manner to deal with everyone from the men working on site to the customers themselves. Neither Neil Frampton nor Moira reacted to him, though, and after the first few weeks Amy's nerves around him had settled. The van left the yard and Amy turned her attention back to Moira.

'Can I ask you something?'

Her only recollection of Moira was like a cardboard dress-up doll where the clothes and the face and hair all have neat edges and it's all precise and two-dimensional. Amy liked the memory; Moira had a precise way of working too and everything she said seemed measured and voiced only after careful consideration. 'Would it be connected to your father?'

'He told me more about the fire.' Amy didn't know what kind of reaction she'd expected. Moira watched her, her gaze steady.

'He's always told me he had nothing to do with it. I doubt that's changed.'

'You say that with conviction.'

'Your father . . .' she paused and Amy wondered whether there was going to be more to the sentence. She rested both elbows on the table top and pressed her hands together. Her hair was neat and straight and ash blonde, just as it had always been and the whole effect was of near perfect symmetry. She blinked slowly. 'Your father burnt down that house. He was guilty, Amy.'

'You were his friend.'

Moira shook her head. 'Meaning what? That I'm not allowed to believe the worst about him? We were friends when we worked together, not when he killed two people.'

'And what if he didn't start that fire?'

'Amy, I knew you'd want this conversation at some point, but I don't. Neil wants you to have a job and that's fine, but don't drag me into any discussion about your father or that fire. There's no point going over it.'

'Not for you.'

'Or for Stan. Drop the subject around us.'

'I know he didn't do it.'

Moira's expression darkened, 'No,' she snapped. She stopped, took a breath and then continued more carefully. 'You're his daughter, you'll see him in a different light, but the Robert I knew wasn't the straightest arrow. He worked hard as a last resort; if he saw a shortcut he'd go for it.'

'That doesn't make him guilty, does it?'

'He blurred the boundaries. He ran up debts that the company had to pay.'

'It was his company.'

'Half his company,' Moira corrected, 'but not his money to screw around with. He was always pushing, living it large as they say.'

'It doesn't mean . . .'

'I used to turn a blind eye to his behaviour; he had charm and I liked to think he'd never do anything too serious. But, looking back, I can see that something had to give. And that house fire would have paid back a substantial hole in company funds.' Moira's expression was resolute. 'I'm sorry, Amy, but I really think you need to let it go.'

Amy looked away. Nothing in the room moved apart from the persistent click of the second hand as it marched around the clock face. 'So you believe he was capable of murder?' she asked quietly.

Moira's voice softened again. 'It's hard to believe that someone you've trusted could do that, but I'm sorry, that is what I think.'

Amy's view of the yard took in three one-and-a-half-storey, red-brick walls broken only by a tight gateway. It would have been more than wide enough for the horses that had originally hauled carts loaded with sacks of coal for delivery to the local houses. She often pictured them standing obediently in this airless rectangle, their lungs thick with the coal dust that had impregnated the brickwork and still left dust shadows on her Portakabin window.

Their vans struggled through the gateway. The entrance gate was striped by gouges and paint scrapes from being clipped by bumpers and wing-mirrors but those horses and their soot-faced drivers were what she pictured whenever she wanted respite from the continual paperwork.

Right now the other desks stood empty, the vans had returned for the night and the halogen lamp over the doorway would shine from dusk. Dusk came sooner to this yard than to the rest of Cambridge.

Her phone vibrated and her gaze slid from the window to the word 'Mum' flashing up at her from her desktop. She let it go to voicemail but after that her thoughts returned to their earlier conversation.

She worked for less than ten minutes after that, but noticed how the darkness was closing in on the yard. She needed the overtime but right now had lost her appetite to be here and on her own. She shifted the invoices to the back of her desk; she'd worked through less than half and done nothing on the other paperwork. 'Shit.' She shook her head. She felt spooked and tried to convince herself that the feeling was irrational; there had been plenty of times when Stan and Moira had left her alone in the office. Why should loss of daylight be a big deal? It was only a little after six. Early evening.

Fifteen minutes, she told herself.

She found the keys to the filing cabinets and rolled open the fourth of the sixteen drawers. She removed a bundle of papers from halfway through the suspension files and took them back to her desk. She read each page. It had taken a while for Moira to leave her on her own in the evenings but each hour of overtime now included quarter of an hour of searching the next document available. She wasn't sure what she needed to find but as long as she worked here then there was the chance of finding something.

But not tonight.

She relocked the filing cabinets then double-checked the storeroom door, knowing that it too would be secure but telling herself that it still needed to be tested just in case.

In the kitchenette she washed the mugs. She had always washed her own but never left anyone else's dirty either and over the past months she'd become the only one who seemed to bother with Stan's. She liked the routine and the feeling that she'd achieved a task, no matter how insignificant, before the end of each day. Her ritual was to leave straight afterwards, to pick up her bag and coat, to scan the room once, turn out the light and lock the door behind her. It felt symbolic although she never understood why.

She pulled on the handle and forced the key to turn. A ripple of movement reflected in the half-glazed door, the distorted shape of a man loomed close behind her. She turned sharply. 'Stan?' Her tone fell halfway between surprise and guilt.

'You're leaving already? I thought you wanted the extra hours.'

'I do.'

He eyed her carefully, as he often did. His expression stayed neutral and, as usual, she found herself trying to guess which way the conversation was about to head. He never wanted her here, she was always conscious of that and maybe that was why speaking to him always felt forced. Sometimes tense and forced, and other times polite but still forced. This time she felt on edge and she was aware of the illogical urge to say the right thing.

'I can come in early tomorrow.'

'What time would you have billed for today?'

'Just the hours I worked, Stan.'

'Because we're happy for you to do the overtime but that doesn't mean we're happy to be taken for a ride.'

She turned so that she faced him more squarely. 'Is that really something you think I'd do?'

'The problem is, I don't know what you will do. Questioning Moira was a mistake. Don't do it again, Amy.' He stepped aside. 'I'll see you tomorrow then.'

'Goodnight, Stan.'

She was halfway across the yard when he called after her, 'There's nothing here for you.'

She kept walking towards the gateway and the street lights on the pavement outside.

CHAPTER 11

Goodhew sent Gully a text, 'Would you help me with something?' And as soon as he received her one-word reply he knocked on her door. He knew where she lived but had never been to her house. She shared with two others but he had never met them either.

A slim woman in her mid-twenties opened the door; she had purple-tipped hair and matching eye shadow and held a pot of Häagen-Dazs. The spoon protruded from her mouth. She stepped aside to let him in.

'I'm a friend of Sue's.'

She pulled out the spoon. 'Gary, right? I'm Zoe. She said it would be you. She's in the kitchen.' She waved towards the far end of the hallway.

Gully was crossing the kitchen with two mugs of coffee, and she set them on the table. 'Or there's beer?'

'This is fine.'

'I didn't say yes to helping.'

'You said "*what?*" and that means you're curious.'

'You could have just phoned. Or did you need to see me in person to check whether things are awkward between us?' She lifted the mug but paused before taking a sip, watching for his response.

'Are they?'

'I think we should keep working together until they're not.'

He barely smiled but could tell she'd recognised that he felt the same. He took a slip of paper from his pocket and passed it to her. 'This needs to be discreet but I want to find this woman.'

Gully read the note then frowned. 'Melanie Franks or Jane Williams?'

'They're the same person. Melanie Franks was a pregnant student in 1991. My grandparents helped her disappear and from then on she used that alias.'

Gully's frown deepened. 'I don't understand.'

Goodhew drew a deep breath and began to explain about his grandparents' work. He was only a couple of sentences in when Gully stopped him. 'Now I get it,' she grinned, 'I always knew your grandmother had a past.'

'Their work was very low-key apparently.'

'I bet it wasn't. So what's this Melanie's story?'

'My grandmother didn't know too much at the time. They relocated Melanie to Hereford and that should have been it but, after his death, my grandmother – Ellie that is – I need to call them Ellie and Joe now – Ellie found a note in his handwriting and she thinks Melanie may have been in touch with him.'

'That's a long shot.'

'I hoped you'd help me track her down.'

'What do you know?'

He flicked the note. 'That's about it. She was studying history and her child would have been born in 1991.'

'And that's it?'

'Pretty much. I'll find her family. They never reported her missing so she may have kept telephone contact.'

'And what exactly do you think I'll be able to do?'

'There's more leeway to look for information while Marks is here. That gives me until next Friday to trawl through as much as possible. You're great with databases and you know your way round the archives.'

She blinked. 'Who told you that?'

'You did.'

'When?' She'd tried to sound casual but there was an unmistakable edge to her voice.

He pretended not to notice and replied lightly, 'When you spotted Joe's case.'

She drained her coffee mug and turned away to put it in the sink. 'Of course I did. I suppose I have a rough idea of the layout.'

She rinsed the mug thoroughly then refilled it with cold water and sipped that as she returned to sit at the table. 'I can look but I'd need a starting point.'

'I know you do. I'll let you know as soon as I find something, then will you search?'

'Yes, and in the meantime, I'll check health and employment databases. Anything I can sneak a peek at.' The pink that had risen in her cheeks subsided again and, to anyone who didn't know her, she would have seemed unperturbed.

'Do you need help searching for anything?'

She had regained full control of herself and didn't react. 'Like?'

He eyed her carefully. 'Whatever took you to the archives in the first place?'

She brushed it away. 'It was a pet project, a diversion. It doesn't matter now, I've finished.'

'If you're sure?'

'I'd rather chase this.' She folded the piece of paper he'd given her and tucked it under her mug. 'I'll start tomorrow. And I'm on earlies so unless there's anything else?'

'Actually, there is.' He passed her the bangle. 'I need to trace this.'

She held it above her head so that the light from the ceiling shone through it. 'Trace what exactly? Who it belongs to or where it was bought?'

'Either. Both.'

'There's no kind of maker's mark. It could be a cheap mass-produced piece. Too late for fingerprints, I suppose?'

'I checked for prints as soon as I got it. I found some but I guess they'll turn out to be my grandmother's.'

'Ellie's.'

'Yes, Ellie's,' he repeated.

'How soon will you get them back?'

60

'I'll give them to Finn in the morning. He might find something but I'd say it's too late.'

'Yeah, maybe.' She continued to study the bangle, squinting at it now. 'Have you looked under a magnifying glass?'

'I photographed it, then enlarged the shot.'

She screwed up her nose. 'That's more this century, isn't it? And?'

He handed her his phone with the zoomed-in image filling the screen. 'What do you think?'

She held it a few inches from her face and moved her finger across the screen to bring different sections of the picture into focus.

She was studying the 2 mm filaments that were trapped within the acrylic, then looked up, puzzled. 'They're all tiny and pretty much uniform. It looks like hair, but is it?'

'That's what I wondered.'

'Not mass-produced then.'

'Hopefully not. Have you come across anything similar?'

'Locally? No, but I know there used to be a fashion for insects suspended in Lucite. This is the same kind of thing. And Ellie gave it to you?'

'Found it among Joe's possessions.'

She handed it back to him. 'Why ask me what's inside when you already know?'

'I wanted a second opinion before I broke it apart.'

CHAPTER 12

Finlay Beavan had given up on contact lenses; his hours were too irregular and he'd never mastered the right routine. After three months of red eyes and irritation he'd made peace with his heavy-framed glasses and accepted that it was time to embrace his own nerdiness. Contact lenses hadn't been a secret for success with women either. Right now, though, he and his glasses were close to falling out. He dumped them on the workbench and closed his eyes. With his elbows on the work surface he covered his face, using the heel of his hands to block out every intrusive ray from the stark artificial light.

He must have dozed because he heard nothing before he snapped his eyes open at the sound of a familiar voice.

'Finn?'

His blurry vision readjusted. 'Hold on, Gary, hold on.' He found his glasses. 'I dozed off again. I was working but I think over a problem, rest my eyes and bam. Out like a light.'

'Maybe you should go home at night? Being first in and last out doesn't prove anything.'

'I know.' Everyone from his mum to his boss told him the same. 'And it leads to mistakes and depression and loss of the social life that I never had anyway.'

Finn spotted a paper bag in Goodhew's hand, 'What have you got for me today?'

Goodhew passed it across. 'From Sue.'

Finn tucked the bag in the drawer without needing to look. She sent him chocolate digestives as a bribe to fast-track results. He couldn't open them in the lab so it was her way of making him get fresh air and take a five-minute break. A sisterly-type gift, he'd concluded, when the contact lenses had failed to work on her. He still appreciated the biscuits, though. 'Does she need me to do something?'

'No, I do, but she sent them anyway.'

Goodhew took two evidence bags from his jacket pocket and placed them side by side in front of Finn. 'One has some acrylic pieces and the other has the prints I lifted from it. I think they'll be recent. Prints couldn't last twenty years on a surface like this, could they?'

'If the resin hadn't quite set . . .'

'No, after that.'

'Not unless there was a residue of some kind on the fingertips.' Finn repositioned the bag on the work surface and shone a magnifying lamp onto it. 'I'll take a look.'

'I know it's a long shot.'

'This was some kind of bracelet, right?'

'Yes. And I have to level with you, this isn't evidence, it's something I've been given . . .'

'As a gift?'

'If you like. And I want to find out whether it could be evidence.'

'So this is personal?'

Goodhew nodded.

Finn grinned. 'Cool. I never get to do anything that bends the rules.'

'This doesn't.'

Finn's face fell. 'But it might?'

'At a push.'

Finn peered through the magnifying lens at the bangle that lay in three pieces inside the bag. The breaks were clean. 'It's been broken recently. Did you do it?'

'Yes, to see whether it was possible to extract the hairs. Are they human?'

'I believe so. I can extract a sample, put it under the microscope. I can't tell yet how the polymer has bonded to the hair itself. How much analysis are you hoping for?'

'What's possible?'

Finn didn't reply immediately. He knew that Goodhew would sit quietly while he worked. He opened the evidence bag and used a scalpel to scrape away at the plastic until a single hair became free. He studied it under the microscope for a minute or two before risking any kind of answer. 'The hair has been cut at both ends, which will limit some of my analysis. Morphology, for example, may be difficult.'

'Which is what?'

'The growth phase the hair was in when it was lost. There may be no skin cells attached either.'

The hair sample was thin, a pale translucent wisp. 'It's fine hair.'

'I thought that. A child's perhaps?'

'I can't speculate. It might not be head hair. It might turn out not to be human.'

'And what about DNA?'

'Everything's possible on *CSI*. Here, I just do my best.' Finn used several variations on the same comment. Goodhew usually smiled but today his thoughts seemed elsewhere.

'And if it is a child's, can you identify the parents?'

'Familial DNA? Like I said to Sue, it is most conclusive when there is more than one sample.'

'She asked you?' Goodhew asked quickly.

'She's a few weeks ahead of you with that question, though.'

'Why did she want to know?'

Goodhew was studying him a little too closely now and Finn was glad that he didn't have an answer. He wouldn't have wanted to betray Sue's confidence but he wasn't much of a liar either. Finn picked an answer that he hoped was sufficiently vague. 'Just whether two samples would prove a relationship between two people, and I told her, "It depends."' He held up the portion of bangle. 'I'll find what I can but it won't be fast.'

'I know.' Goodhew reached for the evidence bag. 'If I take most of this you'll still have plenty to work with?'

'The more you leave, the more chance there is of a usable hair sample. Your call.'

Goodhew left the two larger sections and slipped the third back into his pocket. At the same time, he pulled out an envelope and handed it to Finn. 'I took my grandmother's prints for elimination.'

Finn double-blinked. 'So this is connected to your grandfather's case?'

'Depending where it leads me.'

This time Finn didn't take the envelope. 'I don't need it. I know Ellie Goodhew's prints are on file.'

'Really?'

'Look.' He moved to his PC, rattled through a couple of menus then pulled up the relevant records, a close up of Ellie Goodhew's right-index fingerprint filled the screen.

'Any idea why it's there?'

Finn shook his head, 'It's from 2009 but was last accessed in October.'

Goodhew didn't comment and there was no sign from his expression that the answer revealed anything. His attention stayed on the display, his gaze darting across it as if checking each whorl, lake and bifurcation.

'Can you print it?' he whispered. 'Not the image, the whole record.'

'Better, I'll email it,' Finn replied and in a couple of clicks it was gone.

CHAPTER 13

A lone coach idled in the bus bays at Drummer Street, the few pedestrians he could see looked unhurried and it was possible to pick out single sounds from the hushed city.

He checked his watch for both day and time. It was Sunday and a little before twelve. No wonder Finn had been working alone.

Goodhew picked up a takeaway coffee from Savino's but didn't attempt to drink it until he reached the market. He could remember when the market square had stood empty and the cobbled area in front of the Guildhall had always looked black and bleak on an overcast day. The current market had begun in a small way, opening for tourists and Sunday browsers; back then it had been more about antiques and curios than everyday needs. Now, it was a permanent fixture, bright striped canopies over fresh food stands and local craft stalls. He often bought fruit and artisan bread here, once he'd bought a painting too, and today he searched the rows until he spotted Kimberly Guyver's work. She drew pen-and-ink backgrounds of Cambridge scenes with women in the style of Al Moore or Gil Elvgren painted in the foreground. Her friend Mule usually looked after her stall but today it was Kimberly herself who stood next to the canvasses. She was one of the most beautiful women he'd ever met and could have modelled for pictures like these but she was only happy behind the easel. She kissed him on the cheek and hugged him. 'How are you? I heard about Ratty. I'm sorry.'

'Thanks. How's Riley?'

'At school and behaving most of the time. He's cheeky, but no vices, no virtues, right?'

'And Anita?'

'The best stand-in grandmother a kid could have.'

'Please give her my best wishes.' He paused for a moment to let the reminiscences drift away. 'I didn't expect to see you here. I thought Mule would be looking after the stall and it was him I was hoping to see.'

'He's back in Wellington for a month, fed up with our weather. What's he done?'

'Nothing. I'm looking for someone who could make a piece of jewellery, with something embedded in it.'

'In a setting, like a stone?'

'No, no.' He handed her one section of the broken bangle. 'Like this, acrylic or resin, or Lucite with the item preserved within the plastic.'

'Is the person who made it in trouble then?' Her dark eyes stared into his and she had a hint of a smile. 'I can't just blab to the police even when it's you.'

'Old habits and all that? And no, he or she isn't in any trouble.'

Kimberly brushed her hair back from her cheek then turned her head towards the Cambridge University Bookshop on the corner. 'You want Crystal; she'll be on the craft market, the one in Trinity Street. She's about my height, in her fifties and usually in the furthest corner from the gate.'

'What's her last name?'

'How would I know? Her first name's not Crystal either, it's a nickname because of what she sells. Like Mule because he makes shoes. Be nice to her,' she winked at him, 'and it's good to see you again.'

Lorraine Martin's best investment had been the workshop at the end of her garden. She'd forgone a car and had cycled to work for two years until she'd saved for it because borrowing the money had been an impossibility. That had been almost fifteen years ago and now she tried to ignore the places where the paintwork had flaked and damp had seeped into the wood, where the grain had swollen and the window no longer fitted the frame. Her plan last spring had been to wait for the summer, then to sand and fill the wood, repainting it with a weather-proof coat again. The last had been guaranteed for ten years and that had flown in the blink of an eye. But the summer had passed and good intentions had achieved nothing.

It was another reason to feel disappointed with herself; her workshop was her place of comfort, and it deserved to be cared for. Being alone had never been her strength either, but she never felt it here. Solitude yes, but not loneliness. Here, she could lose herself in her work, enjoy the silence, concentrate without listening for the doorbell and without hanging around within grabbing distance of the phone.

She always kept the windows clean though and the step outside brightened with planters, currently filled with lilac and white winter pansies.

Inside measured eight foot square, smaller than she'd originally wanted but just about affordable to heat. She worked in outdoor clothes whenever possible and only turned on the fan heater when her feet ached or her fingers became clumsy. It housed moulds and chemicals, a buffing wheel and an old map cabinet whose shallow drawers she'd filled with an assortment of bezels, clasps and decorative scraps that she thought she might one day have a need to use.

In the corner facing the door she'd squeezed in an armchair draped with woollen throws and sometimes, like last night, she'd fallen asleep to only wake at first light, the windows misted with condensation. She'd wiped them first because she never blocked the view of the garden.

It was bloody cold, but not as cold as standing still for hours at the craft market. She pitied the traders that left warm homes; at least she was acclimatised to it. She packed two boxes into her car; she had time to spare but she still skipped breakfast.

She sprayed herself with deodorant, unable to face the idea of stripping off to wash until she could soak in the bath later. She glanced at the side door that opened into her kitchen; it would be sensible to make up a flask but in truth, even going inside for the essentials held no appeal. Her own home yes, but she had been right to take no part of it into her workshop, to buy someone else's armchair and bench rather than use her own.

She pulled out of her driveway and glanced in her rear-view mirror; it had become her habit to watch her house shrink behind her.

The craft market was located in All Saints' Garden. It was fenced off from Trinity Street by wrought iron railings that flapped with laminated posters advertising local arts events and lectures.

Lorraine's stall was at the back; people generally browsed all the stalls, walking in a circle either clockwise or anti-clockwise. She'd deliberately positioned herself halfway round, hoping to catch customers when they were most immersed.

Lorraine made three sales within the first hour, then nothing for the next few. She bought hot chocolate from the coffee cart and watched the pedestrians on Trinity Street, willing them to come through the gate. A man in his early thirties caught her attention. He didn't meander like most, wasn't laden with tourist shopping or walking with a companion. He was tall and lean and wove between the stalls, glancing at the items for sale but barely pausing.

There was nothing overtly familiar about him but she sensed that he was there for her. She straightened her pile of business cards then continued to fiddle with her display until he reached her.

He picked up a paperweight, turned it over a couple of times before replacing it among the other items.

'They're all handmade,' she told him. It was one of her most used opening lines.

'By you?' He looked up from the table and seemed to study her carefully.

'Of course.'

'Said with pride,' he observed. 'I'm not a customer.'

She didn't respond but she didn't feel threatened by him either. At least, not by him specifically. But her hands were back in her pockets now, with the nail of each thumb digging into the side of the corresponding index finger. She waited for him to speak, trying to keep her mind clear of any panic, even though she had no reason to worry.

'My name's DC Gary Goodhew.'

'Police?' He didn't look like a policeman. He looked like someone's brother. Someone's son. She shook her head at her own lack of logic. He asked for her details but she must have seemed suspicious or bewildered or maybe just slow because he showed her his ID before asking her again.

She murmured her name but was fixed on his. She hadn't registered until she saw his identification. GOODHEW. It could have been a coincidence but for those same green eyes.

She studied him, trying to recall the features too, but failing.

'Are you all right?' he asked.

She nodded, clutching at the thought that his face seemed kind. 'What's happened?'

In answer he held out a section of a bangle. She wasn't sure if she was meant to touch it but reached for it in any case.

'I'm trying to find the person who made this,' he said.

The bangle had been snapped and she ran her thumb over the broken surface.

'Is it one of yours?' he asked.

The last time she'd held this it had been whole, unmarked and barely worn. Would it be surprising if she didn't recognise it now? Or had this young detective spotted the involuntary widening of her eyes and the way her winter-red cheeks must have paled at his name.

'Yes,' she replied, 'it's one of mine.'

'You hesitated.'

'I wasn't sure,' she lied. 'It's so badly damaged. What happened to it?'

He took it from her and was about to speak when he stopped himself. For a moment he looked beyond her, past the railings and along All Saints' Passage.

'I'm not here officially,' he told her. 'You don't have any obligation to answer my questions and this,' he tapped the bangle, 'this isn't evidence yet. But I'm hoping you'll help because . . .'

'Because of your grandfather?' she replied.

And it was his turn to look startled.

The photographer on the adjacent stand had agreed to watch Lorraine's jewellery and they'd retreated to the nearest café. Goodhew noticed that Lorraine Martin often hesitated before she answered questions, long enough to rehearse the answer silently before trying it for real.

The current pause was the longest so far.

'I met your grandfather once, shortly before he died. He brought that bangle to me because he wanted to find its owner. I was shocked when I read about his death.'

'In the paper?'

'Yes, in the death notices. I had promised to contact him if I came across anything. I didn't realise he was ill.'

'He wasn't. It was an assault and I'm hoping to shed light on it.'

'It's a long time ago.' She took a few seconds to consider her own comment. 'But not so long when it's your own family.'

'What do you remember?'

She stirred her coffee and her gaze wandered outside. Memories could prove stubborn after twenty two years but sometimes the truth was stubborn too. Goodhew needed her to cooperate.

'Obviously I have my grandfather's notes,' he lied, 'but only up to when he spoke to you.'

'I can't remember word for word.'

'As much as you can then.'

'The bangle was a gift, ordered by a girl named Melanie.' He sensed that Lorraine was testing him now.

He leant closer and tried hard to look unsurprised. 'Melanie Franks? Yes, he mentioned her. Go on.'

'He said he needed to find her.'

'Why?'

'I don't know.'

'He could have asked you that without bringing the bangle. Why was it significant?'

'Because I made it, I suppose. I don't know.'

'Maybe because of what's in it? Child's hair or baby hair?'

Lorraine's eyes flickered for a second then met his gaze again.

'Melanie was pregnant.'

'And it's her baby's hair?'

'Yes.'

He wasn't buying it. 'Did she have a boy or a girl?' He fired the question back at her.

And again she hesitated. 'A girl, I think.'

Goodhew's expression hardened. 'I thought you knew her?'

Lorraine sat back in her chair and clasped her hands together in her lap. 'Not really,' she murmured.

'You see,' Goodhew continued, 'according to my grandfather's notes she'd left Cambridge before her child was born.'

It seemed obvious to Goodhew that Lorraine Martin had been quick to give him a false answer but wasn't an accomplished enough liar to sustain the story. 'She phoned me, I suppose.'

'And what? Posted the hair so you could make the bangle? You know that doesn't add up.'

Lorraine knew she'd been caught. She fell silent and chewed her bottom lip.

'It's not her baby's hair, is it?' he pushed.

'No, it's Nadine's baby.'

'Nadine who?'

She shook her head and stared at him thoughtfully. 'I'm sorry, the truth is I can't remember the details. Melanie cleared off and I was hoping you'd let slip about where she'd gone.'

'So let me get this straight.' Goodhew leant across the table and lowered his voice. 'I turn up over twenty years later and you suddenly have the urge to catch up on an old friend? Why would you?'

Lorraine gave a small smile but Goodhew knew he was just supposed to see the sadness behind it. 'For old time's sake, I suppose.' She held out her hands, palms upwards. 'To know she's OK. She was terrified before she left.'

'So the bangle didn't belong to her, did it?'

Lorraine could have stuck to her story but, instead, she was quick to back down. 'No, I made it for her friend Nadine. And, before you ask, I don't remember the rest of her name, but Melanie would.'

'One more question, was this before or after Melanie left the area?'

This time Lorraine's reply was immediate. 'Afterwards.'

Goodhew continued to watch her after they'd parted company. He wondered whether her first action would be to call someone and tell them about his visit. Instead, she stood with her back to the railings and stared at the dwindling numbers of potential customers with no apparent interest. She hung around until the market closed at four then shook herself from her stupor and began to pack away, methodically at first but then with increased haste.

Goodhew grabbed a taxi and sat inside, watching her until she was ready to leave. He'd checked her address by then and followed her to make sure that was where she was headed. He then asked the driver to drop him further along her street. He walked back and waited a little way along from her house. He watched her enter her house, turn on the lights, come back outside to unload her car and then, half an hour later, dim the lights in the front room. The only movement from behind the thin curtains was the perpetual dancing of the light from the TV screen. He walked to the nearest shop, bought a sandwich, then walked back along the street one more time. At 7.30 p.m. he headed home.

CHAPTER 14

Lorraine poured herself a tumbler of red wine and took it and the rest of the newly opened bottle through to the front room. She turned on the TV and channel-hopped for several minutes but despite all the choices there seemed nothing to watch. She left it playing the news channel, hoping it might throw up an item to distract her until the wine took over, but instead her thoughts stayed with Goodhew.

Both Goodhews.

The elder had come to see her and then, just a few days afterwards, he'd died. She'd always wondered about the timing and the rumour that he'd been beaten. If she'd triggered that attack, then she could endanger the grandson now.

If.

And if it had been a coincidence, then keeping quiet to the younger Goodhew now would be a mistake.

If.

And what if she could pass on enough information for Melanie to be found?

Another if.

An hour later the bottle had gone. She went to the kitchen and returned with a second. She remembered Nadine so clearly, not like Joe Goodhew or like Melanie who both existed in her memory as sketches. Nadine had remained a defined image. She'd had old-fashioned features: round face and large dark eyes, small heart-shaped mouth and slender girlish figure. The kind of looks that might have been in vogue in the 1920s or '30s. Lorraine could still see the way Nadine played guitar, leaning back in a chair, picking the individual strings, her small fingers deftly making the shapes of the chords. Lorraine looked at anyone who played and only sometimes spotted that same degree of rapt concentration. Maybe guilt had burnt it into her brain like that.

She phoned her sister then as she always did when she needed comfort. 'I'm going to sleep in the workshop,' she told her. 'Fuck the house.'

'Come to mine. Stay the night.' Her sister tried to sound upbeat and neither of them mentioned the six-plus glasses of wine that had begun to interfere with Lorraine's sentences.

Lorraine could hear herself becoming emphatic, trying to be logical. 'No,' she told her. 'I spoke to Joseph Goodhew and then he died. And what about the fire?'

'Not everything is a conspiracy, some things are just what they are. Bob set that fire.'

'I can see how other people benefited. Even you.'

'Lorraine, listen.'

'I have listened, but who has ever listened to me?'

'Lorraine?'

'I'm going to bed. But I'm not letting it drop. Not this time.'

'Straight to bed?'

'Promise,' Lorraine replied, but her sister's mothering was enough to send her in the opposite direction.

She ended the call. 'Fuck you and your perfect life,' she muttered to no one.

Several minutes passed before she picked up her mobile again. She began to dial but changed her mind and threw it down beside her on the settee. She wanted to be face to face, not fobbed off via the phone.

She grabbed her jacket and house keys and headed towards the city centre. She hurried, head down with her thoughts on everything she needed to say. She imagined the conversation, rehearsed her responses and found Neil Frampton, just as she guessed she would, at his desk in his private office in St Barnabas Road. She tapped the glass and he glanced up from the PC screen. His expression darkened when he saw her, but he gestured for her to wait. It had been a while since she'd seen him but at first glance he looked almost the same; he'd aged but wore the same clothes and the same hairstyle. Still trying to emulate the easy style of the City boy dressing down for the country even though he was too old and the clothes were too tight.

It seemed like a full five minutes before the front door opened. In the hallway light she saw him more clearly. He had more jowl now and an unnatural lack of lines. It might have been a couple of years since she'd seen him last. It might have been longer.

She thought she'd be allowed inside but he held it open by a foot's width. 'Why are you here?'

'I know something about Melanie.'

'What?'

She smiled knowingly.

He ran his tongue around his teeth as though trying to dislodge something unpleasant. 'You're pissed.'

'I know something,' she insisted. 'It's that detective.'

'What detective?'

'The one who died. His grandson came to see me.'

'I don't know what you're talking about.'

'The grandson is in the police. He came to see me.'

'What has that got to do with Melanie?'

'He knew her name and he had Nadine's bangle. I could have told him everything but I didn't. But I want to know something from you.'

'What?'

'Was it because of what I told him?' She could tell by his expression that she wasn't being clear. 'Back then you asked me questions and straight afterwards this policeman's grandfather died. I can tell him that but it depends on you.'

'There's nothing to tell. Go home. Sober up and keep quiet.' He shook his head. 'It's all history and we're not going back there.'

He closed the door and the small pane of glass at the top darkened as he drew the curtain behind it. She swayed a little but, apart from that, didn't move for several minutes as she debated whether to knock again, or shout, or just head home.

This wasn't right. He'd missed the point.

She banged several times on the door with the flat of her hand. 'I know,' she shouted. '*I know.*'

She felt drunk, but within the fuzziness of alcohol there was a crisp clear kernel of sense. A sober eye of her drunken storm, a place where she could see herself with complete clarity. She wasn't a bad person. And that wasn't a new thought. She was a weak person and she knew that too. She continually made herself promises and always broke them because she habitually abandoned good intentions to jump at the easy route. She'd lost count of the number of opportunities that she'd traded for quick money or short-term gains.

But this was a different kind of drunk from her usual slide into stupor. Holding that bracelet had galvanised her. She remembered so clearly when and why she'd made it.

Nadine had been one of the early ones.

She felt in her pockets and pulled out the miniature pen that always hung from her house keys and then found a single business card. She wrote quickly across the back of it then cut through onto Argyle Street with her hands clasped together and the card pressed between her palms

She was close to the other end when she became aware of a car behind her; its headlights lit the road ahead but it had slowed and seemed to be keeping pace with her. There were few spaces between the parked cars; she passed one gap and expected the vehicle to pull in. After a few yards more she glanced over her shoulder; the boxy silhouette and high wide headlight beams came from of some kind of 4x4. She kept walking, careful to be steady, unhurried, not to panic.

She passed the next parking space and listened carefully, relieved as she heard it swing in and the engine still. But just a moment later the door slammed and a familiar voice called her name.

'Wait up,' he shouted.

She scowled at him but didn't walk away. 'Why are you here?'

'Just passing. Do you want a lift?'

'If I had two broken legs you wouldn't drive me home.' She folded her arms and waited for Stan to respond. He came closer without speaking. She tried again. 'What do you want?'

'Keep away from their house, don't turn up like that again.'

'But they should have listened to me; I wanted to help them.'

'They don't want to know.'

She stepped towards him but wobbled slightly, steadying herself on the nearest house wall. 'I've only ever tried to do the right thing.' She heard the tone of her own voice become more insistent. 'I don't understand why you have a problem.'

'Because *you* are a problem. Nothing is ever left in the past with you.'

'Well, I'm not going anywhere because I know that one day they'll listen.' She waved her finger at him. 'They can turn me away all they like, but one day . . .'

'You haven't got anything they want.' He moved closer and the air around her seemed to still. 'It's Melanie's address or nothing and you don't have it.'

She broke the silence that followed with a short laugh, 'And when I get it? Then they'll change their minds, I suppose?' she shook her head as she stepped away, 'Forget it, I won't bother them again.'

'And I can tell them that?'

'Be my guest.'

She walked away without looking back. After a few seconds of silence, she heard the 4x4's door slam shut and its engine turn over. She held the business card a little more tightly and kept walking.

CHAPTER 15

Amy had worked at Frampton's for enough time to recognise people on her way to work. One or two of them smiled at her now and she smiled back, occasionally said good morning. She could spot anomalies in their routines; the days when the woman in the blue coat from ten-to didn't cross paths with her until five-past. Or when the nervous man wasn't at the bus stop or the lady with the red setter failed to appear from Mill Road cemetery. Mondays were days when people were more likely to run late but this time everyone had been on cue and the day felt comfortably normal until she turned in to Cockburn Street and spotted the first pulse of blue emergency lights from the far end of the road. She could pick out just a single police car at first, parked at the corner of Argyle Street. Her route. Cars still moved freely past her but access to the side road had been barred.

When she reached the junction the officer blanked her at first. His head was tilted as he spoke into his radio; an indecipherable stream of crackling words came back at him. 'No update,' he replied. He glanced along the street behind him and added a comment that she couldn't catch even without the static. Beyond him, at about the furthest point visible, there was another police car and a cluster of activity. The officer finished on the radio and then spoke to Amy. 'Can I help?'

'I work in Argyle Street, can I get through?'

'Where exactly?'

'At Frampton's,' she told him.

'The yard?'

'Yes.'

'Hang on.' He consulted his radio. 'You can go down there, but no further. We will be canvassing local homes and businesses. When were you last here?'

'Friday.'

'OK.' He stepped aside to let her through.

No one she recognised was out on the street now. A few house-holders stood in open doorways and shadows moved in some of the windows. The street was hushed and her footsteps fell noisily. Ahead of her, maybe a hundred yards beyond the entrance to Frampton's, the police had sealed the road. An officer stood facing her, his back to the cluster of vehicles and the people milling between them. A single ambulance had been parked on one side of the street, and opposite it she could see the white top of a tent. She tried not to stare, pretended disinterest for the last few metres before the gateway, then stole a final glance at the scene before turning in to the yard.

Stan stood at the window facing the entrance, Moira a few feet behind him. He actually opened the door for her too. 'What's going on now?' he asked. 'Any developments?'

'I don't know what was happening before, do I?' Amy hung her coat on the back of her chair. 'Just a lot of people behind a cordon.'

'There's a body in an alleyway,' Stan replied. 'The first car was already there before I got in and it's been lights and sirens ever since.'

'Same when I turned up,' Moira added. 'Luckily I decided to leave the car at home today. I'm not sure I would have been allowed to drive into the street.' She held a pile of envelopes and stacked them on the end of Amy's desk. 'At least the post got through.'

'Yeah,' Stan added, 'thank God it wasn't the postie that copped it.'

'Someone did, though.'

Stan moved to his own desk but repositioned his chair so that he was within sight of the window. 'You don't lighten up much, do you?'

Amy grabbed the post and didn't reply at first. She knew from the envelopes which were invoices, which contained cheques or remittance advices. She blotted out the next few comments too. Stan gave them an update each time an official vehicle of any kind passed the gateway.

Moira ignored him too.

Finally, Amy spoke. 'What if we're not interested, Stan?'

'What happened to your dignified silence, Amy?' he smirked.

Her finger was inserted into the next envelope. She ripped it roughly. 'It's none of our business.'

'I bet you looked at what was going on, same as the rest of us.'

'I looked down the road,' she conceded, 'but I'm not standing with my nose pressed to the glass.' She removed an invoice. Mixed with the post was a clutch of advertising literature, the usual supermarket offers and leaflets for solar panels. One of these, an advert for replacement windows, had been folded into a makeshift envelope. 'AMY' was scored into the shiny paper with heavy blue biro. 'I'm surprised you're not out there holding up the police tape.'

Moira shot a warning glance in Amy's direction. Stan leant forward with his elbows on the desk. 'It's not a problem, Moira. No harm done.'

Amy didn't bother replying; shutting up and staying quiet was the best response to his glibness but she'd lost all interest in that conversation anyway

'Amy.' He had to repeat her name twice before she looked at him.

'What?'

'I'm sorry if I hit a nerve,' he told her. She studied his expression for any sign of sarcasm and saw nothing.

'I was too young to remember much.'

'But even so . . .' he replied, his words petering out mid-sentence, but she knew what he was trying to say.

'Thank you,' she replied.

The 'envelope' contained nothing but a business card. That happened sometimes. Usually a plasterer or a plumber angling for work. But never delivered like this. And this card was ornate, not functional, foil-printed on heavy stock, in an embellished script that read 'Lorraine Martin Designs' and a mobile number. She thought the name meant nothing but a chill ran along the back of her neck. She turned it over. 'Amy, ring me' was scrawled across it in smudged blue ink. She glanced at Stan and Moira but neither had noticed her startled reaction.

She opened the pen tray in her desk and placed the card, logo upwards, among the paperclips and staples.

CHAPTER 16

Gully caught up with Goodhew in the corridor leading to the briefing room. He shot a glance at the closed door in front of them. 'What do you know about this?'

'Suspicious death, female body found in an alleyway in Argyle Street.'

'That's all?' he queried.

'Why, what do you know?'

'The same.'

She didn't reply but they both knew it had to be more than just accident or misadventure.

They pushed open the door. Marks stood at the front of the room and to Gully's surprise there were only a few officers present. She was the only uniformed officer but Marks had warned her this would be the case. The others were out already, going door to door. Maybe he thought being the least experienced officer and the only PC might intimidate her. It didn't.

She'd worked with them all before. DCs Sandra Knight, Kev Holden and Jack Worthington were all old hands but relatively new to Marks's team, Aaron Clarke was on his first day back after a brief secondment to London and, of course, there was Kincaide. DS Kincaide. The DS still made her feel slightly nauseous.

He'd marched through the door a few paces ahead of them and stood to one side of Marks holding papers and an envelope. He probably thought it gave him authority; in her opinion he looked like the magician's assistant.

She and Goodhew took the nearest available seats.

The board behind Marks held two items. The first was a section of map showing a close-up of Argyle Street and its adjoining roads. The location of the body had been marked with a circle of tangerine highlighter. Next to it was a single photo, a crime-scene shot of a woman's body abandoned in a narrow brick passageway. Sue knew the street and could picture the gap that ran between two terraces.

The woman was half lying and half sitting, like a puppet where the strings had been cut, her limbs folding to the floor, her flaccid neck dropping her chin to her chest. In the corner of Gully's vision she saw Goodhew lean closer. She turned in time to see curiosity grow to consternation.

Marks had taken the pages from Kincaide and had just begun to speak as Goodhew cut in. 'Do we know her identity, sir?'

Marks caught his expression immediately. 'Do you recognise this woman, Goodhew?'

'From that picture? I'm not sure.'

Marks turned over the sheet in his hand and held a 10x8 photograph out to Goodhew. There was plenty of time for Gully to look at it too. It showed a close-up of a woman in her mid-fifties. She had tired eyes and deep lines around her mouth. Her hair was mid-brown and shoulder length, badly cut in a style that hadn't suited her and had made her thin face look even thinner. None of that mattered now.

She looked up from the photo in time to see Goodhew nodding. 'It's Lorraine Martin,' he told Marks.

'How do you know her?'

She glanced around; this conversation had an audience.

'She had a stall on the craft market, in All Saints' Garden. I met her there yesterday.'

'Yesterday?' One eyebrow flickered. 'Regarding what?'

'I was asking her advice on an item of jewellery.'

Someone sniggered. It wasn't Marks. He just exhaled slowly. 'A little more information would be useful, Gary.'

'It's a bangle that Lorraine Martin made.'

'And where is it now?'

'Finn Beavan has most of it. I have the rest.'

'It's broken?'

'It is.'

Marks tipped his head in the direction of the door. 'A word?'

Goodhew followed him into the corridor and through the frosted panel in the door Sue could see the dark and unmoving shape of Marks standing with his shoulder close to the glass. They spoke very briefly, then they returned and Marks addressed the room: 'Goodhew will be making a statement.' Then to Goodhew, 'What can you tell us about yesterday that is relevant to this briefing?'

Goodhew explained his conversation with Lorraine Martin. 'I'm sure there was more than she was admitting.'

Marks studied Goodhew carefully throughout. It was an expression that Gully knew well and it didn't miss much, then she saw his expression suddenly change. He stepped back and held out his hand for Kincaide to pass him the rest of the papers. He turned over several sheets before he found the page he was looking for. 'Ms Martin was a divorcee living alone in a house in Selwyn Road. Her only known relative is a sister living in Cambridge and formal identification of the body will take place within the hour. Initial enquiries with the neighbours have produced two independent witnesses who report seeing an IC-1 male, aged around thirty, in the street outside her house at around 7 p.m.' He tapped the page, 'The exact words are "about 6 feet tall, thin and a little unkempt. But too old to be a student." Is this you or an actual person of interest?'

Goodhew winced. 'It's me. I followed her home. I had a feeling she wasn't telling me everything. I thought I might find out more.'

'By stalking her?'

'I didn't. When it looked as though she'd settled down for the evening I left.'

Kincaide stepped forward, 'A word, sir?' Gully wondered whether he thought that echoing Marks's own words gave him some kind of authority. She sensed Marks bristle, although that may have been wishful thinking. Kincaide stepped forward and spoke quietly. She couldn't catch any of the words but Kincaide eventually nodded curtly and stepped back again with his jaw set hard.

Marks looked down at the papers as he turned to another sheet. He read it silently for a few seconds and when he spoke his tone had adopted its usual evenness. 'Preliminary examination indicates that the victim died from strangulation. There were superficial injuries, minor abrasions to the hands and one ankle as well as bruising and further abrasions to the head and face.'

He paused to pass Kincaide another photo to be pinned to the board. The upper half of Lorraine Martin's face filled the entire shot; the skin on her forehead had been scored by two patches of rough grazes. Gully guessed that the victim had hit the brickwork as she struggled. A small amount of blood stained her skin at the hairline.

Marks continued, 'As you can see I received these details only minutes before you all arrived. The alleyway is a fairly confined space and forensics will tell us whether she managed to make contact with her assailant or only with the wall.'

'What was used to strangle her?' Sue didn't look around but knew the voice was Kev Holden's. Gruff and blunt.

'A ligature of some kind. Nothing was recovered from the scene,' Marks replied.

'Definitely not manual then?'

'No.'

'No chance of fingerprints; that's a shame. What about motive then?'

'Nothing conclusive as yet.'

'Unless Gary did it.' Worthington quipped.

'Thank you, Jack, but let's assume it wasn't DC Goodhew, shall we?' Marks didn't appear amused and Gully wished he would glance over his shoulder in time to see Kincaide's expression break into a predictable smirk. 'However, we do have to look at any possible connection to Ms Martin's conversation with Gary. I am no fan of coincidence but it may be just that. As always, pinpointing her movements in those last hours will be key, so Gary's statement will be valuable. Aside from that we will be looking at the possibility of a random attack, possibly sexually motivated. Forensics will be looking for evidence of sexual assault but we already know that her underwear had been disturbed.'

Kincaide's smirk broadened into a grin. 'Couldn't get a date, Gary?'

Marks kept his steely glare aimed at the rest of the room and Sue was certain that no one else dared to smile. 'Gary, stay behind.' He wound up the briefing swiftly then, allocating tasks to everyone else before dismissing them.

Kincaide and Worthington were behind her in the corridor. 'I was only kidding,' Worthington laughed.

'I wasn't. Someone as tightly wound as Goodhew's got to get his kicks somehow. I'd love to pin it on him.'

'Or we could catch the bastard that did it . . .' Worthington grunted before disappearing into a side office.

Kincaide drew alongside her and nudged her elbow. 'Don't mind us, Sue.'

She smiled coldly, 'I don't mind Worthington.'

'You should lighten up, we were just having a laugh.' Kincaide lowered his voice, 'But it wouldn't hurt to put distance between you and Goodhew either.'

She didn't respond but Kincaide carried on in any case.

'He's been unravelling for months, he's become reckless and unstable. He's not going to last in here. If he doesn't get himself killed, he'll be sacked. You watch; he will crash and burn. And then where will you be?' They walked down the first flight of stairs. She hung back to see which direction he would head, planning to choose the other. Instead, he stopped and motioned *after you*, then followed her. A few seconds later he tapped her arm and then lowered his voice again. 'I need to talk to you about something, we'll go to your desk.'

They walked side by side; he was silent until they turned into an empty corridor. He still glanced over his shoulder before he spoke. 'I know why you visit the archives,' he said. 'So how's it going, the search for your dad?'

She glanced at him sharply but he just looked ahead. Thoughts rushed through her mind but none were coherent enough to be spoken. She needed a reply, to show he hadn't shaken her. She managed to say, 'It isn't any of your business,' but her voice sounded fragile and her throat had become tight.

He glanced to his right and saw that the nearest room was empty. He put his arm behind her and seemed to sweep her inside. 'I think it is,' he continued. 'I went down there and checked out your paper trail. It took me a while but it was easy once I saw your mum's name and the date she was attacked. And your date of birth of course. The thing is, I work with you and I'm finding it hard to see you in the same way. I keep thinking of rotten fruit falling from rotten trees.' He screwed up his face. 'Unpleasant, isn't it? And how do you think everyone else will feel about you? Docs Gary know?'

Why was this happening? She pressed her lips tight and gave an almost imperceptible shake of her head.

'I didn't think so. Of course, on the face of it, we'll all be understanding. Logically speaking it's hardly your fault.'

'Stop it, Michael.' She kept her voice low; as much as she hated this it was better here than out in the corridor. 'Stop.'

'I read the files, the rape of your mother was extremely violent. Degrading.'

She backed up a little, her brain still scrambling for words. 'There's anonymity for rape victims.'

'Not from us Sue, you know that; we're the ones looking for the bastard.' He grinned. 'The bastard that's your dad. And there's your problem; it isn't your fault but how many of us will, hand on heart, be able to see you in the same way? Nature versus nurture and you can't escape your genes.'

She looked past him to the door.

'You're tainted,' he murmured.

Sue knew she was close to breaking down, but she wasn't going to allow it. Not in front of him. 'What do you want?'

'Just for you to know that I know. To think about how it will feel when everybody looks at you differently, when Gary pretends to feel the same but you know he's secretly repelled. Haven't you had that feeling about yourself?'

She shook her head even though it was true; her parents had made her feel completely loved but her own feelings of revulsion had always lurked.

'Once it's out, Sue, it can't be undone.'

'So what do you want?'

'You should think about your future here. That's all. Like I said before, Gary will crash and burn and I want you to stand clear. I want you to distance yourself from him.' Kincaide opened the door for her then followed her back out into the corridor.

She wanted to reply but found herself retreating wordlessly.

'Don't burn your bridges, Sue,' he called out as she walked away.

CHAPTER 17

The door hadn't finished closing when Marks began to speak, 'Can I see it?' Goodhew handed him the broken piece of bangle. Marks pressed his lips together, narrowing his eyes as he studied it, 'And you broke this, I suppose?' He didn't wait for an answer. 'It needs to go into evidence at once.'

'I know.'

'How did it end up with you, Gary? I'm guessing there's a connection to your grandfather?'

Goodhew hadn't explained it during the briefing but filled Marks in on his grandmother's revelation.

Marks ran back over it, paraphrasing what Goodhew had told him. 'So it was an item that was unfamiliar to your grandmother when she found it in his desk?'

'That's correct.'

'And Lorraine Martin and your grandmother both knew the name Melanie Franks?'

'Is it enough to link the two cases?'

'Tentatively. It's certainly too much to ignore.' He pinched the bridge of his nose and tapped his forehead lightly with his index finger. 'There doesn't seem to be anything in what you did yesterday that could have triggered this attack. But it can't be treated as a random assault.'

Goodhew and Lorraine had stood in the open together at the market. Perhaps someone saw them together then or in the café. Or spotted him standing outside her house. But it would only be relevant if that person also thought that Goodhew posed some kind of threat. He didn't buy it. 'She must have contacted someone.'

'I've made the phone records the highest priority.'

'What about email and social media?'

'No smartphone, no tablet, no PC. Not even Wi-Fi in the house so it was text, phone call or face to face. The old-fashioned way of communicating, not like this,' Marks jiggled the mobile in his hand. 'It's buzzing like a news wire.' He placed it on the seat of the chair next to him. He suddenly stilled. 'Is there anything else you're not telling me, Gary?'

'Such as?'

He didn't reply but didn't look convinced by Goodhew's reply either. 'The files relating to your grandfather's case are up from the archive. I had them sent to Sheen's office, safer there than most other places in this building.'

Sergeant Sheen guarded his desk and accumulated paperwork carefully; Goodhew was the only person Sheen ever accused of snooping around up there and Goodhew suspected that he only got away with it because Sheen let him. 'That's a good idea, thank you, sir.'

'And I want Sheen there when you go through the files. If there's anything that's pertinent to this case, then it needs to be flagged up immediately. As soon as we officially connect the two cases then you are also a witness in both. You weren't acting in an official capacity when you questioned Lorraine Martin so your position on the team is something that has to be handled very carefully. In fact, I'd move you on to something else right now if we weren't so desperate for resources. Don't put a foot wrong. Do you understand?'

'Yes sir.'

'Get that bangle into evidence and your statement done before anything else.'

Marks was right; there was nothing Goodhew wanted more than to start going through those files. But, as Goodhew wrote his statement, he felt himself being drawn elsewhere.

It took him thirty minutes to walk to Lorraine Martin's house in Selwyn Road. There was a patrol car parked in the street opposite her house and a police Transit van blocking her car in her driveway. It was a mid-terrace, built, he guessed, just after the war. He'd seen that much last night but it had been hard to make out the detail then. The daylight revealed that the house was tidy but tired, the once white uPVC window frames were stained to grey, weeds had broken through the sparse gravel and the brickwork had been discoloured by rainwater and the spread of algae.

He hadn't come to look inside, at least, not yet; he kept walking towards the location of her body. There were several routes she might have taken and they only shared the first half-mile. For the rest he chose the route that kept to well-lit roads and avoided the footbridge that crossed the train-line. The route he chose was the one that might have seemed safest to a lone pedestrian. It was busy; easy for her to have made her way unimpeded through to Argyle Street. Despite all that, it was still a two mile walk so taxi services were being checked too. He made a list of every commercial premises that looked likely to have CCTV capturing footage of the streets. There weren't many, and he knew that it was too soon to know that this was the route she had chosen but he figured that if she had walked this way then people must have seen her.

The junction with Mill Road held promise. Cambridgeshire City Council had its own cameras at several points along the road, pointing in the right direction and recording – providing the spending cuts hadn't switched them off.

There was nothing remarkable about Argyle Street. Like the other backstreets, houses clustered up to the pavements and cars hugged the kerbs leaving narrow channels for vehicles and pedestrians alike. But, unlike the others, access was blocked by a single patrol car. A few bunches of flowers leant against the road-closed bollard. PC Ted Moorey stood to its right clutching a clipboard.

He grinned very briefly when he saw Goodhew. 'How's it going?'

'That's what I came to find out.'

Moorey was of slight build with a teenage complexion and just-out-of-bed hair. 'I was doing door to door but we swapped over and now I'm freezing my nuts off here.' He looked like he should have been at sixth form.

'Any results so far?'

'Nothing much, plenty of residents have gone to work. The family who live opposite the alleyway have a new baby, and when she woke they heard some kind of scuffle, put it down to cats scrapping, but they reckon that was after twelve.'

'That figures. If it had been much earlier I'm sure someone would have alerted us and she wouldn't have been out there all night.'

'It's a narrow alley, though, and plenty of people walk around oblivious.'

Goodhew knew there was a great deal of truth in that. 'Anything on the CCTV front?'

Moorey pointed behind Goodhew to the head of the street, 'There's a shop on the corner with a dummy camera above the door, two that monitor just their entrances so there's a slim chance there and a street cam on the city side of the junction. I logged the number of that one and I'll put in a request for footage from the council as soon as I get back.' Then he turned and faced in the direction of the body as he spoke, his words less audible, 'One down there but they reckon they don't pick up the footpath.'

'You sound doubtful, Ted.'

'Just that it's a builder's yard and it looks like the camera's angled onto their gateway, which would catch part of the footpath too. I'd want a good shot of the entrance if I was them.'

'I'll take a look. What else?'

'The body went a while ago. I relieved Tommo and he's doing door to door with Dawn at the other end of the street.'

Goodhew walked towards the spot where Lorraine's body had been found. An officer he didn't recognise stood outside the tented area that screened off the site of the body. Their investigation had sliced the road in two. Some way in the distance he could make out the shapes of PCs Charlie Thompson and Dawn Marsden as they stood side by side at an open doorway. There was little point in walking down there just to ask if they wanted to double-check that CCTV. Or to find out that they already had. Easier to do it himself.

Goodhew backtracked as far as the yard. A flatbed truck was parked just inside the gateway, dwarfed by a Portakabin that dominated the space. A man stood at one of the windows but he turned away as soon as he saw Goodhew approach. There were a few items of small plant machinery lined up to one side; perhaps there wasn't much to steal but the yard was totally enclosed by a robust and high brick wall. Moorey was right; they had CCTV and no reason to point the camera anywhere except at the entrance and the footpath beyond.

The man introduced himself as Stan Mercer and the two women in the office as Moira Trent and Amy Laurence. Mercer stood between Goodhew and the women and clearly would have preferred to stop the conversation there. 'We've already had some of yours around. That body had been found before any of us arrived this morning.'

'You told my colleague that the CCTV doesn't capture the entrance area. That's exactly where it seems to point. Would you mind showing me some of the footage?'

'He got the wrong end of the stick.' Stan shifted his weight and pushed his hands into his pockets, 'I said it wasn't much of a shot.'

'Can I see?'

'There isn't anything. The camera was switched on but the disc drive is full so nothing was saved.'

'Really?'

'It stopped recording a month ago,' he shrugged. 'I hadn't realised.'

Goodhew stepped forward and Stan had little choice but to let him through.

Moira was a slim woman, probably in her mid-fifties. She smiled, either in greeting or because Stan's failure to keep him out had amused her. Amy glanced briefly. She was younger and as soon as he made eye contact she looked back to her paperwork.

'Who arrived first today?'

'I did,' Stan replied. 'It was cordoned off by then.'

'And prior to that?'

'Friday. I left around six.'

'You didn't come in over the weekend?'

'No.'

Moira spoke next. 'Amy and I left just before that, at a guess, 5.30?' She looked to Amy for confirmation and Amy nodded. 'And we weren't in over the weekend either.' She glanced across again, but Amy had shifted her attention back to a clutch of invoices. 'Well, I wasn't,' Moira added. 'Amy?'

'Sorry, what?'

'Before today, when were you here last? Friday?'

'Yes, I thought I just said that?' Amy seemed slightly puzzled as if she hadn't been completely listening but around her neckline her skin had changed to mottled pink and she held the sheets of paper with rigid fingers.

Goodhew addressed Moira. 'Does anyone else work in here?'

'No. The main office is in St Barnabas Road. We're the overspill,' she added wryly.

Goodhew continued to track Amy through his peripheral vision and waited for her to turn away again. Stan was close to the window, clearly split between not wanting Goodhew there and his own curiosity.

'Mr Mercer, are you aware of any suspicious activity in the area that may have gone unreported?'

'Nothing during the day. I'm rarely here at night. We get takeaway wrappers and cigarette ends left in the gateway sometimes but that's about it. No one's pinched anything from the yard for a couple of years. We heard it's a woman's body.' He paused just long enough to lean in closer to Goodhew. 'Was she local?'

'It's too soon for formal identification.' Moira was watching them. Goodhew glanced at Amy and the way she turned from invoice to invoice seemed mechanical. Stan waited expectantly. It wasn't appropriate for Goodhew to make any comment before the facts were made public. 'There's nothing more I can tell you at this stage,' he said.

'Nothing?' Stan asked sharply. 'You must know what happened to her.' Stan turned to look through the window again. Moira's gaze followed.

'There will be a statement when there's more information.'

Amy glanced at the other two then back at Goodhew. Her gaze was slightly unfocused, as though her thoughts were elsewhere and he was irrelevant. She dipped her head, giving herself the smallest nod then focused properly on Goodhew as she spoke. 'Do you have a card? Just in case anything springs to mind?'

Stan scowled, 'Like what?'

'If I knew what, I'd tell him right now, wouldn't I?'

Goodhew handed a card to her. 'Anything you think of, OK?'

'OK.'

Goodhew thanked them for their time, and left with the feeling that they were still watching him as he walked back across the yard.

CHAPTER 18

Goodhew woke early the following morning, walked across Parker's Piece to swim his regular hundred lengths and still arrived at Parkside for seven. He headed straight to the second floor, and had reached the cul-de-sac of floor space that Sergeant Sheen had commandeered to house his archive of local information when he heard DI Marks yelling his name.

He turned and found his DI close to his heels, bearing down on him.

'Neil Frampton,' Marks announced. He didn't slow but grabbed Goodhew's arm and pulled him out of the corridor towards Sheen's desk. Sheen looked mildly surprised but didn't speak.

Goodhew moved quickly but his expression felt frozen. Frampton's Builders, the yard he'd visited – he made that connection immediately, but Marks didn't know he'd been there. So the name was clearly supposed to mean something more to him. Nothing sprang to mind but Marks had been driven up here by some imperative that obviously related to Goodhew.

'Does the same person get struck by lightning twice?' Marks asked.

Goodhew was baffled. 'Maybe. If they chase storms.'

Marks glared. 'Rarely or no would have done.'

Sheen looked up, his gaze flicking from Marks to Goodhew and back again.

'On the night she died, Lorraine Martin visited Neil Frampton. Do you know who that is, Gary?'

'Frampton's Builders? Apart from that . . .' Goodhew shook his head. 'I don't think so.'

'Neil and Carolyn Frampton?'

Again, Goodhew drew a blank, but he saw Sheen stiffen, then lean back in his chair, poised to witness whatever was about to unfold. Marks's attention was fixed on Goodhew as though he was waiting for him to betray some kind of telltale emotion or admission. 'Lorraine Martin phoned her sister, then went to pay a visit to Neil and Carolyn Frampton. They own Frampton's . . .'

'Builders.' Goodhew completed the sentence. He could picture the livery of their vehicles, white vans and small trucks with the company name in turquoise and black. 'I stopped by their yard earlier in case they had CCTV footage of the entrance. The foreman wasn't keen to help, but nothing stood out.' And, although he couldn't put his finger on it, something that could have been a childhood memory about Frampton's nudged at the edge of his thoughts.

Marks continued, 'Lorraine Martin gave you two names in connection with that bangle, one was Melanie Franks, and the other?'

'Nadine.'

Sheen uttered something that Goodhew didn't catch. Goodhew looked away from Marks to find the sergeant looking stunned. Sheen stared at them both, 'I said Romsey Terrace.'

Goodhew felt mystified. 'What am I missing?'

Without being asked Sheen replied, 'In March 1991 there was a fire at a house in Romsey Terrace. Two people died, they were boyfriend and girlfriend.'

Marks took over, 'Theo Frampton was Neil Frampton's son with his late wife Louise, and Nadine Kendall was Theo's girlfriend. It was arson. Neil Frampton's business partner, Robert Buckingham, was convicted.'

Sheen cut in. 'He'd been poaching money from the firm and the business owned that property. He could have covered up the theft if they'd had the payout.'

'In addition, he'd had an affair with Nadine and she'd threatened to tell his wife.'

They both watched Goodhew as he pulled a chair closer. He sat, and for a couple of minutes was too busy thinking to be concerned about Marks or Sheen. 'So,' he said finally, 'the fire occurred before my grandfather died. The fire involved the Frampton family, and Lorraine Martin's death does too. I saw her about an item in my grandfather's possession.'

'And hence the lightning question,' Sheen added.

Goodhew felt cautious. They all knew from experience that it was easy to head down the wrong route by misinterpreting information. 'Everything does seem to be linked.' And he also knew that it could put his grandfather's case back into the spotlight. 'We'd need to find a link between the fire and my grandfather.'

'I have that already,' Marks said.

'What, in the last twenty seconds?'

'Faster than that.'

Sheen cast a wary look at Marks. The sergeant stayed silent but it was clear to Goodhew that he was the only one in the dark here. 'It's something from before my time?'

Marks gave a humourless snort. 'Only in one sense. From 1989 until your grandfather's death, your mother worked for Neil Frampton.'

'Really?' He had a vague memory of his mum working part-time while he was at primary school. Something in an office. And she'd taken time off during the school holidays. 'I don't really remember.'

'Do you have up-to-date contact details for her?'

'Somewhere.'

'Keep them ready, we'll need them.'

CHAPTER 19

Amy lived in a top-floor flat of a four-storey purpose-built block. It had been designed like a wedding cake with each tier smaller than the floor below, using the leftover roof space to provide a balcony. Some residents used theirs to store bikes and pushchairs, or sun loungers, rusting kettle barbecues and other items that would have wintered unseen in most people's garden sheds.

She often woke earlier than she needed, roused by a sick feeling that balled in the pit of her stomach. Or by the feeling of falling. Or by her heart. She couldn't feel it thump or race; instead it would flutter weakly like the dying moments of a moth at the glass. Today, it was in her gut. She was too tired to move. The idea of proper sleep – restful and dreamless – taunted her. She lay immobile for over an hour until she managed to convince herself that there was no possibility of catching even the briefest nap. Ten minutes later and she was out on the balcony, still wearing her pyjamas and shrouded in her duvet. She stood her mug of tea on the corner of the safety rail and let the steam rise and the drink cool in its own time.

She switched her thoughts to work and let the office conversations between her, Stan and Moira play out in her head.

If she'd met Stan in the street she would have guessed that he might be ex-military, not in the officer-and-a-gentleman way, but in the ex-bouncer, ex-squaddie, stubborn-featured way. He was thickset but probably not as hard or as fit as he thought he was. Even so, she'd noticed that when the other Frampton employees came into the yard they took instruction and held out paperwork with deference. They had minutes in the man's company; she and Moira had all day, every day.

And she was glad of Moira, who diffused Stan's ill temper, brushing it away when Amy would have homed in on the bad atmosphere that he generated and tried to sort it out or, worse still, let it wind her tight with tension.

She knew that feeling responsibility for other people's moods was a weakness. She'd grown up testing the air for her mum's bad days, and more recently had been feeling like the barometer of Stan; between herself and Moira she always seemed to be the first to know when his mood was changing. Yesterday he'd taken too much interest in that dead body and the police activity along the road. She'd prodded at him until he'd finally responded.

He'd torn himself away from the window; what she'd wanted all along was for him to stop drooling at the glass. To anyone else the fascination might have seemed natural but she'd been on the other side of it. She knew how it felt to be on the receiving end of prying eyes and sly gossip.

She'd expected confrontation from him but instead he'd shown the only glimmer of warmth she'd seen from him. Eventually he'd turned to the window again but didn't offer any further comments and she'd tried to busy herself with the mail. She found herself torn between staring at his back and wanting to snatch another look at Lorraine Martin's business card that she'd hidden in her drawer. She'd wished she'd hidden it in her bag instead; it would have been safer there. She slid the drawer open just enough to see one corner of the card. She reached towards a pen, then glanced at Stan. He hadn't moved. Her fingers crept further across and withdrew the card, and then she leant down to transfer it into the side pocket of her bag. She looked up to find Stan staring at her.

'Why are you here, Amy?'

His usual abruptness had returned. She'd slid the drawer closed again. 'I told you, I needed a job.'

And he'd moved closer and stood at the end of her desk, blocking her view of Moira and the rest of the room. 'None of us are daft, Amy, not even Neil. We all know you want more than that.'

'I don't,' she'd begun but Stan had simply shaken his head.

'I thought maybe you were like him and would be trying to screw money out of Neil, but no. It is something, though.'

'My dad was your friend.'

'No, turned out I was his and he was an arsehole . . .' He'd corrected himself, 'Is an arsehole, and you're either a great actress or you have a lot to learn about your old man.'

Amy had pinched her top lip between her teeth and then avoided his gaze and felt ashamed for doing so. He'd left then, slamming the door behind him and she'd stared helplessly at Moira with a lump in her throat and a long pause before she'd risked trying to speak.

'Well,' Moira had said it as if the one word covered everything, then crossed the room to pass Amy a box of Kleenex. 'Stan always had a soft spot for Nadine. He would go over to the main office on any pretext. And he always looked up to your dad and, even though your dad was older, he did think of him as a friend. Imagine the impact the case had on him.'

'I get that.' Amy had thought it over for a few moments. 'Were Stan and Nadine ever a couple?'

'No, they were poles apart. Stan just didn't know it.'

She took her tea and wandered back inside. The flat felt stuffy by comparison with the fresh morning air. She tossed the duvet on to the settee and sat beside it. Her iPad lay on the armchair closest to her and opening the news app was faster than turning on the TV. She wanted to read the latest on the body found in Argyle Street and, after her anger towards Stan for his own prying, she guessed that made her a hypocrite, but that was tough.

She entered her postcode on the BBC site and switched to the local news stories. An involuntary 'oh' escaped her as she read the headline. 'Murder probe after body find'.

Murder.

The photo at the top of the article showed the view down the street from before Frampton's Yard, pointing towards the location of the body. Apart from the police car parked in the foreground the view looked similar to the way it looked every other day.

Police are appealing for witnesses after the body of a woman was found in an alleyway in Argyle Street. The woman's body was discovered early on Monday morning. The body has not yet been identified and a post mortem examination has been arranged.

She scrolled down the page. Two local residents made comments about 'hearing nothing' and it being 'a lovely street to live in'. Until the last line she read nothing that she didn't already know, then a name jumped out at her and she had to rewind to the start of the sentence to be sure that she understood.

Although police have yet to make a formal identification, the victim has been named locally as Lorraine Martin.

'Shit.' Amy said the word out loud and it sounded harsh as it hit the walls of her empty flat.

To Amy, Lorraine Martin was nothing more than the name on the card, but a connection somehow existed. The woman had known where she worked. Anyone who cared enough could have followed her and found out but it was far more likely that someone had told her, and Amy could count on one hand the number of people who knew where she worked: Moira, Stan, Neil and her parents. And possibly Carolyn Frampton if Neil had gone as far as telling his wife. OK, that made six, so not an average hand but still a finite number.

If Moira or Stan had known anything, they hadn't let on, and she'd never heard Lorraine Martin's name from either of her parents. That left Neil, and possibly Carolyn.

Neil had made it clear that she was to work in the yard and to stay in the yard, but within ten minutes Amy had dressed and was heading towards Frampton's main office.

Back in the days when her father had been a partner, when it had been Buckingham and Frampton, the business had bought a large but run-down detached house in St Barnabas Road and used it as their base. Another lost asset, as Amy's mother had been pointing out since before

Amy had been old enough to know what an asset was. Once it was no longer theirs, the house prices had risen, the neighbourhood had been rejuvenated and the Framptons had moved in. The office stayed put, but the vans and equipment had been relocated, tucked out of sight in the Argyle Street yard.

The last time she'd walked past had been several years ago in the summer; the wide pavements were baked and the trees and privet hedges were the only signs of life in the heavy silence. She hadn't slowed as she reached their offices but glanced up at the building for enough time to notice that they'd renamed it Frampton House, sandblasted the brickwork and replaced the aluminium-framed windows with traditional hardwood.

And now it was pretty much as she remembered it. Neil's F-Type Jag was parked in the driveway alongside a Porsche Cayenne and a Suzuki Bandit motorbike. She texted Moira to let her know that she'd be running late. 'Gone to St Barnabas Road, I'll be back as soon as I can.' She switched her phone to silent.

CHAPTER 20

From outside the house, it seemed to Amy that two rooms at the front were used as offices, portioned off from the private, residential part of the building, which had a separate entrance around the side. The door to one of the office rooms was closed, the other open with a desk positioned close enough to the entrance for the woman sitting at it to greet any arrivals. She was in her late forties, tanned and lean in an I-do-yoga kind of way.

Carolyn Frampton.

It took a few moments for Amy to recognise her. She'd seen the wedding photos where Carolyn at twenty had looked like a teenager while her husband had looked old for thirty-seven. She remembered her mother bumping into her on occasion and introducing her as 'Auntie Carolyn' but, apart from that, she hadn't seen her since her father's conviction. Carolyn was still blonde and sporty but now looked mature and womanly rather than girlish.

It was her mannerisms that gave her age away first, the tilt of her head, the way she moved her long fingers when she spoke, the double blink whenever her expression broke into a smile.

'I'm looking for Neil. Is he here?' Amy stepped forward and cast her gaze around the rest of the office. There were two empty desks, one tidy and the other strewn with building plans.

'He's not,' Carolyn replied. 'Can I help?'

'Not really, I just came to see Neil.'

'And you are?'

Carolyn's smile was polite but her expression had the kind of authority that left Amy feeling that she had to answer. 'I'm your temp. From the yard.'

'Amy?' A small 'oh' formed on Carolyn's lips.

'Yes, Amy Laurence.' Amy hesitated; this wasn't how she'd planned it.

'What happened to Amy Buckingham?'

'My mum reverted to her maiden name.'

'Of course she did.' Carolyn seemed suddenly lost for words.

'I know Neil planned to tell you I was working for you.'

'He did, kind of, I just didn't register.' There was a hard edge to the silence that followed, then Carolyn found her voice again. 'Did Neil tell you to stay away from here?'

'Not at all,' Amy lied, 'but I've never had a reason to come over until now.'

'And now with Moira off and Stan out on site . . . I see.'

Amy didn't see but stayed quiet as Carolyn stood.

'Take a seat.' She gestured in the general direction of the other desks and Amy did as she was told and chose the closest chair. Carolyn picked up a couple of pens from in front of her and returned them to the pen pot that stood alongside the telephone, and then tucked her chair back under the desk before leaving the room.

A few moments later, a young man in a heavy plaid shirt entered. He nodded but didn't speak. He crossed to the plan-covered desk and sat with his back to her.

Amy watched the back of the man's shaved head. He had a spreadsheet open and had begun entering data. 'So Neil is here?' she asked perhaps too quietly since he didn't reply. She felt too awkward to ask again and she wasn't sure why Carolyn had left her there or how long she might be. She took Lorraine Martin's card from the side pocket of her bag. If she couldn't see Neil, she'd ask Carolyn to explain about the card; even if it was nothing to do with her, she would see whether Lorraine's name produced a reaction. She held it discreetly and waited.

Everything was different here to the Portakabin where mud scuffs routinely stained the grey nylon carpet and the only item decorating the wall was a laminated year planner. Through this window there was a view of a quiet suburban street and the interior décor included original mouldings, embossed wallpaper and carpet that sprang beneath her feet.

A few more seconds passed, then, from somewhere on the other side of the wall, she heard raised voices. The urgent staccato of a woman. Probably Carolyn. The low rumble of a man's voice. Then shouting. Both voices now. She looked down at her hands folded over the card in her lap and pretended not to hear.

Plaid Shirt's fingers stopped tapping the keyboard. She looked up and this time he turned fully towards her. She guessed he was about her age, maybe a little younger. His shirt sleeves were rolled up above his elbows and a tattoo of a Chinese dragon dancing in red flames covered his left arm, a tiger snarled on the right. 'We can both pretend to be deaf if you want but they're still shouting.'

She screwed up her face. 'That's Neil's voice? I might have caused it then.'

'Flirting with Dad?'

'I'm sorry?'

'That really wouldn't amuse Mum.'

'You're Carolyn's son?'

'You're sharp. No wonder you got the job.' He smiled suddenly; a broad grin that lit his face. He leant forward to shake her hand, 'I'm Alex Frampton.'

'Amy. I'm the temp from the yard.'

'Amy the Temp? Is that double-barrelled?' Then the smile vanished again and his dark eyes studied her for a few seconds. 'So how have you caused that?' He cocked his head in the direction of the shouting. 'Shame the walls are too thick to hear the words. They don't usually fight, you know. Most days they don't even speak.'

'Do you know the name Robert Buckingham?'

'Of course.'

'I'm his daughter.'

'Woah, fuck me,' he gasped. 'No wonder they're pissed.'

'I came here to see Neil. I didn't think it through.'

He leant forward, elbows on knees. He seemed more curious than annoyed even though the row still reverberated in the other room. 'And Dad gave you this job?'

'He did, but after I asked him for it.'

'Just like that?'

'Pretty much.'

'How often have you spoken to him since?'

'Not at all. But I'm sure Stan and Moira would tell him anything he wanted to know.'

'Well, you're not dumb, are you?' Alex shook his head. 'My dad still keeps tabs on your dad, you know. He's not going to lose sight of him.'

Amy almost asked why, but Alex answered for her.

'It's an unsettled score. However long your dad spent in prison wasn't long enough in his opinion. He thinks there might be a day when the books get balanced so to speak. He doesn't want to do anything himself but wants fate or the hand of God to step in.'

'Seriously?'

He raised his eyebrows. 'Yes, seriously. I've grown up with it. I know it chapter and verse.' He hooked his thumb in the direction of the door. 'Moment of truth, then,' he said before turning back to his spreadsheet.

Amy stood up when Carolyn reappeared, ready to flash the business card if Carolyn told her it was time to leave. She called Amy over. 'It seems that losing a stepson doesn't give me the same right to complain about you being here as it would if I'd been Theo's mother.'

'I'm here because I needed to speak to him, not cause trouble.' Amy raised her hands in surrender. 'And I'm sorry I've upset you, but I'm not my father. What happened when I was four isn't my fault.'

Alex gave a grunt, 'I wasn't even one. There's no lower age limit.'

'Keep out of this, Alex,' Carolyn snapped and turned back to Amy. 'He'll see you now.'

Neil Frampton was at the window when she entered his office. 'How are you?'

'Fine. I thought you might check up on me, though.'

'I don't need to. I thought you would come to see me when you were ready, and here you are. Do you know what I trust more than any one person, Amy?'

She shook her head.

'My gut. I'll make decisions based on experience but, as soon as my gut tells me something different, I listen. Your gut tells you what your brain's too slow to process.'

She wasn't sure how to respond so she took a step closer to him, ready with Lorraine Martin's card.

'Asking me for a job wasn't just about you needing work as much as you needing something else from me. Your father's heart attack was a trigger and you turned up with the idea that I felt guilty.' His mouth contorted as though the words tasted bitter. He swallowed. 'My first reaction was to throw you out of the car but my gut told me to take a chance and to see where it led.' He cocked his head at the window. 'Now the police are on their way over and here you are. That's not a coincidence either, is it?'

Amy shook her head. 'I don't know anything about the police coming.'

Her bewilderment must have been obvious; enough to make him hesitate.

'The body in Argyle Street?'

'Yes,' she replied, but didn't mention the card or Lorraine's name after all.

'Her name was Lorraine Martin and she's Moira's sister.'

Amy felt herself draw a sharp breath and heard herself say, 'Oh.' Then add, 'I'm sorry, I had no idea.' She smelt the dust and mud from the yard as she felt the crisp edges of Lorraine Martin's business card. 'Why would that be anything to do with me?'

He studied her expression carefully for a few seconds. 'Perhaps it's not,' he conceded. 'It's just my gut that says otherwise.'

She wanted to tell him that he was wrong but she just gripped her bag more tightly and headed for the door.

Alex caught up with her as she stepped onto the pathway outside. 'I'll give you a lift.'

She shook her head. 'I don't think your mother would like it.'

'Are you OK? You look shaken.'

'I'm fine. I need to get back to the yard.'

'Then I'll drive you.'

He reached for her elbow to prevent her from walking away. She scowled at him. 'What are you doing?'

'Please don't walk off. I'm pleased you're here. We need to get to know each other.'

She still scowled and kept moving. 'Why?'

'We have things to talk about, we're like estranged relatives, people who can fill in the picture that the other one doesn't know.'

She didn't stop walking but she slowed, 'Go on.'

'Like I said, I was only months old when my brother died and I don't remember anything that happened, but I know what I've grown up with.'

'Which is?'

'Curiosity, I suppose. Questions I asked that weren't ever answered. Other kids' parents used to stare at me sometimes, but if I caught them they'd look away again.'

'Yeah, I had that too.' Amy stopped and turned to face him. She remembered the expressions at school pickup, the parents who seemed to look straight through her and tried too hard to make small talk when she had walked within earshot. She'd wondered when they whispered to one another whether they had something new to discuss or were just dragging the story out for a fresh audience. She'd thought she had been the only child feeling that way. 'What do you want to ask?'

'Why you think he did it.' He was studying her closely now.

But she was watching him just as closely as she replied. 'I don't,' she said. He didn't look surprised. 'But is it fair to say that to you? Your family don't need to hear it when there's no proof yet.'

'Yet?'

'That's not why I'm here.' She shook her head, then lied. 'I just needed a job. But if there's anything you do know . . .'

'That my parents have never doubted the verdict?' His eyes hardened. 'That your father's as guilty as?'

The spark of camaraderie vanished as quickly as it had arrived. She didn't argue, there would be no point.

A car carrying two men pulled up to the opposite kerb. She recognised one of them as the detective who had visited the yard. He was looking directly at her and she could tell that he'd recognised her too. 'The police are here,' she told Alex, then walked away.

CHAPTER 21

As Marks and Goodhew pulled up outside Frampton House, Goodhew saw the man and the woman walking away from the building. She glanced in his direction and he recognised her immediately. She kept walking but the man with her crossed the road and approached them. 'I'm Alex Frampton. Are you here to see my parents?'

He took them into the building and introduced them to his mother, Carolyn Frampton, who, in turn, took them towards a closed door. Its heavy gloss paint and round, darkly varnished metal handle reminded Goodhew of the formality that still hung in the corridors of local government offices like Guildhall; they might have been modernised but the residue always stayed. And the inside of the room was no different.

Neil Frampton shook their hands, rising from his chair to not quite his full height in order to do so. He was over six feet tall. Carolyn Frampton had to be close to five-eight but she seemed much shorter than that when, very briefly, she stood alongside him. His skin was a blotchy pink, hers lightly tanned. She had a wiry leanness, he had the build of a man who'd made a gradual but dedicated slide towards obesity. He wasn't quite there yet, but it was on the menu.

'Do you want me to stay?' she asked him.

Marks replied, 'It is both of you we've come to see.'

She drew up another chair, placing it at one end of the desk rather than alongside her husband.

Neil Frampton's gaze had settled on Goodhew to begin with, but now he switched his attention to Marks and opened the conversation with a single word. 'So?'

'We're investigating the death of Lorraine Martin,' Marks began. Goodhew watched Mr and Mrs Frampton closely; if Lorraine Martin had been close to them, or they'd been unaware of her death, Marks's approach would have shocked them. Neil Frampton's expression revealed nothing. 'Her sister, Moira Trent, works for you, is that correct?'

'Yes, it is. It was how we heard of her death this morning.'

'And what was your relationship with Lorraine Martin?'

'Casual.'

'How did you meet her?'

Neil Frampton watched his wife answer the first few questions. None of her answers were mirrored with any corresponding nods or murmurs of agreement from him. Some people just weren't emotive, others chose to keep their feelings under wraps. Goodhew was pleased when Marks changed direction. 'Mr Frampton, on the night of her death, Lorraine Martin visited you. Can you tell me about that?'

'I was in here. She banged on the window.'

'What time was this?'

'I don't know. Late. Around ten. I should have been in the house by then but weekends are always spent playing catch-up.' Frampton's gaze strayed from Marks to Goodhew and back again.

'And she banged on the glass?' Marks prompted.

'I opened the front door but just to get rid of her . . . Make her go, that is. She was drunk, virtually incoherent. And she'd phoned Moira too, before she came here, I think. But she didn't say anything much. And then she went.' He stopped as though he hoped that answer would be enough. Marks tilted his head back a little and studied Neil Frampton without comment. Frampton didn't seem quick to take the hint and his wife just studied the desktop.

Goodhew leant forward. 'Mr Frampton, we need to know what she said.'

'She wasn't making sense, she rambles when she's drunk.'

'You've seen that in the past then?'

'Moira has told us,' Mrs Frampton cut in, but too slowly since her husband was already nodding by the time she'd started to speak.

'Mr Frampton?'

The big man rested his elbows on the desk and pressed his face into his hands. He blew a long, unhurried breath out through his mouth and dragged his hands back as far as his temples, stretching out his fleshy features. 'Theo and Nadine. You know all about what happened to them.' He closed his eyes and spoke slowly as though to himself. 'I didn't know what to make of her at first. She wasn't the girlfriend I imagined for him. But what do the parents know? We're the only ones who see our children the way we do and he'd liked her for such a long time before he asked her out.' He paused to inhale then exhale, slow and controlled. 'She worked for us for a while, then moved away. I don't know whether she stayed in touch with Theo, whether he encouraged her to come back even, but at the time we were just pleased to have her working here once more.' Again the breathing. 'She met Lorraine when she was working here the first time. Through Moira, I imagine. I never saw them together when Nadine came back though.' He opened his eyes and sagged back in his chair. 'It was a few months after the fire when Lorraine first turned up drunk. She rambled on about Nadine mostly, how Nadine should never have been at the house, and kept telling us about her weird theories.'

'Such as?'

He shook his head slowly. 'Some comment that Nadine had once made, or a random news item that she'd seen that had meant something to her. She'd piece things together like people do when they're trying to prove a conspiracy theory. Twisting things to make them fit.

'I could see she was struggling – mentally, I mean – but it wasn't my problem. No one else's problems are all that important when you've lost a child. She was erratic; when Robert was arrested Lorraine said she knew he'd done it, but after the court case was over she came and asked me whether Theo had been depressed, whether it could have been a suicide pact. I stopped listening to her then, I couldn't hear it any more. From then on, as soon as I saw her I became angry and I don't know what she said this time, last time or the time before that.'

'Luckily Moira understands.' Carolyn Frampton smiled wearily. 'She intervened as quickly as possible when Lorraine behaved like that. Apart from those times, Moira managed to keep her work life and her private life very separate.'

'Unlike us?' he sighed.

'Yes, unlike us.' She echoed her husband's words and the tension between them seemed to settle. 'I imagine Lorraine's behaviour was hard for her to deal with.'

Marks turned to a fresh page in his notebook, 'Lorraine Martin's body was discovered in Argyle Street, very close to your yard. Do you know of any reason she would have been in that area?'

They both shook their heads. Neil Frampton looked at his wife and she took the cue. 'None. But saying it's a coincidence doesn't make sense either. We don't know why she'd be anywhere near it.'

Goodhew spoke. 'You have three employees there?'

'Yes, plus others that come in either to pick up plant or file paperwork, timesheets for example . . .'

'And how many here?'

'Just us, and our son, Alex.'

'And the woman I saw in the office when we arrived?'

'Amy?' Carolyn replied. 'She is the third person at the yard.'

'Forget Amy,' Neil Frampton cut in. 'She had no idea that Lorraine had any connection to us. And no one would have been at the yard on a Sunday night.'

'Unless she arranged to meet someone?' Marks suggested. 'Who has a key?'

'Moira, Stan and spares here.'

'Stan Mercer?' Goodhew checked, 'What was his relationship to Lorraine Martin?'

'None,' Carolyn replied before Frampton had the chance, but he took over immediately.

'He knows who she is, he's crossed paths with her like we all have. All of us from the time of the fire that is. Don't discount Robert Buckingham, will you?'

Marks shook his head slowly, his expression patient. 'We have no reason to connect Robert Buckingham to the death of Lorraine Martin.'

'Theo and Nadine are the connection. Lorraine didn't have much that wasn't connected to the past. All she ever did was get pissed and rehash events from twenty-plus years ago.'

Marks spoke next. 'To your knowledge, did Robert Buckingham ever threaten Lorraine Martin?'

Frampton scowled but shook his head. 'I wasn't implying that he had. I was just saying that you should speak to him if you haven't already. Moira, the fire, Frampton's; everything that connects us to Lorraine Martin connects to him too. She probably pestered him the way she pestered us.'

Carolyn glanced uneasily between Marks and Goodhew. 'She hadn't turned up like that in a long time. My husband's exaggerating.'

'I'm not, I've said it how it was.'

'Do you have any of the previous dates?' Goodhew asked.

'No,' Frampton snapped. 'It had been often enough.'

'But not this year,' Carolyn added quietly.

Frampton lowered his voice and leant in closer to his wife, 'Something set her off this time, Carrie.' His eye contact remained direct and his voice slow. She didn't look away 'Lorraine might as well have been left on our doorstep. That's the work of someone who wants to cause problems. Primarily to me and my business. Don't dismiss what I'm saying.'

Carolyn's expression didn't waver. She broke eye contact first and addressed Marks instead. 'My husband seems to think that he is the focus for everything that happens to us.' She stood and offered her hand for Marks to shake. 'Disagreeing with him isn't allowed and, if it was, I wouldn't have let him hire Robert Buckingham's daughter as our temp. I'm going back to my desk as there's nothing else I'm allowed to add.'

'Carolyn,' Frampton began, but she had left the room too quickly to hear more. 'That's not what I meant,' he finished.

'Maybe not,' Goodhew conceded, 'but it was exactly how it sounded.'

CHAPTER 22

They left Frampton House and headed back towards Parkside Station. Goodhew spotted Amy walking quickly among the pedestrians in Mill Road. They drove past her without comment and Marks didn't question Goodhew when, a few seconds later, he asked if he could make his own way back. 'Don't waste the day' had been his only comment as Goodhew got out of the car.

Goodhew turned towards Argyle Street, ahead of Amy. He waited at the final corner, wishing for a phone box or some other prop that would have allowed him to loiter without the risk of a new call to Parkside Station about his suspicious behaviour.

Her tumble of curly hair had been swept to one side and bobbed on her shoulder as she hurried towards him. Her attention was on the pavement in front of her and she didn't seem aware that there was anyone near her until he spoke.

'Amy Laurence?'

The sound of her name stopped her in her tracks. 'Detective Goodhew, right? Were you waiting for me?'

'Can we talk?'

'What's it about?'

'Your father.'

'And his supposed sins? And my sins? Or neither or both?' She studied him as though she were expecting to see something particular in his expression. 'Do I have any choice?'

'You do.'

She nodded to herself then seemed to make a decision. 'OK, but not here.' She checked her watch. 'I need to go to the yard first. I'm going to make my excuses and take an early lunch.'

'I don't need long.'

'I need it.' She took a couple of steps forward then paused again. 'Does Carolyn Frampton know you want to speak to me?'

'No.'

'And this is informal?'

'At this point.'

She smiled at that and her cheeks dimpled. 'Keeping your options open?'

'Of course.'

'Good. Can you meet me at half past? At Clowns?'

'In King Street?'

'Yes. Now I really have to go.'

Goodhew remembered Clowns from his childhood and often when he walked past the thought occurred to him that it never seemed to change; the bulbous lettering of the signage had never been updated and the building nestled into the terraces along King Street as if the other businesses had grown up around it. It reminded him of the cafés he'd visited on trips to Florence and Livorno, filled with lively banter and the smells of pasta dishes drifting through the hatch from the kitchen. It felt like Italy, but he couldn't imagine it anywhere else apart from Cambridge.

He'd arrived half an hour early and chose a table at the back with an audience of clowns. By the time Amy had joined him, the café had begun to fill and the surrounding tables were occupied.

'It's busy. We can go somewhere else if you like,' he said.

'No need, it's like the tide in here, people flooding in then out again and I'm sure that no one takes any notice of anyone else.' When she sat she seemed to sag into the chair and he noticed for the first time how tired she looked. Her eyes were a deep brown, and, in the soft light, seemed almost as dark as her pupils. She looked at him intently and it was the only indication that she possessed any energy.

'Have you eaten?'

She shook her head. 'I'm fine.'

'Coffee then?'

'I'm OK.'

'It's no problem, I'm having one anyway.'

She glanced across at the counter then back at him. 'Cappuccino, please, one sugar.'

A couple of minutes later she was stirring her drink and staring down on the dusting of chocolate as it rotated. He waited and, finally, she looked across at him and spoke. 'So you know I'm Robert Buckingham's daughter. What else?' There was no edge to her voice, just curiosity.

'I know a little about his case and about his connections to Frampton's.' He hesitated. 'I've taken a guess about you, and, if I'm right, I think you might be able to help me.'

She withdrew a little, moving her hands from the table and dropping them into her lap, glancing past him to the next table, then across to the exit. 'How?' she asked.

'I think your job at Frampton's is connected to your father somehow.'

She half shrugged, half nodded. 'That's not any great deduction.'

'And either that's on your father's behalf or it's your decision and you're trying to satisfy a personal goal of some kind?'

She didn't reply.

'So I wondered what might have prompted this. I checked back and discovered that your father had a heart attack and was admitted to Addenbrooke's shortly before you started working at Frampton's . . . I'm guessing that was somehow a trigger for you?'

She tried to look calm but he could see tension tightening her shoulders. She glanced towards the exit again.

'I'm sorry, I'm not trying to make you uncomfortable.'

'What then?'

'My grandfather was murdered in 1992 and I've found evidence that his case is linked to your father's.'

'What do you mean by linked? I don't want anyone trying to put anything else on my dad.'

'Amy, that's not what I'm implying.'

'What then?'

'I need to see where it all leads; my grandfather's killer has never been caught.'

There was sympathy in her expression. 'But you're not allowed to investigate a crime linked to your own family, are you?' she asked.

'Not officially. But it's an old case and I've been allowed some leeway.' Amy didn't respond, just waited expectantly until he conceded a little more. 'I'm not to actively investigate but I have access to the files.'

'So this is what? A chat on your own time?'

'It's borderline,' he admitted. 'And I haven't seen the case files yet. I won't until I'm back at Parkside, but I've followed my nose and ended up here.'

'At Clowns?'

'At this connection.'

'When twenty-odd years of investigation didn't?' She shook her head. 'That makes no sense.'

'There was an item withheld.'

'What item?'

'I can't comment, but it led me straight to Lorraine Martin and, from there, to Frampton's.'

'So you had contact with her before she died?'

'I did.'

'And you're now investigating her death?'

'I'm part of that team, yes.'

'And here I am in the middle of both investigations.' She studied him, her expression shrewd. 'What do you think you want from me?'

'I had a feeling about you when I saw you in the Argyle Street yard, then again at the office. Then I discovered you're Robert Buckingham's daughter and I knew I needed to speak to you.'

'You thought we had a connection?' she asked.

'Something like that.'

He saw an amused look cross her face. 'It's a crap chat-up line.'

'That's obviously not what I was getting at.' His reply was out of his mouth before he'd had the chance to see she was joking.

119

'Obviously? Thanks.'

'I didn't mean it like that either.'

She gave a small smile. 'I think I'm safe in here. They know me and I'm sure Genni,' she pointed in the direction of the owner, 'would *know someone who knows someone if you know what I mean.*' She said the last part of the sentence in a patchy Italian accent, then gave a short laugh. 'Sorry, I've been so tense. I don't know the last time I found anything amusing.'

'You're not working at Frampton's at your father's request then?'

She shook her head. 'How do you know?'

'Because I get the feeling that you're keeping everything to yourself.' He leant back in his chair and imagined himself in her situation. It wasn't so hard. 'It must become a strain, a burden and sometimes you wonder whether you're making mistakes because there's no one to ask.'

Without warning, her smile crumbled. 'I've made no progress whatsoever,' she whispered. 'When I started out it was simple. I found out that my dad didn't start that fire and I just wanted to get inside Frampton's and find something that would prove it.'

'I don't understand why they want you there.'

'They don't. I told Neil I was desperate for work. He's a strange man. He helped my mum out when my dad was in prison. He told everyone I was there except his wife; Carolyn found out about me this morning.'

'You weren't supposed to turn up there, I take it?'

'I had no idea that he'd never told Carolyn. My mum switched to her maiden name when she divorced Dad, changed mine too of course. If I'd been Buckingham then Carolyn would have realised sooner.'

Goodhew took another sip of his coffee. 'What did you think you'd discover?'

'How should I know? I even went through their filing cabinets but, of course, there's nothing. It's too long ago and no one would tell me if they did know anything. Why would they? Anyhow, I started off so worried that I might be wasting my time that I didn't realise I don't mind Moira and actually like the work.' She sipped her coffee. 'I don't know how the hell you think I can help you but go ahead, convince me.'

Goodhew explained the background to his grandfather's death,

120

careful to keep to details that were already in the public domain. 'His death came after your father's conviction . . .'

'So Dad's not in the frame for it?'

'No, but that's not what I was alluding to. My mother worked at Frampton's from before the fire until my grandfather died. Your dad must have known her.'

'What's her name?'

'Paula Goodhew?'

She shook her head. 'Doesn't ring a bell, but I was small. Is that the connection?'

'No. What about the name Melanie Franks?'

Again she shook her head. 'Who was she?'

'The details are sketchy, but we know that Melanie knew Nadine Kendall.'

Amy's expression became wary for a second and her voice sharp. 'And?'

'Why the change of tone?'

'Hearing Nadine's name. I don't know, association, I suppose.'

It seemed as though she was fighting to contain some emotion.

'An association with what?'

'Isn't it obvious? I know it wasn't their fault they died, but it was Theo and Nadine's deaths that wrecked my family.'

'And your dad must have been well known to both Nadine and Theo Frampton?'

'Everyone knew Theo. I don't remember but apparently I acted like he was my big brother whenever I saw him. Nadine worked at the office so I know they knew one another but I was too small to remember anything first-hand.'

'So you didn't know there was a connection between Nadine and Lorraine Martin?'

'Oh.' Amy's tone changed again; shocked but muted now. 'No, I didn't.' Her gaze slipped away from Goodhew's and dropped towards the table top. She watched the tips of her fingers tap out a rhythm on the surface. Her lips remained pressed together and even in the artificial light he could see that she'd paled. He didn't hurry her but her concentration seemed so complete that he started to wonder whether he

121

needed to nudge her. 'Shit,' she muttered finally. When she looked up at him deep furrows puckered her forehead. 'Look, I'm going to take a chance on you. Don't be flattered, I just don't know what else to do.' She grabbed her shoulder bag from the floor, hoisting it onto her lap. 'I hadn't decided what to do with this.' She passed him a business card. 'It was delivered to me at work – it arrived by hand the morning that her body was found. I didn't know who she was then, of course.'

It was in Goodhew's hand before he'd had a chance to refuse it, he'd left prints but managed to bag it without handling it further. 'She wanted you to call her. Do you know why?'

'No.'

'When did you receive it?'

'Monday morning.'

'And did you try calling her?'

'No, I was wondering about it when I heard that the body had been identified. She was dead before I could have read it, wasn't she?'

'By hours I believe.' He stared through the evidence bag at the card, the writing on it was small and the three letters unevenly spaced. 'Dropping this in at Frampton's was more than likely the last thing she did. This will need to be logged properly. You'll have to make a statement too.'

'I understand.'

'This complicates things. Your connection to Lorraine Martin will form part of the investigation.'

'There isn't a connection.' She looked at him steadily.

'There's something. Something that Lorraine Martin either wanted from you or had for you. How well do you know Moira Trent?'

'Dad mentioned her over the years and I think I remember her from when I was a kid, but it's only since I started at Frampton's that I've had any contact. And I only found out today that she and Lorraine were sisters.' Her gaze flicked past him. 'Can I tell you why I wanted to meet in here?'

'Go on.'

'It's where I've always come. My mum would see our solicitor, or the police or whoever, then bring me here to cheer me up. It was our thing for a while. She gave up coming but I carried on.' She turned her head to look at the clowns on the shelf to her left. Some of them were ugly – caricatures with distended features or exaggerated expressions. She pointed to a Venetian mask of a woman with liquid eyes and a heart-shaped face. 'She's my favourite. I wanted to be her.'

Of all the clowns this one looked most like Amy. Goodhew didn't comment.

'Some kids have an imaginary friend, I used to make up stories about her. She looks serene today. Sometimes I looked at her and saw a gleam of excitement. Or fearlessness.' She studied Goodhew thoughtfully. 'I'm not fearless, though. I thought I'd achieved nothing since I worked there but since this morning I've been scared.'

'Of what?'

'That I stirred up something that got Lorraine killed.'

'It doesn't work like that.'

'We've both had contact with her and then this? Aren't you worried that it was you?'

He was, but shook his head and lied. 'No, I'm not.'

CHAPTER 23

Goodhew returned to Parkside Station and filed a report on his meeting with Amy, passing the information straight to Marks who passed it straight to Kincaide. Goodhew made his way up to Sheen's desk where the files from his grandfather's case waited. Sheen glanced from his one-finger-one-thumb keyboard skills long enough to greet Goodhew then made a point of turning his full attention back to the computer.

The case files were held in a series of heavy card document boxes. In his mind's eye Goodhew could not have envisaged a situation where he wouldn't have pushed everything else aside to look through these. Instead, he'd followed other leads first. He knew that the contents held the potential for everything or nothing and, even now, felt a reluctance as he opened the box marked '1/5'.

There was no puff of dust or smell of age and it took only a few seconds to see that the contents were in no discernible order. He opened the other boxes too and rifled through the paperwork, trying to find the earliest document. Eventually he found the transcript of the initial 999 call. His grandmother had called it in. Of course, there was no indication of tone, just the words. He could imagine her voice though: precise, determined and taut with pain.

> Operator: *Ambulance emergency. Hello, caller, what's the emergency?*
> Ellie Goodhew: *My husband's been attacked. I need help.*

She gave her address. *I need an ambulance. They've tried to kill him.*

Op: *It is on its way. I will help you until it arrives. Is your husband conscious?*

EG: *No. He's been hit.*

Op: *I need you to check whether he's breathing.*

EG: *He's not, I know he's not.*

Op: *Check in his mouth for any obstruction. Are his airways clear?*

EG: *They're clear. I already checked.*

Op: *You need to start chest compressions.*

EG: *I have. I'm doing them but he's not breathing.*

Op: *You need the heel of your hand . . .*

EG: *I know how. That's what I'm doing. Nothing's happening.*

Op: *Is anyone there with you?*

EG: *It's not helping.*

Op: *Is there anyone there who can take over?*

EG: *No. Where's the ambulance?*

Op: *It's on its way. You're doing well, just keep trying. Two compressions per second.*

EG: *That's what I'm doing I'm not stopping.*

The operator continued to reassure Ellie, to encourage her to keep going even though his breathing hadn't restarted, even though she had to be exhausted. The transcript ran for another two sheets. Goodhew turned the final page.

Op: *The ambulance is outside now. They need access to your building.*

EG: *We're on the second floor. I don't want to leave him.*

Op: *You have to let them in. Just do it as quickly as you can.*

EG: *Tell them I'm coming. But I think it's too late.*

Goodhew straightened the sheets and read the first page again. *They've tried to kill him.* He leant forward and sifted through the uppermost sheets in the box; there seemed to be no order to any of it and he needed the chronology.

Sheen cleared his throat then pushed his keyboard away, 'You need to unpack them, then spread it all out, like you would with any other pile of information.'

'Have you looked through these boxes?'

'Yes, they're chaotic. That's what happens when people keep poking around taking one more look.'

'People?'

'Marks went over it again when you started here.' Sheen had a broad Suffolk accent and often spoke slowly with long pauses between his sentences. Some of the officers held the opinion that he wasn't that bright; anyone who'd worked with him knew the opposite was true. Sheen just liked to double-check his facts before rushing to speak. 'I think seeing you around here bothered him. We went through everything but we didn't find anything new.'

'I see.'

'And in my opinion you shouldn't be let loose on it now; you're too close to it. Even your mother's name's come up, Gary. Marks should transfer you out into the Fens somewhere until it's all done.'

'And I need to read everything I can in case that happens.'

Sheen shook his head. 'Read or photograph, Gary?'

Goodhew gave Sheen a lopsided smile, 'Are you leaving the room for a couple of hours?'

'Long enough to get coffee and then I'll be back, but I don't really think I need to supervise you, Gary. I'll pretend you have been sent to Littleport or beyond and mind my own. What are you having? White coffee with one?'

'Yes, thanks. And can I borrow the flip chart?'

'As soon as two cases were linked I thought you'd be drawing a diagram; when we reached three it was inevitable.'

Sheen returned with the drinks and continued talking as though there hadn't been a five-minute gap. 'I've always been curious about the situation with your parents.'

Goodhew placed his coffee down on the carpet. Sheen hadn't asked a direct question and Goodhew could have brushed it aside, but he had too much respect for Sheen to ignore him. 'I used to spend a lot of time with my grandparents, at their house,' he began. 'Then I was ill, off school for a full term of primary and I spent most days with my grandfather. I carried on going round theirs after I went back to school.'

'Parkside School?'

'Yes, so it was just across the road.'

'And now here.' Sheen's eyes widened as if he'd had enlightenment. 'You haven't strayed more than about 500 yards.'

'I wish. My parents split up after my grandfather died, after they came into his money that is.' It struck Goodhew then that it was easy to talk to Sheen and he wondered why the sergeant had spent so many years behind a desk. 'My mum lost the plot with it and sent us to boarding school.'

'And your father didn't have a say?'

'Dad worked away.' Goodhew had never bought that explanation; there had been enough money for his dad to have worked locally and to have brought up his children at home. He still felt anger at both of them if he dwelt on it for too long. 'That's it,' he added.

He meant it to be the end of the conversation but Sheen didn't take the hint. 'So where's your mum now?'

'On the outskirts of Sydney. When my sister moved out there, my mother followed.' It didn't really hurt to talk about his family after all, he realised, not when Sheen had probably read every detail of his grandfather's murder. 'She remarried a few years back but I haven't met him.'

'And your dad?'

'He's a decent bloke.' Goodhew screwed up his face. 'But we're not interested in my dad, are we?' Goodhew patted the box of documents. 'You're not going to tell me that he's in here too?'

Sheen shook his head. 'No, but there is this one other thing. It might not come up but, then again . . .' For once Sheen seemed to have started talking before he'd thought it through. He paused, made a fist and pressed it to his mouth.

'You can't stop there.'

'I know. I was looking for the words.'

'Sometimes you just have to jump in.'

'You don't say.'

'Sorry.'

127

Sheen continued in his own time. 'We suspected Neil Frampton of having an affair. It wasn't relevant to the investigation, but it's relevant to you and if it comes up again I'd rather you'd heard it from me.'

'Go on,' Goodhew said. It was obvious what was coming next but he needed it spelt out in any case.

'Frampton hit the booze when his son died. His wife, Carolyn, was busy with their baby and home seemed to be the last place Frampton wanted to be. At least, that was my take on it, and he seemed very close to your mother, Gary. I'm not accusing her, I'm just saying what we all saw.'

'Thanks.' He had only just found out that his mother worked at Frampton's, had never heard of Neil Frampton until Lorraine Martin's death, but believing the story was not a problem. He lifted a pile of documents on to his lap and glanced across at Sheen. 'How well do you remember my grandfather's case?'

'At the time I was pretty well versed. And I've had a little refresher now and then, but no doubt there's plenty that I've forgotten.'

'Did my mum . . . feature?'

'Feature?' Sheen raised one eyebrow, 'Just as the deceased's daughter-in-law,' he assured Goodhew. 'Nothing more.'

'Good. And no, I don't suspect her of anything, I just wanted to understand whether the investigating officers had missed the opportunity to link the two cases sooner.'

'It was that bangle you turned up with that made the link. Without that, it wouldn't have been looked at twice.'

That was true, when combined with Neil Frampton's name it had produced an instantaneous connection for Marks and Sheen. The implication unsettled Goodhew; inadvertently or otherwise his grandmother had helped to ensure that the two cases remained detached from one another. He switched subjects. 'How long before the Romsey Terrace files come up?'

'They'll be here this afternoon. It's connected to an active case now so it'll be quick.'·

'Can I ask you a question?'

'Quid pro quo, Clarice?' His accent and attempt at Hannibal's psychotic grin both fell short.

'What is Sue searching for in the archives?'

Sheen's smile faded. 'I don't know.'

'She hasn't told you?'

Sheen shook his head. 'I have an idea but it's not my business. Or yours.'

Goodhew ignored the hint. 'But you've guessed? You've worked it out, right?'

'Yours isn't the only family with baggage. Just leave it alone.' Sheen added, 'Would you tell her everything, Gary?'

He liked to think that he would but, in truth, there were things he'd never shared with anyone; Sheen had a point. Goodhew changed the subject. 'I just met with Robert Buckingham's daughter.'

'Amy?'

'Yes, Lorraine Martin attempted to contact her. Amy had no idea who she was and there's no hint to what she wanted so I'm guessing that it's connected either with Frampton's or Moira or, most likely, Amy's father.'

'That third one's a leap.'

Goodhew shook his head. 'Not really, Amy's been working at Frampton's trying to prove her dad is innocent.'

'There's many forms of innocent and I don't think Robert Buckingham qualified. He's served his time, what difference would it make now?'

'You sound like Kincaide.'

Sheen waggled a finger at Goodhew. 'I'm ignoring that.' He turned and pulled a file from the shelf above his desk. After a brief search he passed Goodhew a press clipping. 'That's not how he usually looked. Buckingham loved himself, he was a cocky bloke back then. And too old to be acting like he did.' The photo showed Amy's father as he was led into court. The photographer had caught him looking dishevelled and disorientated, the flash seemed to make his eyes bulge.

The way Sheen had said it made Goodhew expect to see a man in his fifties, a candidate for mid-life crisis. Goodhew studied the picture and then took a guess, 'Mid-thirties?'

'He liked teenagers. And always had to be seen to be doing well.'

'You knew him personally?'

'I met him a few times, the first when he came in here to make a statement. He always dropped things into the conversation that were intended to impress. You know the type?'

It was a rhetorical question; they all knew *that* type.

'They eventually convicted him on a manslaughter charge because there was no clear evidence that he knew the property was occupied. That angered plenty of them here. The end-of-case beer felt more like an end-of-case shandy; watered down and flavourless.'

'What's he doing now?'

'Small-time builder, I believe. He's been out for a while but I don't know where. Of course, his wife divorced him and he lost his stake in the business so I doubt he's as cocky now.'

'And Lorraine Martin? Did she play a role in his conviction?'

'I don't think so. In fact, I don't remember her at all.' Sheen frowned. 'Wait for the Romsey Terrace files and, until then, I'll find you that flipchart.'

But something else had just struck Goodhew. He reached for his jacket, 'Actually,' he replied, 'I don't need it right now.'

CHAPTER 24

Marks had told Goodhew not to waste the day but he had to work with Kincaide at some point. Kincaide was at his desk and, with no one else in the room, he'd rearranged the furniture again, this time so that he was closest to the display board. All the other desks faced his and he was furthest from the door. His desk was clear apart from a neat pile of papers stacked under a container of half-eaten takeaway sushi and a new mug, printed with a picture of handcuffs and the slogan, 'Feel safe at night, sleep with a cop'. Kincaide glanced up long enough to scowl. 'Where have you been?'

'Lunch break,' Goodhew replied, 'and before that I met with Amy Laurence.'

'The admin girl from Frampton's?'

'Yes,' Goodhew echoed, 'the admin girl.' He sat at his desk and powered up his PC. He knew Kincaide was waiting for him to explain but, then again, he was waiting for Kincaide to ask.

Kincaide's patience gave out first. 'So what did she want?'

'I'm about to email it to you.'

'Email what?' Kincaide snapped.

'My report,' Goodhew's voice sounded calm to the point of being inflammatory. It was deliberate but he didn't care.

Kincaide strode across the office then. It was a small space and three or four reasonable steps would have done it. Instead, the carpet between them was swallowed in a couple of strides and his hands slamming down on Goodhew's desk seemed to be his braking method. 'Do you have any idea how much pressure we're under on this one? The fact that you're still on this case when you're involved with the murder victim just shows how fucking under-resourced we are . . .'

'There was no involvement . . .'

'You were meeting up with her and stalking her the night she died.'

'I met with her once in connection with a cold case. A case that Marks knew I was following up.' Which wasn't quite a lie. 'Even you know I had nothing to do with her death, Michael.'

'So what report?'

Goodhew turned to his PC and clicked the screen a few times. 'I've just sent it.'

Kincaide returned to his desk and opened the file. By Goodhew's estimate he'd be fuming by the end of page one. It actually took about six seconds. 'What the fuck?' Kincaide grunted.

'You read quickly.'

'She's Robert Buckingham's daughter and you didn't report it?' He read on. 'And she had material evidence and the first I know is after lunch when you decide to email me?' He spun his chair back to Goodhew. 'What the hell are you playing at?'

'Marks knows all about Amy Laurence. I kept him posted. He said I should update you and I have.'

'You,' Kincaide's index finger made tiny jabbing motions, 'you are someone that needs to get out, out of this department, out of this job.'

Goodhew shook his head, 'You like to threaten people when there's no one else around, don't you?'

'That wasn't a threat, it was a fact. You're reckless.'

'I don't care what you think I am. I care what you do and you threatened Sue.'

'That's bollocks.'

'You told her to keep away from me. That she didn't want to burn her bridges. You shouldn't stand in a stairwell; sound travels.'

Kincaide's eyes had darkened to blackened pips. He rose from his chair and again took a couple of steps in Goodhew's direction. He opened his mouth to speak but Goodhew cut in first.

'Enough. Don't let me see you bully anyone.' Goodhew held his glare then deliberately walked past Kincaide to the board displaying the case photos. 'When's Moira Trent being interviewed?'

There was a lengthy pause before Kincaide answered. Goodhew could feel his eyes boring into the back of his head. He guessed that Kincaide's fists were clenched at his side, his body tense. 'This afternoon,' he eventually hissed.

'I'd like to go.' Goodhew turned slowly and watched Kincaide fight to hold his temper.

'I'm sending Sandra Knight. She'll take someone, but it won't be you.' Kincaide shook his head. 'You don't make the decisions, Gary. You can spend the rest of the day in here following paper instead of people.'

'That's fine.'

'I'll email you as you seem to prefer computers to humans.' His smile was bitter, 'Bank details or phone records?'

'And I thought you didn't love me.'

Kincaide fiddled with his computer for a few seconds then gave the mouse a final double-click. 'You have them both,' he smiled coldly, 'and I'm going with Knight. Email me as soon as you have anything. And email me if you don't, I want you in here until I get back.'

Kincaide left in a cloud of machismo. Point made. Subordinate humbled. Goodhew opened both files and then crossed to the window, looking down in time to see Kincaide and Knight drive out of the car park for their five-hundred-yard journey to Clarendon Street.

He checked the time, ten past two. At worst he reckoned he had an hour.

He slid the papers out from under the sushi. The pile was about three inches thick and, as he'd guessed, contained everything that Kincaide had been copied in on throughout the day, with Lorraine Martin's phone records and bank statements at the top.

'What did you do to Kincaide?'

He glanced up to see Gully in the doorway, leaning on the frame, her arms crossed. 'I might have upset him,' Goodhew replied flatly.

Sue crossed the room, her attention focused on the paperwork in front of Goodhew. 'Did you just manipulate him out of the building?'

'It ended up that way. I really wanted to speak to Moira Trent but Kincaide wasn't having any of it. The best I could do was hope he went too.'

'I was talking to Sandra and he grabbed her by the elbow and practically hauled her out to see Moira Trent.'

Goodhew looked rueful. 'I let him get to me first, though.'

She looked blank. 'Why now?'

'Little things.' And some that were not so little.

She nodded. 'Actually, I wanted to talk to you.'

Goodhew had continued to flick through the papers. He separated a bundle and placed them down on the table in front of Sue. 'What's up?'

'You know I want to become a detective?' She didn't need to wait for an answer, they both knew how much it would mean to her, 'The thing is, there's an opportunity for secondment to the Met.'

'As a detective?'

'No, but attached to a unit dealing with organised crime; primarily people trafficking and forced labour. There's potential for promotion and I'd gain more experience . . .' She fell quiet.

'I understand.' He wanted to ask, *Is it because of us?* Except there was no 'us' and he doubted that Sue thought about him the way he thought about her. 'What about your family?'

She hesitated. 'I was thinking of them, that's why I went for London; it's closer than some of the other options. I just wanted to let you know what I was doing.'

'If you're sure?'

'I think so.' He saw her redden before abruptly turning her attention to the papers, spinning them round so they were the right way up. 'From Kincaide's desk?'

'Ignore bank and phone, he's given me those already.'

'What are we looking for?'

'The best angle for knowing Lorraine Martin better.'

'FORM?' It was an acronym Sue had discovered on a website. It was designed to give topic ideas for making conversation: family, occupation, recreation, money. It worked for building a picture of dead people too and they never objected to personal questions about their finances.

'Yes, and don't think too hard. Just anything that jumps out at you.'

'Uh-huh.' She was already reading. He followed suit and half an hour passed in silence before she pushed several sheets towards him, 'Her medical records going back five years.' She pointed to the medication history, 'She'd been on antidepressants throughout. Plenty of people are, but look.' She turned to a page that contained the standard patient information, a header record with gender, date of birth and NHS number. Below this was a row of short dates with initials beside them. 'This summary sheet dates back much further. These same fields appear on the screen when I visit my GP, so I know that those,' she pointed to the dates, 'represent significant events. The headlines if you like.' There were three entries; 21/06/92 MHA S2, 15/9/01 MHA S2 and 23/1/06 DEPR. 'I'll need to check these abbreviations but that looks to me as though she was sectioned twice then diagnosed with depression in 2006.'

He mulled over the dates. 'Nineteen ninety-two, 2001 and 2006. I wonder if they're significant in any other way. No details, though?'

'Like I said, just the last five years.'

'I'll put in a request for the historic records and hope they haven't been mislaid or mislabelled.' Goodhew was close to the end of his pile of papers. 'You've done better than me.' But his voice slowed at the end of the sentence, his attention settling on the last but one sheet. 'Although . . .' He began to read.

'Gary? It's almost quarter past, we need to stop.'

'OK,' he agreed, then quickly used his phone to photograph the document. He bundled the pages back into their original order, straightening the pile and returning them to their position on Kincaide's desk and crowning the pile with the pot of sushi.

'What was it?' she whispered.

'Last year a neighbour, a Mr Gilligan, made a complaint against Lorraine Martin. He alleged that she was verbally abusive towards him and his wife. He claimed she'd been a problem in the past and that he'd finally had enough. It's worth a follow-up.'

'And what will you do about Kincaide? You can't just go behind his back on either one of these leads.'

'I'm thinking.'

Sue pulled a second chair up to Goodhew's desk. And when Kincaide returned they were poring over bank statements.

'What have you found?' he asked. His tone was reasonable now, filling the post-argument silence with fake politeness.

Goodhew did the same. 'Nothing yet. What about Moira Trent?'

'Says that Lorraine rang her drunk on the night she died. Was shouting about *they* and *them* and sounding paranoid. Not the first time she'd been that way.'

'Michael, I need a word,' Gully reddened a little but carried on. 'I came in looking for something to work on, and I assumed that those papers,' she pointed to his desk, 'weren't restricted since they were out in the open like that. Anyhow, Lorraine Martin was sectioned twice, in '92 and '01, and last year her neighbour made an antisocial behaviour complaint against her. I'm sorry if I did the wrong thing.' She smiled apologetically then pressed her lips firmly together.

Kincaide's expression had darkened instantly. 'One's a dead end. Mr Gilligan passed away three months ago. I didn't know about Lorraine Martin's mental health but her full medical records are on their way to us, so I would have been fully informed by tomorrow. You know what assuming does, Sue, so, for future reference, remember my desk isn't fair game.' Then, as an afterthought, 'Don't do it again.'

'You owe me, Gary,' she said under her breath.

She started trawling through the phone records and Goodhew carried on with Lorraine Martin's bank statements. Her account revealed more by the details that weren't present than those that were; no mortgage payments and few deposits. The money she earned came in infrequently, cash in hand by the look of the modest and irregular deposits. She'd covered her bills and little else.

Goodhew looked over at Kincaide, 'Michael, what did her sister say about her employment status? Was the jewellery her main source of income?'

'Apparently. She said that for spells Lorraine had hosted foreign language students but had knocked that on the head a couple of years ago to work full-time on,' he paused to make quote marks in the air, 'her art.'

Kincaide liked making quote marks so Goodhew made the signs himself and asked, 'Were those wiggly fingers yours or Moira's?'

'Hers. She called it "my sister's hobby". I don't think she approved but then she is an accountant. She wouldn't have seen that as a proper job.'

'Is that what she said?'

'That's what her expression said. Have you found something?'

'Just a lack of income. Is anyone questioning the other stallholders from the market?'

'Worthington's on it.'

'Or the neighbours?'

'Uniform went house to house. What's wrong with deskwork, Gary?'

Goodhew considered the little he knew about Lorraine. She'd owned a tatty Ford KA panel van, tiny with a 1.3 engine. It might have been just large enough to carry her jewellery displays to craft markets and fairs but it was definitely a budget option. The outside of her house had been less than pristine too but he had no way of knowing whether it was down to lack of funds or lack of motivation. He'd met her, of course, and he hadn't seen any sign of money then; her skin had the capillaried look of outdoor living, her hair had seemed unstyled and her clothes more practical than chic. But then again, he wouldn't have known expensive clothes from high-street knock-offs.

'About this deskwork?'

Kincaide had returned to his own paperwork and was reading. Only his eyes moved towards Goodhew. 'Go on.'

'I need to visit her house.'

Kincaide scowled, 'Explain.'

'She either lived very frugally or was receiving other money on the quiet. From her car and what I've seen of the outside of her house I'm guessing the first but I need to be sure. If I find any evidence that her spending outstripped her income, then we'll need to keep looking.'

'You sound like the Inland Revenue.'

'I'd just like to look.'

Goodhew expected him to dismiss the idea out of hand but, instead, Kincaide remained expressionless. 'You'll need to curb that attitude if you ever want to make it to DS.'

'And if I don't?'

'Take the keys and knock yourself out.'

CHAPTER 25

Mr Gilligan had lived in the house facing Lorraine Martin. A two-bedroomed mid-terrace that would have been identical in style to all the others on that side of the street before most people began to update with aluminium then uPVC replacement windows, new roofs and fancy doors. Goodhew remembered biking around these roads when he'd been ten or eleven, sometime in the year before his grandfather had died. Selwyn Road was supposed to be the coldest street in Cambridge. The last place the snow would melt. Back then the best thing to do with a day had been to explore the back alleys and end up at Newnham or Jesus Green or Cherry Hinton Hall. He might have cycled past here then and it might have looked exactly the same with the original windows in sky-blue frames, fussy net curtains and a potted hydrangea on the window sill in the lounge.

He rang the bell and immediately saw movement in the single ground-floor window. After a few seconds the door was opened by a chubby-faced woman in her fifties. Goodhew introduced himself, 'and I realise Mr Gilligan has passed away but I wondered whether his wife might be able to help me?'

'That's Mum. I don't know whether she'll talk to you or not.' She leant close to Goodhew and lowered her voice. 'She's just been diagnosed with Alzheimer's,' she told him and then raised her voice to a conversational level. 'Come in, we can ask, can't we? I'm Maggie,' she added and led Goodhew through to the sitting room.

Mrs Gilligan looked close to ninety and, while there was a strong resemblance between the two women, the mother was daintier. She wore a long-sleeved dress and sat straight with her hands clasped in her lap.

'Mum, this is Detective Goodhew, he's a policeman.' Maggie spoke slowly but without raising her voice.

Mrs Gilligan smiled up at them both. 'Is this about Lorraine? Poor girl.'

'Yes, that's right. I'm hoping you'll be able to answer some questions.'

'And you say you're a policeman?'

'I am.'

'It is only the police that have been in and out of her house so far. I'm waiting for the others to arrive, the young men and women. I have always thought they would one day.'

'Which men and women, Mrs Gilligan?'

'The young men like you. I thought you might be one of them. I'd like to help you but there's nothing to tell.'

'I'm from Cambridgeshire Police.'

She studied him for a moment, her eyes bright. 'Are you looking for your mother, lad?'

Goodhew squatted down near her chair. 'No, I'm a policeman.'

'So you told me.' She pointed at him with a trembling index finger. 'Some will still flourish on rocky ground. And I always thought that would be the case. You seem to have done well.'

'I'm here about Lorraine Martin, your neighbour.' Goodhew glanced at Maggie and she mouthed *sorry* back at him. 'Mrs Gilligan, do you remember your husband reporting her to the police? He claimed she'd been verbally abusive to both of you.'

'Of course I do. Derek said that it was my fault that she lashed out the way she did but I was trying to help her. I thought if she could confide in someone . . . Instead she began screaming obscenities at me. She threatened me, you know, and although Derek thought I was wrong to interfere he always stood up for me, so he decided to have a word. I told him not to but he'd got himself all riled and he wouldn't listen. She came right back at him, screaming and shouting foul language. I

140

tried to pull him away. "Leave her," I said, "she's off again." But he wouldn't let it drop entirely so that's when he phoned you and made a complaint.'

Goodhew nodded. 'What did you mean by "She's off again"? Were these outbursts a frequent occurrence?'

'It had happened before, then other times she was very polite.' Mrs Gilligan's gaze wandered past Goodhew as she thought back. 'I'll tell you something, I went over there later that day and she started crying and I wasn't at all surprised. That's just how it went with her.'

'How long have you lived here, Mrs Gilligan?'

'This house belonged to Derek's parents and we took it on in the fifties so we've been here longer than she has. And how old are you, twenty-something?'

She was a few years out but he didn't correct her

'Which means,' she continued, 'that we'd seen it all over the years and I knew she was heading for it again. She'd been out the front all morning that day, playing her wireless too loudly and shouting on her telephone. She kept pacing and I went over to see her, not to ask her to turn it down, but to ask her if I could help.'

'You thought she was having some kind of breakdown?'

'I don't know the name for these things but I knew she wasn't right. Derek didn't see eye to eye with all of that, he just saw her anger as an attack on me, thought she should have been able to control herself.'

'Did you have much contact with her after that?'

'Not before my Derek died. I would still say good morning when I saw her, not that that was very often. Then she bought me flowers for the funeral. She was kind underneath it all, you know.' She stared across the street then, reflecting on what she'd just told him.

'And how had she been more recently?'

Her expression brightened. 'There was a man standing in the street the night she died. I saw him and I told the police. I thought he might be one of them too.'

'One of them? Can you be more specific, Mrs Gilligan?'

She shook her head, 'I didn't get a good look at him but I'd say he was your height but younger.'

Goodhew didn't bother admitting that it was him that she'd seen. 'But what do you mean by *one of them*?'

'Lorraine's children, the ones she gave away.'

'Mum! There's no proof.' Maggie had remained in the background until then and Goodhew had been aware of her from the corner of his eye. She'd seemed on edge the entire time: fidgeting with her hands or moving her restless feet, caught between staying silent and the urge to interrupt. 'I grew up on this street, lived here until I was in my twenties and of course I've been back ever since.' She began picking her words more carefully. 'Lorraine always had lodgers, often students, and Mum was a bit nosey. I never thought there was anything strange going on. And I've never listened to this idea of babies. Lorraine didn't have children.'

'So you say, Margaret, but I saw her.' Mrs Gilligan sounded determined. 'I saw her and that's why she went like that from time to time.' She tapped on her temple with her index finger. 'It's all very well thinking that there are shortcuts in life but there's always a price to pay.'

'Which shortcut did Lorraine take, Mrs Gilligan?'

'She should have kept that baby, but she took in those girls and paid off that house. Thought she'd got it free when the rest of us had to slave for it.' She shook her head sadly. 'She paid in the end though, didn't she? Poor, poor girl.'

Goodhew tried asking her more questions but Mrs Gilligan only repeated snippets of everything she'd already told him. Maggie stepped outside the front door with him as he left. 'Mum's clear in her own mind but she's never explained the specifics to me. I've heard these kind of stories time and again but I never had any concerns about anyone but Mum.'

'How long had this been going on?'

'It started after I left home.' She touched her thumb to successive fingertips as she counted back the years. 'That was in the late eighties, I suppose. I can't give you an exact year. It just seemed like nosiness or gossip at first. I thought she was spending too much time at home with an idle mind so I dismissed her as a bit depressed, a bit of a fantasist maybe. And Dad felt the same, bless him. That sounds harsh, doesn't it?'

'A little,' he conceded.

'And I never saw Lorraine with a baby. It all sounded too far-fetched, but since Lorraine died, I'll admit it feels as though there must have been something wrong . . .' Her voice trailed off and her expression became more solemn. 'You're taking Mum seriously aren't you?'

'We're taking everything seriously.' Goodhew shook Maggie's outstretched hand. 'Please call me if she says anything else.' His gaze rested on the house opposite. 'And please thank her again, tell her that she's been a great help.'

CHAPTER 26

The hallway was carpeted in brown with a pattern of cream boxes framing pink roses. It reminded him of a seaside hotel, of more lucrative days now long gone. It was good quality but old, thinner in the centre and faded in the patches where light had fallen through the glass-paned door. The walls were decorated with a heavy embossed paper coated with layers of magnolia emulsion. There were no pictures on the walls, no side table, no curtains at the landing window. And as he walked around the house he found that the rooms were the same; clean but sparsely furnished, the décor good quality but worn and each room tidy because it stood so empty. It was obvious from the start that there was no hidden wealth in the house unless it had been burnt on drugs, alcohol or some other secret obsession.

He wore gloves and began in Lorraine's kitchen. Her freezer and larder were well stocked, her fridge bare apart from milk and cheese. She'd liked soup and pasta and had frozen several kilos of cheese when it had been on special offer. She hadn't been a vegetarian but ate little meat. She'd cooked food in batches and froze them in single portions, bagged and labelled in black pen.

It was a strange way to get to know a person but, from experience, he knew it worked.

He moved from room to room, gathering details and photographing everything he touched even though the crime scene officers would have taken similar shots. It wasn't until he reached the bathroom that the items became distinctly personal. He guessed that when Lorraine Martin had let rooms out to students the entire downstairs had been a communal area, so perhaps she'd never quite re-established herself there.

She had kept her medicines in the bathroom cabinet; here there was an accumulation of prescription blister packs, most were painkillers or antidepressants, some part-used, others untouched. An unfinished course of antibiotics, two years out of date. Two condoms and a small selection of complimentary shampoos and shower gels brought back from hotel stays, all coated with a thin but stubborn film of dust.

The dust continued to her bedroom where the surfaces and handles had been fingerprinted but the curtains and bedspread were dull, their fibres clogged with it. She hadn't been a fan of ornaments or pictures; the only exception he'd seen stood on her window sill; a heavy glass paperweight, hexagonal and set with dried flowers inside. It hadn't been dusted for prints but he could see finger marks on the sides. He turned it over. There was no maker's mark underneath, just the words 'MADE IN ENGLAND' etched into the base. He placed it back down and photographed it, suddenly registering how it had felt in his hand, warmer and with a softer smoothness than glass. Dust-free too.

Lorraine Martin had stood at this window with the paperweight in her hands. This might have been the object that had inspired her jewellery. He looked down on her garden, the barely tended rectangle of grass, the narrow strip of concrete path that looked as though it had been rolled out and dropped on top. Everything about the garden mirrored everything about the house apart from the last few feet before the fence.

The far left corner was occupied by a quarter circle of flowerbed, the far right by a garden building, not quite a shed but not a summerhouse either. It reminded Goodhew of a beach hut with its tongue and groove sides and dark blue window frames that contrasted with the main duck-egg blue body. He could see from the window that the décor of the shed was no less worn than around the rest of the house but, even from upstairs, it was easy to see that the glass was cleaner and that the step outside the door had been kept swept and clear of dead leaves. Plant pots stood either side of the door; one was an old teapot, and the other an enamel saucepan, both brimming with white and lilac winter pansies.

The same pansies filled the flowerbed, too, as though she'd bought too many and they had been planted to use up the surplus. The extras were in the pots, he decided, the others had been planted at regular intervals and provided a dense carpet around the base of a small concrete bird bath. The edge had been made with old house bricks, tilted at a forty-five-degree angle and embedded in the soil.

Goodhew glanced behind him at Lorraine's bed, then stepped back and sat at the pillow end. The window sill was just below his eye level and, from the bed, a large proportion of the view was sky and skyline. And the only part of the garden he could see from there was the beach hut and the flowerbed.

He stayed there for several minutes, trying to see both the room and the view through Lorraine Martin's eyes. Trying to imagine her life in this house, her struggle with depression and how she felt about the home that seemed to have gradually faded around her. Wondering whether anything here had helped her battle the personal ghosts that had visited her for the past twenty-five years.

Are you looking for your mother, lad?

He phoned Kincaide. 'Is there any record of Lorraine Martin having had a child?'

'There's no next of kin apart from her sister.'

'What about a child she lost, or gave up?' He explained Mrs Gilligan's comments.

'And how old is this woman?' Kincaide grunted.

'Old enough to make a reliable statement. Lorraine Martin paid off her mortgage and I'd like to know when. It's been years since this house has been cared for and years since she first suffered from mental health issues, both of which date back to the approximate time of the fire in Romsey Terrace. In my opinion we need to look back that far. If she also gave birth back then . . .'

He was interrupted by another grunt from Kincaide. 'That's all in hand, Gary. What's the situation with her income? Remember that's what you went to look at.'

'There's no money here, she's lived on a shoestring.'

'Come back then.'

'I haven't finished.'

'If the finances check out, then you have.' Kincaide hung up.

Goodhew straightened the bed covers and walked slowly downstairs. He wasn't too old to be Lorraine Martin's son and Mrs Gilligan had also said, *I thought you might be one of them.*

He phoned Gully. 'Who's doing Lorraine Martin's pm?'

'Sykes.'

'Can you phone him for me?'

'I thought you were coming back. Can't you phone him yourself?'

'I've looked over the house but not the shed in the garden, I want to do it first and Sykes will be gone by then.'

'So what do you want me to ask?'

'Whether there's evidence that Lorraine Martin had a child, or children.'

'When?'

'Not recently. The neighbour asked me if I was looking for my mother and she thought I was *one of them.*'

'Meaning what?'

'She wasn't specific but she said I was about the right age so I'm wondering whether there might be an estranged child out there somewhere.'

'Or more than one?'

'I know, sounds unlikely, but I can't leave it either.'

'To be your mother she would have been a teenager.'

'Mrs Gilligan thought I was younger.'

'I see, so a pregnancy that was twenty-odd years ago?' Then added dryly, 'I like the timing.'

'I spoke to Lorraine and she also tried to contact Amy Buckingham; I believe her death is related to at least one of those events. But I'm not just homing in on things that date back to 1992.'

'Of course you are. Marks is looking for a connection to your grandfather, so why don't you just tell him what you're thinking?'

'I will, when there's something to tell.'

Goodhew thought she was about to say something and waited but there was silence from the other end of the phone.

'OK,' he said finally.

'I'll phone Sykes then,' she replied before they both hung up.

By the time he returned the phone to his pocket he'd already made it to the beach-hut-shed. The bunch of keys for the house included one for this door too, but the wood was old and the lock rudimentary; it would have been just as easy to open it with a screwdriver.

Inside was small, square and incredibly cluttered. The furniture consisted of a chair heaped with cushions and rugs and a workbench crowded with jars of paints, empty moulds and chemical bottles. The floor was piled with the boxes and display cases of jewellery she'd taken to the craft market. The air was heavy with the smell of solvent and the untreated interior wooden wall nearest the workbench was stained with splashes of pigment; the other walls were covered with bangles and pendants, hanging on tacks from knee height up to the ceiling.

Here there was no dust.

The electric light was concentrated on the workbench and the daylight from the windows was fading; Goodhew had a torch but used the flashlight from his phone to study the items on the walls so he could snap photos too if the need arose. Each piece of jewellery had an item encapsulated in the Lucite, just like the paperweight on Lorraine's window sill and just like Nadine's bangle too; dried flowers or small hand-painted motifs seemed the most popular. He guessed that Lorraine had made them all.

He looked more closely and found that some were visibly flawed with air bubbles locked into the acrylic. He didn't know what he expected to find but still worked his way, item by item, around the first two walls. It was only when he glanced across to the nearest window that he noticed something familiar about the way the light caught one of the bangles hanging there. He photographed it in situ then took it from its hook; he didn't need to magnify it this time to know that tiny filaments of hair were suspended in the Lucite.

Baby hair.

When Goodhew had taken the first bangle to the lab, Finn had only suggested that it might be a child's hair but now Goodhew knew in his heart that this hair was identical and that it had belonged to a baby. He held the bangle in his palm and the grey light of late afternoon fell onto it from the window, then he dropped it into an evidence bag.

When he looked up, he realised that the window was facing the flowerbed squarely. First, he tried sitting in the armchair and then he stood at the bench. Both times, the crowd of mute pansies stared back at him.

He opened the workshop door and drew a couple of deep breaths of the untainted garden air. He could feel the importance of this spot, that it had been Lorraine's sanctuary, but now he was sure that it was so much more. That the carefully maintained flowerbed that she could see from both her bedroom and her workshop was a tiny shrine. But if she had given birth to a child, and that child was now an adult as Mrs Gilligan imagined, then perhaps there would be no baby buried here.

He made two calls to Parkside Station, to Kincaide out of courtesy and Marks out of necessity. As he spoke to Kincaide he crossed the patchy lawn and took a closer look at the flowerbed. Well-kept flowers didn't make a grave; the care given to this little corner didn't make it a memorial.

But by the time he rang Marks, Goodhew was standing in the gap between the workshop and the fence, hooking out a trowel and a metre-long bamboo cane, a garden spade and a black rubber bucket.

'It's Goodhew,' he said as Marks answered his phone. 'Do you have a minute?'

'What's up?'

'If I had the idea that something might be buried, how much evidence would I need for you to authorise a search?'

'It depends what it is and where it is. You can stop being cryptic, Gary. What's this about?'

'The hair locked in that bangle, sir, I wondered if it belonged to a child who'd died.'

'Based on what?'

'Nothing in particular, I was just thinking.' He felt Marks's irritation, imagined his determined lack of expression betrayed this time by the darkening of his pupils and the tightening of his mouth. 'It really is just that and I wanted to know what it would take for me to convince you to look further.' Goodhew took the bamboo cane and slipped it into the soil. It sunk about six inches with little resistance.

'For a body,' Marks muttered more to himself than to Goodhew. 'Proof that a person existed would be a start. Beyond that? Witness statements, evidence of a crime, a confession, something that resembled a grave . . . Where is this location?'

'I don't have one,' he lied, as he tested a couple more points in the flowerbed. 'It was just supposition, in case I got that far.'

'So where are you?'

'In town.'

'It sounds very quiet there.'

'I'm down on Jesus Green. I've been staring at lists for hours and I needed a break.' He held the cane and waited. 'I'm sorry I bothered you, sir.'

'It's fine. Come up to my office as soon as you're back.'

'I will.' Goodhew wished he'd never phoned Marks when he'd known all along that the answer was going to be the same as it had been on so many other occasions; to trust his own judgement.

He sank the cane into the ground at various points; in the flowerbed the soil was less tightly packed and it slipped several inches deeper without effort. He moved the bird bath onto the lawn. It had left a circle of compressed mud, smaller than a dinner plate. He pushed the cane into the ground, and at first it seemed consistent with the rest of the bed, loose earth where the top few inches had been regularly turned and replanted. It was only as he withdrew the cane that he saw a dimple form in the soil, a subtle subsidence where a cavity underground had given way and crumbled in on itself.

He lifted the topsoil away from the footprint of the bird bath, carefully depositing each spadeful on the grass near the fence. He took the trowel, knelt on the pansies and dug down, filling the bucket with the earth he removed.

He had no idea how long it took. There might as well have been nothing else in the world, his thoughts made everything fall silent. The rhythm of the trowel scooping soil into the bucket, the slowly widening wound in the ground, became the seconds and minutes, the ticking of time.

There was no warning when the tip of the trowel first failed to penetrate more than an inch into the soil. There was no sound of it hitting anything hard, it just came to an abrupt stop. He'd dug to just over a foot below the surface and hadn't expected to find anything this soon. At first he could see nothing but dark earth. He used his bare hands to reach down to the bottom of the shallow hole and pushed his fingers into the mud. His fingertips found the obstruction just below the surface, a fold of something soft, slimy from dirt, strong enough to prevent him from pushing his fingers through it. Some kind of fabric.

His hands were now too filthy for him to stop to take photographs and he silently cursed himself as he worked to clear the soil. He freed up a corner of the cloth and scraped away a small section of the mud that clogged it. The texture became visible before the colour; waffle blanket, the kind they wrapped around new-born babies.

He stood up and allowed a few seconds of silence before he went to wash his hands. He'd done enough and now he needed to tell DI Marks the truth.

CHAPTER 27

Marks had spent a long time cultivating the ability to maintain an impenetrable expression, but there were still times when it failed him. Luckily this occasion had been thanks to a phone call from Sykes so no one had seen him scowl and shake his head as he replaced the receiver.

'Goodhew, bloody Goodhew.' He swung by Sheen's desk on the way to Kincaide's. 'Where's Gary?'

'No idea, he went hours ago. Have you tried Kincaide?'

Marks shook his head. 'What did Goodhew say before he left?'

Sheen leant back in his chair. 'Looked over some of his grandfather's papers. Talked about his family a bit. Asked about the Romsey Terrace fire.'

'That's it?'

'How much drama do you want one person to have?'

Marks smiled weakly. 'And Lorraine Martin?'

'Yep, mentioned her too. Wanted to know if she'd been involved in Robert Buckingham's conviction.'

'Nothing about a body?'

It was a rare sight but Sheen looked genuinely mystified. 'What body?'

Marks shook his head; it was too much to explain right now. 'How long are you staying?'

Sheen glanced at his watch. 'A couple more hours. Going straight to the cinema after this.'

That distracted Marks for a moment. 'Really?'

'My grandson wants to see another superhero film. I didn't know the Avengers weren't Purdey and Steed until last time I took him.'

'Hmm.' Marks took a couple of steps to the window and tapped the glass. 'Goodhew phoned a while ago, asked me how much evidence was needed to dig for a body. He said it was a hypothetical question. He told me he was taking a break down on Jesus Green but now he's ignoring his phone.'

'So you don't know where he is?'

'Hopefully back in the building or, at worst, just taking a night off, like a normal person.' Marks still hadn't decided whether he was reading too much into the conversation he'd just had with Sykes, but taking a night off was hardly Goodhew's style. 'Watch his flat and ring me if the lights go on. He's not the only one who can spy from the other side of Parker's Piece.'

By the time Marks left, Sheen was already standing, coffee in hand, watching for movement in Parkside Terrace.

Kincaide sat at his desk with most of the investigating team back in the room. Marks called him and Gully out into the corridor, 'Where's Goodhew?'

Kincaide replied. 'Following up Lorraine Martin's financials.'

'He's here?'

Gully shook her head and Kincaide shifted his weight and looked uneasy. 'No, I told him to come back. Then I told him that if he had a problem following instructions from me then he needed to speak to you.'

'And where was he then?'

'At Lorraine Martin's house.'

'Why?'

'She didn't have any money in her accounts, said he wanted to check out whether there was evidence of funds coming from elsewhere. He wanted to see her house for himself.' Kincaide's expression remained anxious. 'It didn't occur to me that he was lying.'

'I doubt he was but you should have checked with me before authorising him to search that house again.' Marks glared at Sue. 'Do you know anything different from that?'

'No, but perhaps it's something else he found when he got there.'

'Why do you say that?'

'I don't know how he makes connections, but he must have seen something because he rang me and asked me to ring Sykes, to find out whether Lorraine Martin had ever had a baby.'

'Yes, Sykes just told me and that's what rang the alarm bells. I spoke to Goodhew an hour ago and he was clearly having one of his trains of thought.' Marks turned to Kincaide, 'Michael, how much do you know about this?'

'Nothing, but Goodhew doesn't want to cooperate with any of us, does he?'

'Goodhew has the idea that there's a body buried somewhere. Possibly at Lorraine Martin's house. That hasn't come from nowhere, has it?'

Kincaide's expression faltered, 'I don't know, sir. I don't know anything about a baby and it's not my fault if he can't follow simple instructions. He should be back here.'

'Michael, get over to Selwyn Road, make sure the place is secure, then ring me. I want to know whether anything's been disturbed and whether he's still there.'

'Sir, it would be quicker to ask uniform to check. They'd be there by the time I'm out of the building.'

Marks didn't respond.

'I'll grab my keys,' Kincaide said as he ducked back into the office.

Sue had stepped away from them and now she stood quietly, one shoulder against the corridor wall. She seemed in no hurry to go.

'He's right,' he told her.

'Who?'

'Kincaide. That it would be quicker for uniform to check. Depending who.'

She turned her hand over to show her phone. 'I texted him. Asked him if he was still there.'

'Has he replied?'

'Not yet. He will though.'

'And what are you thinking?' he asked.

'That I couldn't second-guess what he's doing right now.'

154

Kincaide's jangling keys came within earshot at the same moment as her phone quietly buzzed. 'Change of plan, Michael,' Marks told him, 'You're right, uniform will tackle it. And I'm borrowing Sue.'

Gully followed him along the corridor and he could see in the periphery of his vision that she was texting one-handed as she walked. 'What did Goodhew answer?' he asked.

'It was a blank text.'

'Which means what?'

'He's got my message, couldn't reply that second. So I've asked him what's happening and told him to speak to you.'

'And?'

'He just texted back, he's going to ring you.'

Marks stopped in his tracks. 'Well, he hasn't yet.'

'I told him to give you a couple of minutes, you were talking to Kincaide.' She tapped rapidly on her phone screen, 'I've put, *now is good.*'

He held his phone ready to answer.

'I'm sure he wasn't avoiding you,' she added as it began to ring.

Marks turned his back to her as he answered, 'Goodhew?'

Marks could hear the sound of footsteps. They halted and Goodhew's voice replied clear but low. 'You need to come.' In the background Marks could hear the distant sound of voices and traffic.

'Where are you?'

'Barton Road, I decided to walk round the block. I needed to clear my head for a few minutes, to make sure that I was certain before I called you.'

'And?'

'There's a body in the garden.'

'You've uncovered it?'

'No, just come, sir, and I'll explain.'

CHAPTER 28

Once Goodhew had found the blanket in the soil he'd stopped digging. He hadn't known that there was a body but had rarely felt more certain of anything. He waited at the house while the work began, positioning himself near the kitchen window so that he was clear of the forensics team but within sight of the activity as they erected their tent and began the slow process of excavating the area.

There would be criticism for the way he'd disturbed the ground but he knew it had been necessary to ensure that the search happened at all. He included that in the report and typed it up on his phone, emailing it to himself for later. The recovery of the body had taken several hours; he'd been there for three when DS Brosner cracked open the back door. 'You were right,' she told him, 'we've found it.'

He'd returned to Parkside soon afterwards and finished his report. It was another few hours before Marks called him. 'Sykes has the body ready. Are you coming?' Then they drove to Addenbrooke's with little further conversation. Goodhew guessed that what they both wanted to discuss was what they had yet to see.

Each set of remains was different, the injuries and circumstances unique, but every autopsy Goodhew had attended had been in the same familiar surroundings. Today, the sterility of the room sat uneasily with him, the tiny form too fragile to belong in a space designed for the largest of human corpses. Both Marks and Goodhew hung back until Sykes spoke.

'If you're going to stay in here you may as well be close enough to actually see something.'

The bones had been laid out in the same order as a body lying on its back, but spaced out to leave at least a centimetre between each joint. They were heavily discoloured and, at least to Goodhew's eyes, the skeleton seemed incomplete. Sykes liked to deliver information at his own speed so neither Goodhew nor Marks asked any questions, they just waited for Sykes.

'I'm not a forensic anthropologist,' he began, 'skeletonisation isn't my field and there will need to be further tests, but let's start with what we do know. Firstly, yes, these are human remains.'

Goodhew glanced at Marks who was studying Sykes through narrowed eyes. Sykes remained unperturbed. 'People bury pets in gardens and I've had plenty of bones through here that belong to a former homeowner's dog, cat or marmoset. They've been brought in by police officers so you can congratulate your colleagues on this occasion.'

'Good to know,' Marks replied flatly.

'So what do we have here?' Sykes didn't wait for an answer. 'Thanks to the synthetic fibre content of the blanket used to wrap the body the bones have been kept together long after the disappearance of the tendons linking them.'

'About the blanket,' Goodhew began, 'what possibility is there that there will be usable DNA from it?'

Sykes scowled at the interruption. 'A waste of time. Anything body-related would have degraded and become so saturated with mud and minerals that it wouldn't stand out. But we're not here for the blanket, are we?' Sykes made a point of recapping his last sentence before continuing. 'The body has been in the ground for some considerable time, certainly in excess of a decade.'

Sykes pointed to two small and tapered pieces of bone with the gloved tip of his little finger and waited until both Marks and Goodhew drew closer still.

Closer inspection revealed that the bones had the texture of dried cuttlefish, or the dehydrated husks of driftwood.

'These are the bones of the lower arm; the radius and ulna. Notice that nothing remains of the hands and feet; the smaller, softer bones have gone the same way as the soft tissue. I certainly cannot tell you anything related to the cause of death, or the age of the baby or even its sex.'

Marks began to ask a question but Sykes immediately interrupted. 'I can, however, tell you that, from the circumference of the skull and the length of the femur, those measurements are within the normal range for an average new-born.'

Marks spoke again, 'But you don't know whether the death occurred pre- or post-birth?'

'That's correct.'

'What's your best guess?' Goodhew began.

'I don't guess.'

'Estimate,' Goodhew corrected himself, 'what would you estimate as the likely age of this baby?'

Sykes looked down at the bones and only spoke after a lengthy pause. 'Somewhere between thirty-two weeks' gestation and the baby reaching two months old.'

'And DNA?' Marks asked. 'Will you be able to recover enough for any kind of profile, or to prove parentage?'

Sykes pressed his lips in a tighter line and shook his head. 'There's almost zero possibility.' He continued to shake his head. 'In fact, I'd call it zero. With just these bones there's nothing we can do to extract DNA.'

Sykes removed his gloves and crossed to the furthest surface where his laptop stood. He began tapping at keys and as the screen accessed the hospital's records system he added, 'But I can tell you who the mother isn't.'

This time Marks and Goodhew moved closer without any prompting. Lorraine Martin's name appeared at the top of the screen and they followed Sykes's finger across to the right-hand column. It read G0/P0.

'Gravidity 0, Parity 0,' he explained.

Goodhew risked a guess. 'She'd never been pregnant?'

'Never past the first two or three months and had certainly never delivered.'

CHAPTER 29

With few exceptions Cambridge buildings rarely rise above a few storeys high and Addenbrooke's sprawls low and wide across the heart of the Cambridge Biomedical Campus on the south side of the city It took over ten minutes of long corridors and signposted footpaths to make it back to their car. Marks began speaking as soon as they'd left Sykes. 'What made you dig, Gary?'

'Mrs Gilligan wasn't clear but she knew something had been going on at the house, dating back years. She described Lorraine's emotional state and waiting for people to come back . . .'

'How reliable is she?'

'Her daughter says she's been diagnosed with dementia, but the things she said fitted with the picture we have of Lorraine – particularly the emotional outbursts.'

'It's a huge leap.'

Goodhew smiled to himself. The fact was he'd wanted to believe her and he'd tilted what she'd said as a result. Many times he knew it worked the opposite way when the same claims would have been dismissed and, in most cases, that would have been the accurate call. 'I was lucky,' he said, 'her dementia diagnosis is pretty recent and she'd been telling these stories for the past twenty. And you've been to Lorraine Martin's house?'

'I have.'

'Nothing's had more than minimal attention in that time. The only part not neglected was that flowerbed and it was in plain sight of her bedroom and her workshop.'

Marks shot a swift glance in Goodhew's direction. 'Not a case of bury it and try to forget about it?'

'No, it was more personal than that. That's why I thought the baby might be hers. I found another bangle too, it was flawed and kept with other damaged pieces, like a collection of seconds. When I stood where that bangle was hanging I was facing the flowerbed again; I think the baby meant a great deal to Lorraine.'

Marks slowed. 'But why would anyone bury a baby in that way if they cared about it?'

'A concealed pregnancy perhaps. A teenager?'

'But who? And if it wasn't her baby why would Lorraine hide it then treat its grave with so much respect? Why would she choose to look out on it every day unless she was mourning?'

'When Kincaide and Knight interviewed Moira, what did she say about her sister's frame of mind?'

'Little, but that was before all of this. The first thing I'm going to do is visit her again.' He held out his set of car keys for Goodhew. 'You can come if you drive.'

Goodhew took the keys, then neither of them spoke until they were seated in the vehicle.

'Why don't you own a car, Gary?'

'Why do people like that question, sir?' Goodhew slipped it into gear and headed for the exit, 'I drive at work. Apart from that I walk most places and sometimes I use a taxi. It's a valid choice.'

'Don't you feel limited?'

'More like unencumbered.'

'You know people make assessments of others by looking at their car.'

'And that's a reason to own one?'

'Not at all. I was just making an observation; it's just another example of why you're difficult to weigh up.'

Goodhew pulled out onto Long Road and headed towards the city centre. 'Can I ask where we're headed?'

'As in direction or with the conversation?'

'With the conversation, sir.'

'Feels like a cul-de-sac.'

'OK, here's the truth. I've never felt the desire either to buy one or to own one, but that choice seems so alien to so many people that virtually everyone in the department has asked whether I had a bad experience, or can't afford one or whether it's moral or ethical reasons.'

'But it's not?'

'It's not. I just don't have the need for one.'

The traffic slowed and Marks studied the pedestrians who were now able to keep pace with the car. 'I think you feel the need to go your own way, Gary. You don't want to do anything just because it's expected.'

'OK . . . why the analysis?'

'I'd like this closed before I leave. Selfish or not, it would make it feel as though I'd finished at the right moment.'

Goodhew didn't reply; he couldn't see the connection between car ownership and Marks's retirement.

Marks stared at the road ahead although Goodhew had no doubt that he was firmly in his boss's peripheral vision. 'I'm naming the baby Frankie by the way.'

'Why?'

'It's too impersonal otherwise. He or she isn't just a pile of bones.' He let his words settle for a few seconds before he spoke again. 'You found Frankie's body when I told you not to dig.' There was an edge to his voice. 'I trust your judgement, Gary, but if I tell you that I expect you to follow your nose on this one, will you still do it?'

'Despite my personal connection to the case?'

'Despite everything.'

'I'll give it my best.' Goodhew took his eyes from the road long enough to check whether Marks's expression gave any clue. It didn't. 'Is there something you need to tell me?'

'I took another look at Nadine's file. I convinced myself I'd seen that bangle before.'

'And?'

'There it was, in the photos of her flat and in the inventory.'

'The same one?'

'It was in her personal effects, not in the evidence. Her next of kin would have had responsibility for disposal, and the records show that several months after her death all but her family photos were donated to charity. I would like to assume for a moment that it is the same bangle.'

'We can hardly ask Lorraine.'

'Quite.' Marks twisted in his seat and finally looked directly at Goodhew. 'I believe that your grandfather stole it from Nadine's flat sometime between her murder and the disposal of her personal effects.'

'But there's no proof?'

'None, but consider the odds.'

Goodhew already had and Marks was right; Lorraine had admitted that the bangle had been Nadine's and his grandfather had had the opportunity to take it; the probability that Joe had taken it was pretty high. 'How does it help?'

'You tell me. Could he have known of its significance or was it just as the souvenir that it appealed to him most?'

Goodhew didn't know. He pulled up to the kerb outside Moira Trent's house, locked up and was with Marks at her doorstep but still hadn't replied. Marks didn't push for an answer, perhaps he didn't expect one, so they both waited silently at the front door. Goodhew's phone vibrated and he stole a quick glance at the screen, killed the call, rapidly texted Sue in reply and was done by the time Moira appeared.

She wore camel trousers and a cream top, her hair was a muted blonde shot through with streaks of grey. The greyness had seeped into her complexion too. These weren't the details Goodhew usually noticed but the effect was like finding a 1970s colour photo where everything had faded until it was a shade of beige. The interior of the house echoed the same tones. She led them through to her kitchen and gestured for them to sit at the large farmhouse table.

'Thank you for coming,' she said even though their visit had come without warning. She didn't try to smile but pressed her lips tightly shut and waited with her hands resting on the back of the chair opposite Marks.

'Please take a seat, Miss Trent.' Marks waited for her to settle then added, 'You have a different surname to your sister?'

'There's the difference between us inspector; I hated our father and used our mother's maiden name after they divorced. Lorraine hated him but continued to use his name to keep the peace. She was more forgiving.' Moira turned her right hand palm up on the table, 'At school she was the one who volunteered her time, and I . . .' she turned her left hand, 'I didn't. Which also explains why I became an accountant and she lived as she did.' She looked across at each of them in turn. 'We were very different but a bond existed nonetheless.' She leant back in her chair. 'I know there's been activity at Lorraine's house.'

'There's been a development,' Marks said. 'A discovery at your sister's home.'

Moira's shoulders stiffened and her jaw set, and Goodhew wondered whether she would be listening fully; the stillness that descended on her seemed forced and he pondered whether her only thought was 'don't react, don't react'.

'A team of officers have recovered the remains of a baby from the rear of your sister's property' Now it was Marks who became still, watching her, watching him.

She tried hard to show nothing but couldn't help the colour slipping further from her face, or the seasick grey that replaced it. 'She never told me about a baby,' she whispered. She tipped her head back as though she wanted to stare at the ceiling but then closed her eyes. Her lower teeth bit her top lip and she took several heavy, slow breaths. It was a while before she spoke.

'Was it buried near the bird bath?'

'It was.'

'She always kept it so pretty. But I never would have guessed.' She raised herself and then leant forward again, this time resting her elbows on the table and facing Marks squarely. 'I don't know what you're thinking, but Lorraine would never harm a child.'

'We know it wasn't Lorraine's baby.'

'How?'

'Pathology. They can tell when a woman has delivered a child.'

'She wouldn't harm *anyone's* child.' She shook her head. 'Lorraine suffered depression, she lost her job because of it.'

'Which job was this?' Marks asked even though he and Goodhew both knew the answer.

'She was a nurse. At Addenbrooke's.'

'Until when?'

'Maybe 1990, I don't remember exactly.'

The facts matched what they already knew but Goodhew watched Moira more carefully now as he waited for his moment.

'So from 1990 until she began making jewellery, she did what exactly?'

'She had severance pay; it was the stress of the job that had caused her problems. That and the lodgers. I helped her when I could.'

'And you made up her accounts?'

'Yes.'

'So you do have records?'

'Not now. They'd be too old.'

'It will be necessary to search your paperwork.'

'I don't think so.'

'We'll be able to request a search warrant.'

She gave a small, hard smile. 'I have nothing to hide.'

Goodhew leant forward then and they both looked across at him. 'Do you remember any of Lorraine's lodgers, Miss Trent?'

'Vaguely, I suppose. Some Christian names perhaps.'

'Like Nadine?' Marks stayed expressionless. Moira failed.

'What about her?'

'I've just received a message to say that Nadine Kendall lodged with your sister for four months in 1990. Why wouldn't you be forthcoming with that information?'

'I'd forgotten.'

'Really? This is the same Nadine whose bangle is in our labs at the moment, being analysed to see if it contains baby hair. Ring a bell?'

'Of course I knew Nadine. But not the bangle.'

'Are you sure? Because it was made by your sister.'

Moira shook her head. 'I don't know what my sister made.'

'But you know what she used to do,' Goodhew said.

This time her puzzlement looked genuine. So did Marks's.

'What kind of nurse was she?' Goodhew pushed.

And the confusion vanished. Moira's eyes snapped shut then reopened slowly, filled with only part of the light they held before. 'She was a midwife,' she told them quietly.

'So,' Marks replied, 'what can you tell us about the baby?'

She stared into her hands.

'Was it Nadine's baby?'

Again she shook her head. 'I don't know. I know Nadine was pregnant and she moved away. As far as I know she had the baby adopted because when she came back the following year it was just her. I don't know anything else.'

CHAPTER 30

Amy and Alex's paths had crossed every day since their first encounter. He'd found reasons to visit the site office: to check costings, to borrow equipment, to look for missing paperwork. Today was no different and Amy glanced up from her computer to see Alex crossing the yard again.

She continued working until he opened the door. 'We don't see you for weeks, now you're here three days in a row. Are you harassing me?'

'You found me out,' he said flatly. He'd crossed the room and dumped a pile of building plans onto Stan's desk. 'He's out on site, right?'

Amy nodded. 'He's back at one.'

'I'll clear off at lunchtime. I need to get through this and I can concentrate here.' He'd unpacked his laptop and set it up to one side of the desk before rolling out the first of the plans, tacking it to the desk with a short strip of masking tape at each corner and settling down to work the old-fashioned way with a scale rule, pencil and notepad. Amy hadn't meant to watch him but when he glanced towards her it had been too late to look away. 'See, I'm not here to stalk you.'

'That wasn't really my suspicion.'

He grinned impishly. 'Hard work is good for me; working hard in front of my parents feels wrong.'

She tilted her head to one side and studied him for a moment. 'You know, neither of those comments suit you.'

'Why?'

'You have that whole tattooed biker thing going on. You should be a mechanic or a bouncer or . . .' She'd tried to think of a third example.

'A guitarist in a heavy metal band?'

'Yes, why not?'

'Because I'm studying to be an architect, you know, just in case Bruce Dickinson needs a house in Cambridge.'

She guessed it was a joke so she smiled then tapped Dickinson's name into Google. A few minutes later she emailed him across the office, 'I don't know a single Iron Maiden track.'

He emailed back, 'Freak.'

They didn't speak for the rest of the morning but a flurry of short emails pinged back and forth across the office. As he'd packed away his paperwork a final email arrived in Amy's inbox. 'Sorry we got off on the wrong foot.'

She replied, 'Me too.'

Sometimes there would be a lull in the afternoons; no drop in work but a period when they all worked silently and the atmosphere in the room came close to harmony. Today, Amy's keyboard made the only sound as she rattled through each successive email. Stan studied a floor plan, transferring measurements and notes onto a separate sheet of paper. A little later he glanced up and caught Amy watching him. 'Is there a problem?'

'I was wondering how well you knew her?'

'Who?'

Stan frowned as he'd asked but she sensed less impatience than usual. 'Lorraine Martin.'

He placed his pen down then spread his broad hands flat on the desktop. 'Well enough, I suppose. She was a face from the past. Like your father. Like Theo. And Nadine.' He concentrated on his hands, perhaps until he was sure that he had them under control. 'I don't know why they've let you stay.'

'Neither do I, but you know them better than I do. It was obvious that Carolyn wasn't happy, but Neil insisted. I'll carry on at least until Moira's back.'

'I know why Neil gave you the job. I've known all along. He likes to keep an eye on things. He told me to watch you and let him know what I saw.'

Stan's heavy features showed no hint of warmth. This was probably the longest conversation they'd had and Amy already knew she preferred the silences. Despite that she still smiled at the arrival of a sudden thought. 'And now he's told you to talk to me? Or was it Carolyn?'

'I tell Neil. Neil tells Carolyn. That's the way it works.'

'But then, there was nothing to tell until Lorraine died. Was there?'

Amy's keyboard fell silent, replaced by the sound of her pulse throbbing in her ears. She needed to believe that she'd done nothing that would have led to Lorraine's death.

'Why would there be a connection, Stan?' She heard a tremor of fear in her voice and his small, tight reply told her that he'd caught it too.

Then he moved from his desk and sat on the edge of hers. 'What did you do?' he breathed.

Amy shook her head. 'Nothing – I'd never spoken to her, never heard her name even.'

'And your father? Did he contact her for any reason?'

'I don't talk to him about work.'

'Bollocks.' He kept his voice low but intense. 'He's not stupid, he'll be watching everything you're doing.'

'He's not well. He's not like he was before his heart attack.' Stan waited and, when the silence became too much, Amy continued, '*I'm* not stupid. I have wondered about the timings, about Lorraine's death coming just after I started here, but I don't have any information.'

'Lorraine died right here.'

'I know.'

'Had you planned to meet her here?'

'Of course not.'

Had Lorraine known that Amy sometimes worked late? Sometimes started early? These were questions that Goodhew had asked. She looked at Stan levelly. 'You and my dad were friends. Haven't you ever considered he might be innocent?'

Stan shook his head. 'I was his mate. He wasn't mine and it took me a long while to see him for what he was.'

'He always mentioned you, I remember that from overhearing my parents talk. And I know you gave evidence against him at the trial but when I visited him there was never any resentment.'

'And now I pity you.' He rose to his feet, smoothing down the thighs of his overalls with trembling hands. His mouth trembled too, the words percolating close to his lips, anger leaving him torn between an outburst and a physical reaction. He stepped back, his hands dropping to his sides and forming fists, but he was still close enough to over-shadow Amy. The Portakabin floor creaked under his bulk. 'I pity your blind loyalty.'

Amy was out of her chair and face to face with his before she'd had time to think. 'Tell me why you turned against him then,' she shouted at him. He stepped back again and she imagined him leaving before he'd told her anything. She moved forward until she could feel the heat from his face. 'What did my dad do to you?'

'You don't want to know.'

'Do I look like someone with their head in the sand? I'm here until Moira gets back and I can keep this going day after day if that's what it takes.'

'Don't be ridiculous.'

'Am I? I've had weeks of your bad temper. I'm not scared by it.'

Amy could see plenty of signs of Stan's volatility; it bubbled close to the surface, but she could also see how determined he was to keep it in check. 'I think your friendship ended before the fire, otherwise you would have stood by him. In your mind, he let you down.'

'Not just me.'

'Who then?'

Stan ran his tongue slowly across his teeth before he spoke. 'You heard my name in your house because I was his excuse, his alibi for every time he cheated on your mother. "A lad's night with Stan" and I'd see your mum and she'd say, "Stop dragging him out so often, Stan." And I'd apologise and hope she wouldn't ask any questions about where we'd been or what we'd eaten or even which day I'd supposedly been out with him. Is this really what you want to hear?'

'Is it the truth?' she asked.

He bristled at once. 'I'm not fucking around here.'

'I'm sorry, please go on.'

'He used me to ease things over with your mum, and once in a while we'd have a drink together and he'd act like my fucking mate. I forgot the pecking order for a bit – thought we were equals. Not for long, though. He took money from the business, cheated the firm, and cheated his wife. Think about it – he cheated you. He didn't ever have a conscience.'

'He didn't start the fire,' she responded stubbornly.

'Why not? It could have answered all his problems.'

'Like what? Debt?'

'Debt and more. Some of us think it was money. Some of us don't.'

'Us? Like who?'

'Those who were there. Sitting in court day after day.'

'He wouldn't have hurt people – not intentionally.'

'I went to Romsey Terrace the morning after the fire. Neil asked me to go. He stayed home with Carolyn. Alex was still a baby. I didn't know what Neil thought I'd be able to do. The chief fire officer's report explained about the structural damage, about the ongoing risk, likely causes, et cetera. All I remember is the blackened windows and thinking about Nadine and Theo's last minutes.'

Amy kept very still, careful not to do anything that might interrupt him.

'I remember just one word he said. Accelerant. Then I knew it had been deliberate and the only feeling I remember is wanting to kill whichever bastard had done it.'

Stan leant back against the wall. 'In my mind, Theo was just a kid, I'd seen him grow up. And Nadine . . .' His gaze settled beyond Amy and for one unguarded moment she could see his pain. He looked back at her and returned to his usual opaqueness. 'How did you think I felt when I found out it was your father?'

'Devastated if that's what you believed.'

Stan snorted in disgust. 'Have you ever been to a trial?'

'No.'

'Have you even visited a court room?'

She shook her head.

'When you start out you think that all you need to do is get to the

170

end and hear the right verdict. Either Carolyn or Neil attended every day. Theo's mother too until it became too much for her. You end up hearing everything, you relive the final hours over and over. Experts tell you how slowly they died, how they attempted to escape, the cloth they'd held to their mouths, the skin burnt onto the door handle, the two of them huddled and melted. The jury were handed photos we didn't see but we watched their faces. And, throughout, your father sat there. Expressionless. Didn't even have the balls to look any of us in the eye, and none of it shocked him. Did your mum tell you all of that?'

Amy shook her head. 'No,' she replied, 'she didn't.'

CHAPTER 31

Goodhew returned to Parkside, avoiding Kincaide long enough to make it up to the second floor and to the boxes of information on his grandfather's case. This time nothing diverted him and Sheen kept himself deliberately busy while Goodhew made notes and took photographs. When Goodhew stayed late, though, so did Sheen.

'There's no need,' Goodhew told him.

'Someone has to supervise you. For your own good, if nothing else.'

'If there's a complaint because I've been looking through these documents then I don't think you'll be able to stop the mud sticking.'

'Probably not, but I'm still staying. OK?'

'OK.' Goodhew continued to work, aware that Sheen had moved his chair out from behind his desk and was watching him from just a few feet away. He didn't speak again until Goodhew was done and putting the last of the pages back into the final box.

'What happens now?'

'I read and hope I find something.'

'Then cross-reference, check dates, track lines of enquiry?'

'As far as I can.'

'Just like the investigation then, but with fewer resources?'

'You make it sound pointless.'

'Doing what everyone else can is pointless.' Sheen passed Goodhew a flash drive. 'It's the Romsey Terrace case and it contains everything

I could copy in one afternoon. Now you need to step back and do what you do best.'

'Have you been speaking to Marks?'

Sheen shrugged, 'I often do.'

The longest wall of the former study of Goodhew's grandfather was newly painted in a shade that the can described as Sand Dune. The colour chart had promised *classic* and *serene*. It had lied. As it had dried, it reminded Goodhew increasingly of congealed porridge. The good news was that the wall deserved to be defaced; Goodhew found a fat black marker pen and drew three large circles in the formation of an inverted equilateral triangle.

The top left circle belonged to his grandfather's case, the top right to the Romsey Terrace fire and the lower circle belonged to Lorraine Martin's murder. He filled each with names, dates and key facts; it was a slow process and at 1 a.m. he went upstairs to his flat, returning with a pot of coffee, milk, sugar and a mug. He left it to cool and an hour later drank it cold while he surveyed his work. He continued then, underlining some details in coloured marker, drawing lines to interconnect others. By 5 a.m. he was done and in the centre of the wall, in the gap between the three circles, he'd written two names.

He phoned his grandmother then. 'Is it too early?'

She sounded fully awake. 'When is it ever?'

'I'm making omelettes.'

'After staying up all night breaking eggs, I suppose? Give me twenty minutes.'

She arrived in fifteen. Her hair and makeup appeared freshly styled, her pencil skirt and cotton blouse looked newly pressed and she wore an expression which said she'd be missing nothing.

'When do you sleep?' he asked her.

'When the mood takes me. Besides, you know I loathe routine.' She immediately redirected her focus to the wall. 'You've been busy.'

'Joe's case is up there,' he said quickly.

She stood in front of the wall for several minutes without comment. He hadn't thought anything of working in here; it was where he preferred to be. But now he was acutely aware that this was the room that had once been the crime scene, the place his grandmother had held her dying husband. He crossed to the window with the words of the original emergency call reverberating in his head.

The police station looked quiet, the swimming pool unlit.

There was no one on Parker's Piece but he could still picture Sue walking away.

This room connected him to everyone and everything that mattered. He turned back in time to see Ellie reach out to touch the place where Joe's name was written before settling herself on the sofa.

'Well, I didn't like that dismal beige anyway.'

'Sand,' he corrected, 'according to the tin.'

'Proof that you shouldn't believe all you read then.' She pointed at the wall. 'Three cases, three circles, that much I understand, but why the two names in the middle?'

'Nadine Kendall is the common denominator, a victim of the fire, ex-housemate of Lorraine Martin and the owner of the bangle that Joe kept. She is connected in some way to every strand of these separate investigations.'

'Plenty to follow up?'

'Yes, but for Marks, not for me. Lorraine Martin's murder is the primary investigation; the Romsey Terrace fire is a closed case and he'll follow up anything on Joe's case but every resource is stretched.' Goodhew pointed towards the second name. 'I need to find Melanie Franks. As far as the investigation goes, she's nothing more than a name on a sheet of paper. I've looked for her through the usual channels. There's nothing.'

Ellie spread her hands on her lap. 'I've looked for her more than once. I can't find any record of her birth, her university admission or anyone of that name living in Cambridge at that time.'

'I thought you wanted her left alone?'

'I do . . .' She pursed her lips for a moment. 'I thought she might have some answers, but, when I couldn't locate her, I decided to come to terms with that. It seemed safer.'

Goodhew knew that there were personality traits that he'd inherited from his grandfather but there was plenty that had come from his grandmother too; like puzzle solving, doggedness and too much curiosity. 'That doesn't make sense. I could just about understand why you never looked for her but, once you'd made the decision to start, you wouldn't have just given up. And there's that thing you're doing with your hands.'

Her hands had remained palms down, one on each thigh. In symmetry. 'What thing?

'When we play backgammon and you do that, I know there's a play you want me to miss.'

She moved, locking her neat fingers together and resting them in her lap. 'And now I know that I'm so readable, I shan't do it again.'

'So?'

Goodhew knew his grandmother well enough to decipher most of her expressions; right now her thoughts had slipped back into the past and he could see her struggling to find the right place to start. He waited.

'Your parents were totally mismatched from the start,' she began. 'I could see why your dad fell for her, though. She was pretty and exciting and clever and all those other clichés of teenage attraction but, more than that, she had this personality that people just wanted to be around. And you know your dad . . .'

She left the sentence to die. Goodhew could have answered that he didn't know his dad much at all, but that was the point. His father's relationships seemed to be mostly with formulae and computer programs; he stayed absorbed in his work to the exclusion of everything else that Goodhew could remember, apart from the instances when he sat patiently with his son to help him with his maths homework. That habit had continued long after Goodhew had begun to excel at the subject but ended when he and his sister had been sent to boarding school. To Goodhew, his father was clever but remote, neither unkind nor warm, a man with solitary habits and an over-productive mind.

'Your dad looked up from his work long enough to be captivated. I think it was the first time he'd ever attracted that kind of attention.'

Goodhew and his sister Debbie had heard the story of how their parents had met but this time it had a totally different slant.

'They seemed to meet, get engaged and then marry very quickly.

A wedding reception can be full of truths; drinks flow and people's guard comes down. Her father asked me whether we would be buying them their first home – after all, their daughter had married our only child. I don't know how your mum had found out about our wealth, but here we are, over thirty-five years later, and I remain convinced that she chased him for his money.'

Goodhew didn't argue. His mother had gone on a spending frenzy as soon as his parents had inherited after his grandfather's death. His parents' divorce had come at the end of the money and now, according to his sister, her new husband was a wealthy property developer. Goodhew hadn't been to visit her in Australia. 'How does this connect with Melanie Franks?' he asked.

She waved her hand in a just-wait gesture. 'We didn't buy them a house and your parents lived on what your dad earned. He was soon absorbed in his work again and I can see that her life was lonely at times. She found a job when Debbie was a few months old. We looked after you both so it was easy for me to spot the changes in her; late nights, new clothes, different body language. Suddenly she seemed content with the way your dad seemed so detached.'

'She was having an affair?'

'Not then perhaps, but over the next few years there were several.'

'How do you know?' he asked sharply.

Ellie raised her eyebrows. 'I know how to follow people, Gary.'

'But your own daughter-in-law?'

There was a glint of amusement in her eyes. 'Why should family miss out on the perks of the business? She changed jobs multiple times and the last of those was when she started work at Frampton's.'

'Why couldn't I have a normal grandmother?'

She ignored the question. 'You want the truth? Well, this is it. Melanie contacted us via your mother. They worked together and your mum wanted to help her. After the fire it was your mother who began pushing me for information; it seemed as though she'd had a change of heart about Melanie disappearing and was determined to locate her.'

'But why?'

'All she said was that she wanted to make sure that Melanie knew about Nadine's death, but that never made sense. Your mum and

Melanie both understood that Melanie's disappearance meant cutting all ties. She had another reason for wanting to find her.'

'One that wasn't in Melanie's best interests?'

'I'm not accusing your mother of anything but I think it is fair to assume that she knew more than she let on.' She paused and her determined tone softened. 'But you and Debbie had just lost your grandfather, you'd been packed off to that damn school and your parents were divorcing; I was never going to put you both through more without proof.'

CHAPTER 32

Goodhew left his grandmother and went up one flight to his flat. He stood at his window, watching Parker's Piece as he waited for the call to connect. Sydney was nine hours ahead but he hadn't considered the time difference when he'd picked up the phone and felt slightly disappointed as he realised there was nothing inconvenient about his timing.

He wasn't sure how long it had been since he'd spoken directly to his mother, or to either of his parents for that matter, but he immediately noticed that the Australian edge to her accent had developed since the last time.

'So,' she spoke before he'd had a chance to say more than hello, 'are you finally planning to visit? Your sister would love to see you.'

'And I'd love to see her, but my call's work-related.'

'I see.' She wouldn't have liked that reply and he had a mental image of her standing with the phone to her ear, jutting her chin in impatience and flicking the hair back over her shoulder with a shake of her head. 'Go on.'

'Cambridgeshire Police have tried to contact you.'

'I thought I'd hang on until *you* made the effort.' She said it as if there was a question mark at the end of the sentence. It was a habit she had and when he'd been younger he'd tried to guess at the answer and over-explain himself.

Now he kept it short. 'It's partly about Grandad . . . about Joe.'

'I wondered when this would rear its head again. You've been speaking to Ellie, I suppose? I moved to the other side of the world to escape the scrutiny of that woman.'

Goodhew pressed his hand against the cold window pane and caught the moment when the street lamps on Parker's Piece were extinguished for the day; one of the four bulbs on the Reality Checkpoint was broken and the other three going out restored its symmetry. He took a breath. 'It's about Melanie Franks, I need to find her,' he continued, 'and I know you knew her.'

'I wouldn't know where she lives, would I?'

'Please, tell me what you do know. How you met her. Why you helped her. Why you tried to find her after she'd gone.'

'I worked with Nadine Kendall and I met Melanie through her. Nadine died and it's all too long ago, it won't affect anything.'

'You're wrong '

'Gary, I'm not going there,' she cut in before he could add more. 'I know you loved your grandad but you were eleven when he died. Hanging onto it for over twenty years isn't doing you any favours.'

Did she really believe that there was a time limit on grief? On finding answers? Goodhew pressed the glass more firmly. 'You knew Moira Trent.'

'What's that got to do with anything?'

'And her sister.'

'Lorraine? Of course.'

'Lorraine was murdered just hours after I spoke to her about Grandad and Nadine.'

Stillness echoed down the phone line. 'Oh, I see.' She added, 'What happened?'

He explained, filling her in on the same details that had appeared in the local papers, before adding the main detail that hadn't: 'Then we recovered the body of a baby from her garden.' He paused until he'd heard her gasp. 'So your help is important.'

'It's not Melanie's baby.'

'Or Nadine's?'

'No.' Her voice wavered. 'At least, I don't think so. Nadine left Buckingham and Frampton's before she had the baby. I never saw it and as far as I knew she gave it up for adoption.'

'But Melanie kept hers?'

'She left the area when she was pregnant.'

'And they both lived with Lorraine? Or just Nadine?'

'Don't you know that?'

'We have records of Nadine using the address, but nothing whatsoever about Melanie.'

'Yes, they both lodged with Lorraine but I don't see why any of this is necessary, Gary.'

'You can't see why we need to get answers? To identify that child and who killed Lorraine?'

She was pacing now. He could hear the clicking of her heels on a tiled floor. Every time she spoke she slowed or stopped, and then moved on again whenever it was his turn.

'Mum? You liked Melanie and that's why you helped her. If she's in danger now we need to find her as quickly as possible.'

'I don't believe she was ever in danger. I bought into a whole sob story about her fearing for her life, about being desperate to start again with her baby. But there are always two sides.'

'Explain what you mean.'

'Melanie was pregnant, not prepared to have an abortion but being threatened by her ex. Well, that's what she told me and, yes, I put her in touch with Joe and he did what he did. Hang on.' The phone was silent for a few seconds, then he heard her cross the room and the sound of her settling into a chair. When she spoke again her tone had become less abrasive. 'To my mind Melanie was quite dull; she never seemed to like much beyond cookery and museums. I met her because I worked with Nadine and, later, Melanie worked in the office too. She wasn't the sort of person I would have chosen as a friend but work pushed us together and I was fond of them both; I suppose I had the big sister role.'

Goodhew's expression stiffened; at least she hadn't said 'I had the mother role'.

'She latched onto me. She was in debt, perhaps she thought I had money.'

'What kind of debt?'

'She was naive. She just didn't know how to manage and her

spending was out of control. I don't think her parents knew any of it. She said she couldn't ask them for help anyway and if she'd told them she was pregnant it would have been worse.'

'What made you change your mind about her?'

'Do you know Neil Frampton?'

'The man you had an affair with?'

'Gary, it wasn't like that.'

'Really?'

'Neil and I were in a similar position: your father was obsessed with work, Neil's wife with their new baby. We spent hours working together and grew close over the following months. We ignored reality for a while; it was more than friendship but we never slept together. It's the kind of thing that happens when people are lonely.'

'Uh-huh.'

'Do you want to know or not?'

The honest answer was that no, of course he didn't. 'Sorry, go on,' he replied.

'We'd been close like that for well over a year and when that house burnt down and his son died I became the one he leant on. He had problems connecting with Carolyn and their baby. He said he found it too painful to be around Alex. That's when we reached our closest; he needed someone and back then I needed to be needed.'

Goodhew was tempted to stick his fingers in his ears and drone la-la-la until it was over.

She kept talking, 'And that's when he told me that Melanie's baby was Theo's. Theo would never have threatened Melanie but Neil was desperate to find her and bring her baby back into the family.'

Goodhew had seen photos of Theo. He had been strongly built with an intense expression, not a prime candidate for timidity. 'You don't know that, people under duress . . .'

'No. Theo was never wired like that. He was a thinker, he was always measured. And always very kind and giving whether it was deserved or not.'

'On the face of it . . .'

'Gary, if Theo threatened anyone then there are no peaceful people in the world.'

Goodhew didn't think he was naturally cynical but he was finding it hard to imagine anyone who wouldn't issue a threat or two in the right circumstances. He didn't push it, though. 'So you think Melanie had been lying?'

'I don't know the truth but by then I was wishing that I'd never stuck my neck out for her. Neil was distraught when he found out that Theo might have had a child and I knew that Melanie had been twisting the story.'

'How distraught? Enough to attack Joe?'

'Distraught at the loss of Theo. He thought the world of him and I don't know how he carried on.'

'I guess he took a lot of comforting?' Goodhew dropped the sarcasm and carried on before she had a chance to respond. 'Were you surprised at Robert Buckingham's arrest?'

She didn't reply and he was about to repeat the question when she spoke. 'Things shifted after that and by the time of the trial Neil and I had drifted apart again. It was just circumstance.' She changed subject and carried on talking with no pause and it took him a moment to focus on what she was saying. 'I wish we'd been closer, Gary.'

'You and who?'

'Us. I sent you to that school because I thought it was the right thing to do – to give you and Debbie stability and a better education.'

And to push two grieving children out of sight of the acrimony of divorce? 'Do you know anything about Joe's death?'

'Of course not.'

'There's a connection between Joe and Melanie and Lorraine, and if there's anything you know, however insignificant it seems, I need to hear it.'

'Only that I didn't give you the time you needed to get over it,' she told him. 'I made mistakes with you and Debbie, but she and I have worked through it. You could visit, Gary, and the three of us could spend time together. It might fix things.'

He closed his eyes and didn't reply.

'And just so you know, I was the one that broke it off.'

He didn't know whether she meant with his father or with Neil Frampton.

'With Neil,' she added as though she'd read his thoughts. 'I stopped it before it went any further. I don't think I did as much damage as you think I did.'

'OK, Mum,' he muttered, 'but that really doesn't matter now. I appreciate your help and I'll call you again if there's anything else.'

CHAPTER 33

They returned to the storage unit in Hope Street Yard. His idea was simple: if the bangle was a souvenir taken from Nadine's flat then Joe would have collected another item the year before when he'd helped Melanie. Goodhew had only learnt fragments of information from speaking to his mother but his disappointment was replaced by a buzz of expectation as he waited for the door to open. He had the illogical thought that everything might have been removed since their last visit, but of course nothing had changed.

A halogen tube was built into the ceiling and drenched the space in bright blue-white light, but the items that lay in the shadows and cupboards were in almost total darkness. Goodhew used the flashlight on his phone, and his grandmother drew a slim chrome-cased torch from her bag. 'A torch won't time out,' she told him. 'How do you want to do this?'

'Was there any logic to the items he kept?'

'They needed to remind him of the person and the case. His idea was that he'd be able to pick up any one of these mementoes and the whole story would come back to him.'

'He could have just written it down.'

The torchlight caught her face and he saw her grin. 'And where's the challenge in that? Besides, rereading the stories isn't the same as retelling them. I'm sure they improved over time.'

Goodhew opened the nearest drawer. All the items it contained were physically small, the size of a matchbox at most. And there were five of those, two were empty, and the other three held individual items of jewellery; a single earring, a signet ring, a tie clip.

She shook her head, 'It's none of those; I recognise them all.'

Goodhew recalled a few but he didn't see how he would be able to locate anything as efficiently as his grandmother could. She seemed to read his mind.

'Remember, Melanie was a history student. Pregnant. Not local. She can't have had connections to Wales or the West Country or Joe wouldn't have relocated her in that direction.'

'Probably not from anywhere south of here or Joe would have picked the north.'

'Exactly.'

Goodhew realised that he was missing the answer to an obvious question.

'You would have met her, wouldn't you?'

This time she nodded. 'Briefly. She wasn't forthcoming with information. I could see she was scared, or making a good job of pretending to be . . .'

'That's when you and Joe disagreed about helping her?'

'People who are desperate can be dangerous. I didn't doubt that she'd had problems but she wouldn't tell us anything of substance and that wasn't good enough for me.'

She'd opened the next drawer and turned her attention to its contents.

'Her story kept changing. She said the baby was a result of a one-night stand, then that the father had threatened her, that he'd wanted to take the baby but then that she didn't know anything about him. I didn't like the situation but for Joe it was enough that she needed our help.'

'My mother said that Theo could have been the father. Did his name come up?'

'No, never.'

'Can you describe Melanie?'

'After this long it's more of an impression. She was in her late teens, shorter than me, about five-five. Apart from being pregnant she was skinny. Perhaps wiry would describe her better.'

'So not frail?'

'Not at all, more like one of those outdoorsy types. But I don't see how that helps you; she'd be in her early forties now and it would be a long shot to find anyone who hasn't changed shape in that time.'

'It's not that kind of picture I'm after. Which kid would she have been in the class?'

His grandmother then saw where he was heading. She closed her eyes as she considered her answer. 'In my form she would have been Polly Manby. Polly wore shorts and hiking boots in the summer, she cycled everywhere. I suppose we all cycled or walked but only until we had boyfriends with cars. She embraced it. She took her studies seriously too but she wasn't brilliant, just hard-working.'

Ellie closed the drawer and then paused with her fingers hooked through the handle of the next one. She described Melanie in more detail, her reminiscences of one girl triggering a clearer picture of the other. As she finished she gave a short laugh. 'Funnily enough, it worked out differently for Polly than I would have imagined. Last I heard she'd been caught stealing from her employer.'

'Why?'

'No idea. A shortcut perhaps or maybe she just had enough of being responsible. It happens. She studied history too.'

Her description of Polly had illuminated Melanie Franks, perhaps not accurately, but enough for him to begin searching.

It was a little while later when Goodhew placed three items on the desktop.

'Have you found anything?' he asked.

'There nothing I can't identify,' she replied.

'Here's my shortlist.'

She redirected her torch in his direction then killed it when she realised that the items were lying where the overhead light was more than adequate.

He'd picked a smooth stone, an ornament of a bridge and a segment of a black plastic disc. She picked up the pebble first. It was large enough to fill her palm. She wrapped her fingers around it and passed it back to him.

'This was picked up from Rhossili Bay. I was with him. And this

. . .' She held up the plastic, which at first glance might have been a broken piece of an LP but when it caught the light its surface was far more glossy and shone with the full spectrum of colours.

'It's a video disc. We salvaged it from a burgled flat in Wiltshire. Both cases involved young women, though, so you're getting something right.'

Finally, she held the ornament closer to the light. It was a little over an inch high, painted in grey wash and thinly glazed. 'A three-way bridge? I don't believe I've ever seen this before, but the bridge itself I do recognise.'

She returned it to the desktop.

'Do you know it?'

'No.'

'It's in the centre of Crowland in Lincolnshire. It's a small town and I'm sure we never had a connection with the place. But it's less than fifty miles from here and if that's where Melanie came from it would explain why simply moving back home wasn't an option . . .'

'Because she would have been too close to here to feel safe?'

'Exactly,' she replied. 'How long will it take you to check if that's the place?'

'If she went to school there or has family there I should know within the hour.' He didn't need the ornament now but slipped it into his pocket in any case. 'I really appreciate your help.'

She smiled. 'I'm always glad to give it.'

CHAPTER 34

Crowland's bridge had been built in the fourteenth century at the point where the river Welland met a tributary and in a period when the surrounding flatlands had still been submerged. The community had grown around the dry skirts of the abbey. It might have been hundreds of years since the land had been drained but the fields lay so low that Goodhew could imagine the water rising through the soil and the long straight run of Peterborough Road becoming a causeway.

He drove into the centre of town, finding the bridge within minutes. The river had long since dried and the bridge stood as a worn and dusty tourist attraction, spanning a few metres of history. There had only been two listings for the surname Franks; they lived a short walk from one another and a short distance from the bridge. He'd rung G. and S. Franks and left a message but received no reply. The second call had been answered with the kind of cagey response normally reserved for suspected cold callers. 'Mr Christopher Franks?' Goodhew introduced himself then kept it brief. 'I'm trying to locate Melanie Franks.'

'I'm sorry, you have the wrong number.'

'But Melanie is your sister?'

Christopher Franks hesitated for just a moment then relented. 'Yes, she is. But she moved away and we don't have contact.'

'I see.' Goodhew waited for Christopher to comment further: Have you found her? Is she OK? Has something happened? There were none of those.

Goodhew had replaced the receiver and immediately hired a car. When Christopher Franks answered his door, Goodhew continued to speak as though the intervening couple of hours hadn't existed. 'Most people who receive a call about a relative, even if they have cut off contact, will ask what's happened. You didn't. So my guess is that you know she's safe and well.' Goodhew pointed towards the interior of the house. 'I think we should talk.'

Christopher Franks held the door a little wider. 'Go straight through.' He was tall but when he spoke he bowed his head and spoke in a quiet, clear voice. 'You'll need to tell me what it's about.'

Goodhew waited until they were face to face in the dining room. 'It is important that I speak to your sister immediately.'

'I don't know where she is but I can pass on a message.' A slow smile formed on Franks's lips. 'But I'm not doing that unless there's a genuine need.'

'Do you think that she's currently in any danger then?'

'I think the way she lives her life is working out well and if it ain't broke, don't fix it.'

'I believe your sister may have important information relating to a current investigation.'

'In Cambridge?'

'Yes, a recent murder.'

For a moment Franks looked relieved, 'Trust me, you're wasting your time. She has no connection to anyone there.'

'She knew the victim.'

Franks's eyes hardened. 'Twenty years ago, perhaps.'

'Perhaps.'

'No, there's nothing she could add.'

'I need to speak with your sister, it's not optional and if you refuse to cooperate I could charge you with obstruction—'

'Or get a court order and charge me with contempt? Whatever.'

It was obvious to Goodhew that Franks was close to refusing to continue the conversation. 'I'm visiting your parents next: G. and S. Franks, West Street?'

Franks stepped towards the door. 'They won't speak to you and I'd rather you didn't try. They'll worry.'

'It's not optional that I speak to her but why not save us both time and all the legal shenanigans? Try this: send your sister a message, tell her my name, tell her she can trust me to be discreet the way my grandfather was.'

Franks scowled and shook his head but then gave in. 'OK, but that's all I'm going to do.' He sent the text and then dropped his mobile back into his pocket. 'I'll need your number to call you – assuming she replies.'

Goodhew shook his head. 'Thank you, but I'm going to wait.' He stepped towards the sofa. 'Do you mind?' He took a seat without waiting for an answer.

Franks scowled. 'I do actually and I doubt whether she'll reply.'

'We can leave it a couple of hours then try again. I'm not in a hurry,' he lied.

Franks sank into the armchair facing Goodhew and stared across uneasily. 'I'll give it fifteen minutes then I want you to leave. I know my sister and she won't—' He stopped mid-sentence as the landline began to trill. The handset stood on the coffee table beside him and he glanced at the caller display before answering. He listened for a few seconds. Goodhew couldn't hear any of the words but could pick out a female voice and a barrage of dialogue, which eventually paused. 'Only if you're sure.' Franks replied. He studied Goodhew with interest and then held out the handset. 'My sister.'

Goodhew introduced himself and told her about Lorraine Martin's death.

'And Joseph Goodhew was your grandfather?' Her voice sounded artificially calm. 'What date did he die?'

'The eighteenth of July 1992,' he answered automatically.

'Well then,' she replied, 'we need to meet.'

Goodhew phoned Gully and let her know that she could halt her trawl for traces of the existence of Melanie Franks in Hereford; Melanie was only twenty miles from the city but she'd covered her tracks well. It then took Goodhew just over three hours to drive from Crowland to Monmouth. Learning that he would find Melanie in a small and historic town made sense. From his experience people always hung onto something when they switched lives, and not just hobbies or employment in a parallel career where their own skills would still be useful. It was always more than the practical; they would drink at the same kind of pubs, or move to a house with a similar layout, use the same chain stores or feel at home with the same kinds of views as they'd left behind. He guessed it gave comfort and continuity.

She'd given him an address in Monnow Street, a busy but old-fashioned shopping thoroughfare. He parked at one end close to where her flat was located. She lived above a tearoom and just a few hundred yards from the Monnow Bridge. He looked across at it as he locked his car; this one still had water flowing beneath it and was both older and grander than Crowland's, but similar enough to make him smile as he walked towards her door.

She opened it before he had a chance to knock. She must have been watching him and when he offered her his ID she barely glanced at it. 'I can see who you are,' she told him, then led him up the narrow flight of stairs to her lounge. She turned then and held out her hand for him to shake. Her grip was firm and dry and her hands were rough to touch. She looked older than he had expected with pronounced lines around her pale grey eyes but there was also serenity in her expression. She pointed towards one of the two settees that crowded the space, 'Please sit. I've made drinks.' She left the room briefly and returned with a pot of hot water and canisters of tea, coffee and sugar on a tray with milk and empty mugs. 'Actually, it's a case of helping yourself.'

'That's fine, thank you.' He made himself coffee, and she poured boiling water into her own mug but added nothing. 'Do you live here alone?'

'Just me and my cat.' She met his gaze as if waiting for him to ask her about her child. After a beat she relented. 'And my son, Ben, but he's working away.'

She had strong features and a straightforward way of talking.

'Which name do you use?'

'Officially, Jane Williams. Joe did a good job with the papers, but I still call myself Melanie on a day-to-day basis. It's hard to switch. I tried, but people would talk to me and I would ignore them. And it

191

was tough to start again without people thinking that I didn't have any manners.' She smiled enough to make her cheeks dimple. 'Is there any chance this conversation will be confidential?'

'It's unlikely.' Goodhew shook his head. 'It depends what you know and I do realise that's not an incentive for you to answer my questions. Details of your name and address don't need to fall into the public domain but I can't guarantee that they won't.'

'I see. So no false promises?'

'Lorraine Martin's death has led to many questions. I really need your help.'

She cupped the mug of hot water in one hand and pressed it to her cheek. She pressed the fingers of her other hand to her lips and closed her eyes, effectively cutting herself off from him. When her eyes reopened he could tell that she had made a decision. 'It's wrong if I don't,' she said.

'Thank you. Now, I'd like to start with Lorraine Martin. You were her lodger?'

'Eventually, yes. I met her before that, through Nadine.'

Goodhew had never taken a guess at how Nadine and Melanie had met but his subconscious had planted the idea in his mind that they'd been flatmates first and through that had become friends. Finding out that it was the other way around surprised him more than it should have. 'So how did you meet Nadine?'

'I worked at the Boat Race pub, the one on the corner of East Road and Burleigh Street . . .'

'I remember it.'

'Sometimes they'd have jam nights and she would turn up and play. Guitar mostly but occasionally she'd sing. We struck up this odd friendship. In fact, it was the only friendship I had when I was in Cambridge because I really didn't fit in with any of the other students.' She stared towards the window as she remembered. 'It makes sense to me now. I can see that I was out of my depth in Cambridge and I'd barely left Crowland before that. My social skills still aren't the best but back then I was this awkward, geeky girl who was too needy. I was the first one in my family who'd gone to uni and I'd done that against their wishes. I didn't fit in at the pub either. Nadine must have seen that but she didn't judge and it didn't seem to matter.' Melanie looked directly at Goodhew. 'When I tell you what happened you might think she used me somehow, but she didn't. She had her demons but we always looked out for each other.'

'OK, go on.'

'Nadine had told me that she had a boyfriend. I'd never met him but I guessed that there was some issue, like he was already married or something because I never saw them together and he always took her out of town when they did meet. Eventually she told me that he was a man she worked with, her boss and yes, he was married. She loved him, though, I'm sure of it, but we were both kids . . .'

He poured himself another coffee; he sensed she was about to tell him some of the things that she'd spent the intervening years keeping to herself.

'She got herself pregnant. She did it on purpose thinking that he'd leave his wife for her. But of course he didn't, he just dumped her.'

'Do you know his name?'

A small smile touched her lips. 'Robert Buckingham.'

Goodhew nodded, he'd thought as much.

'He demanded that she had an abortion. She wouldn't. I was just on the side lines then but even with all that drama and heartache her life seemed so much more appealing than mine. And I was in financial trouble, behind on my rent and determined not to jack it all in and go home. I remember envying her at the time, I thought she had it all in hand.' She shook her head at the memory. 'I don't know what planet I was on. If Ben ever got himself into a similar situation I wouldn't blame him or belittle him, I'd just want him to come home.'

'But you didn't go home.'

'No, I did something so stupid . . .'

'Please go on.'

'Robert sacked Nadine. She'd kept quiet about the pregnancy but Robert's business partner knew.'

'Neil Frampton?'

'Exactly. And Nadine was approached by the accountant, Moira. She told her that her sister would be able to help. She said she knew a private adoption agency who would pay all Nadine's expenses and place the baby with a new family and that's when Nadine met Lorraine and moved in with her. I would visit, and it still seemed to me that Nadine had landed on her feet.'

'Was she the only one living there?'

'Initially.' Melanie placed her mug back onto the tray. 'Some other girls had moved on I think, and, after Nadine moved in, others arrived soon afterwards. She had five girls in there at one point.'

'Do you know any names?'

'After this long?' She squinted towards the ceiling as she tried to remember, then shook her head slowly. 'Caitlyn from somewhere, Canada maybe. And there was another they called Renee but I think that might have been a nickname. Apart from that . . . no, sorry.' A moment later though she brightened again. 'There is one thing I know; Nadine was the only one who wasn't a student.'

It wasn't the most specific piece of information but it was still significant. 'Do you think that's how Lorraine found them?'

'Lorraine was offering a service. Do you know how many students there are in Cambridge? How many get pregnant where neither an abortion nor a baby is a viable option?'

He didn't think she expected him to reply but he knew that current figures for the university population ran at about twenty thousand, but finding the answer to the second question was impossible.

She replied for him. 'Enough to keep that house busy. And as I spent more time there it all started to seem normal. Then Neil approached me. Theo was the son from his first marriage and Carolyn was his second wife . . .' Melanie was watching Goodhew carefully, the words frozen on her lips.

'Melanie, what did you do?' he whispered.

'She'd had problems when she was a teenager and she'd been told that she couldn't get pregnant. She was fixated with the fact that Neil already had a child, like she needed to outdo his first wife on every front.' She took a breath. 'It seemed to me that she wanted a baby like someone might want a pet, to just go out and get one. So they paid me to do it, to have his baby and hand it over.'

'Surrogacy?'

'Yes, I agreed to do it. I had no interest in children and it seemed straightforward. I told myself it was no different to what Nadine was doing. I inseminated myself. How's this for irony? I wouldn't have sex with him for money but I'd have his baby. I fell pregnant at the first attempt.'

'So their son Alex . . .?'

'No, I conceived and then, completely against the odds, Carolyn did too. She was just a few weeks after me, but I didn't know that straight away. In fact, I don't remember much until the first scan. I thought it would be exactly what it is, a grainy image of a two-inch blob but the second I was in that room I knew I wouldn't be handing Ben over to anyone.' Her grey eyes brightened as she said his name. 'When I found out about Carolyn's pregnancy I thought it would be easy to get out of the agreement, they were having their baby, they no longer had a reason to want mine.' She shook her head. 'Not a chance. Neil wanted his child. I tried to reason with Carolyn but she didn't waver.' The memory still had the power to make her pale. 'They both made it clear that I didn't have a choice. They had me working at Frampton's for a few hours every day – it was their way of keeping an eye on me. I was never out of their sight for more than a few hours at a time. That's where I got to know your mum and, through her, Joe.'

'And where was Nadine during all of this?'

'She left Buckingham and Frampton's first and when I cleared off she was seven, maybe eight months pregnant. I wanted to keep in touch with her but Joe said that if I was ever tempted to make contact with anyone I had to look at Ben and ask myself whether it was worth the risk.'

'So you never did?'

'Never.'

'Do you know what happened to any of the other girls?'

'One baby was born while I was there. Lorraine delivered a little boy. She left with him soon afterwards, the mum cried and then sat in a daze all evening but by the next morning she'd gone. When I left, I heard nothing else of Nadine until the following year when I read about the fire.' Her expression softened. 'It was a pity she hadn't met Theo first; they would have been good for each other. My first thought was that her coming back after hiding away at Lorraine's had tipped Bob

Buckingham over the edge; he must have felt as though he couldn't get away from her. Maybe that's why he snapped.'

'If he did.'

'Well, I don't think he did it for the insurance money.'

'I'm wondering whether he did it at all.'

It took a moment for the shock to fully register and, this time, her colour drained completely.

'Melanie, why did you contact Joe after the fire?'

'Because I read the reports in the paper and none of them mentioned her baby.' Her voice was barely audible. 'It was Robert's child too and he was the one under arrest, so it seemed to me that it had to be crucial to the case.'

'Why not go to the police?'

'Are you kidding? I was living under a false identity and avoiding contact with my child's father. I didn't want to blow all that so I asked Joe for his advice. He said he'd check out the situation before he involved the police. Told me to sit tight. He contacted me a few days later and said I'd need to be patient. I was and heard nothing. I left it for a few weeks then I tried to contact him again, and that's when I discovered that he'd died.'

'Who told you?'

'I phoned his number and your mother answered. She asked me where I was hiding, said that Neil was desperate to contact his son and wanted me to reconsider.'

Goodhew pushed aside the thought that it was another fact that his mother hadn't bothered to share with him. 'What did you do?' he asked.

'I hung up and never called again.'

'My grandfather was attacked and died from his injuries. And I believe it was connected to you because any papers he had that related to you were taken.'

'No one ever found me.'

'I think he was too careful for that.'

She nodded slowly. 'He was such a good man.'

Goodhew had phoned Marks then. The picture was still fragmented but beginning to form and he'd explained the progress that he'd made.

'So we'll need to track down anyone who lodged with Lorraine from Nadine onwards. My guess is that one of them will be the baby's mother.'

'What about Nadine?'

'Possibly. But not Melanie. I'll bring you a full report.'

'That all stacks up,' Marks had told him. 'By the way, we've just received the background on Lorraine Martin's previous employment: she was cautioned for poor performance and eventually sacked when a couple complained that she was drunk when she delivered their baby. Are you done there?'

'A few more questions.'

'Finish them and we'll ask local officers to take the statement, and I know you're off-duty right now but I'd like you back as soon as you can.'

He'd heard a tense note in his boss's voice. 'Is everything OK?'

'The same as ever: problems with resources,' Marks had replied but his tone hadn't changed.

It had taken Goodhew another forty minutes to finish questioning Melanie and now, as he was about to leave, she reached out to shake his hand. 'I liked Lorraine, I think she was doing the wrong things for the right reasons; I think she set out to help those girls rather than make money. She wasn't much of a businesswoman.'

He didn't comment. There were endless examples of kind people doing bad things and it didn't make them any less guilty. 'Can I just ask, did it work out for you and Ben?'

'Yes, thank you. I would never have thought of myself as the maternal type but it has been the best thing.' She smiled warmly and the years slipped from her face. 'Having Ben has taught me so much and we've muddled through together. I work on archaeo-logical digs, the kind that happen before sites are redeveloped, and sometimes he takes a day off and comes along to help. He's honest and hard-working – everything I wasn't at that age and I'm so proud of him.'

She followed Goodhew down to the bottom of the stairs and by the time she opened the front door she had become serious again. 'What your grandfather did for me . . .' She touched Goodhew's arm.

197

Without warning her eyes misted and she struggled to finish the sentence. 'Sorry.' She took a few seconds more before she could finish. 'What he did for me was immeasurable. The greatest gift. And I'm so sorry for your loss.'

CHAPTER 35

Marks and Kincaide arrived unannounced at Frampton's office in St Barnabas Road and Marks was pleased to note the presence of both Neil Frampton's F-Type and Carolyn's Cayenne. 'I'll do the preliminaries then we'll split them up. I'll take Neil Frampton. Remember, keep it tactful if it's in front of the son; we don't know where this is going and it's the wrong time to be indiscreet.'

Marks entered the building with Kincaide close behind Nothing much had changed; Carolyn and Neil Frampton were at their respective desks and Alex Frampton even seemed to be wearing the same plaid shirt. Carolyn Frampton rose to greet them and gave a smile that achieved the right balance between curiosity and warmth.

'I guess this means that there have been developments?'

'Of sorts,' Marks began. 'We have some questions for you and your husband; we are pursuing some parallel lines of enquiry and need more information.'

Her smile faded as he spoke and her expression grew more cautious. 'We are talking about Lorraine's murder, aren't we?'

'Indirectly, yes.'

Alex Frampton had turned in his chair, enough to watch them through a large bevel-edged mirror that hung from the longest wall. Carolyn glanced at her son then back to Marks. 'I'm surprised Neil isn't out here already; an unexpected visit from the police would still get to him, even after this long.'

Marks finally understood the subtext of her earlier question. 'We're not here about the Romsey Terrace fire or Theo's death but we would like some time with you and your husband.'

She looked relieved. 'Of course, come through.' At the doorway she turned back to speak to her son. 'Alex, if anyone calls, we'll get back to them. The diary's on my desk. Can you get Stan to cover for anything that can't be cancelled?'

'How long will you be?'

She glanced at Marks who gestured that he had no idea.

'A while, I guess,' she replied and led them across the hallway to her husband's office.

Marks squinted at Neil Frampton for a few seconds when everyone else was diverted by the need for a couple of extra chairs. He was trying to blur the man's features enough to see what he might have looked like twenty-plus years ago before grief had visited and before over-indulgence had inflated, reddened and visibly distorted him. It wasn't hard to imagine that he'd been a young forty when Theo had died, but he was a raddled sixty-four now.

Carolyn spun a chair round to the end of the desk, almost along-side her husband, but not quite. She wore a sleeveless white shirt that accentuated her toned and tanned arms. Apart from a watch and her wedding ring she was accessory-free, her makeup low-key but perfect. There could have been thirty years between the two of them, not just seventeen.

'As I explained to your wife, our investigation into the death of Lorraine Martin is following several lines of enquiry and one of those relates to the discovery of the remains of a baby at her property.' Marks had switched to his briefing voice, the one he used when he was being careful not to be ambiguous. Sometimes it made people talk more, other times they shut down; Neil Frampton's expression had quickly become opaque.

Carolyn Frampton seemed distracted by her husband. 'We saw it in the local paper.' She looked at him warily. 'It's shocking, isn't it, Neil?'

'I don't think Lorraine put the odds in her favour.'

'Meaning what exactly?' Marks asked.

'It's just a comment; she drank and she was unreliable, therefore she would have been vulnerable to any random nutter and had no one looking out for her.'

'Do you think this was an unplanned attack then?'

'No, I just meant that she didn't avoid risk like most of us do.' Neil Frampton held a ballpoint pen, a cheap one with the name of a plant hire company printed down one side. He studied it intently and waggled it between forefinger and thumb. 'Lorraine came round here the night she died, but you know that already.'

'Yes, we do. According to your statements, she was shouting . . .' Marks paused to read from his notes even though it wasn't difficult to remember, '"I know, I know".'

'She was a pisshead. Practically incoherent with alcohol.'

'Neil . . .' Carolyn cut in. 'Please . . .'

'I find it hard to have sympathy for that woman.'

'What did you think she meant by that remark?'

Carolyn answered first. 'We've both made statements.'

'We did,' Neil agreed without looking up and he continued to fiddle with the pen.

'When Lorraine Martin said those words, "I know, I know",' Marks continued, watching them both closely, 'did it occur to either of you that she may have been referring to the whereabouts of Melanie Franks?'

Neil Frampton's gaze flashed towards Marks as his hand dropped to the desktop, Carolyn's hand shot up to her mouth and then the room stilled. Marks was the only one who spoke. 'We have questions for both of you and, in the interests of confidentiality, we will speak to each of you separately.' They could have refused, demanded to stay together or sought outside support; it didn't mean anything that they did none of those things. He had caught them off guard and splitting them up was simple.

Kincaide left the room with Carolyn Frampton, Marks stayed in the office with her husband. There had been an instant change in the man and it went beyond the immediate physical response; the stunned expression, the wave of paralysis as time froze then the sudden lurch as it thrust to catch up again.

Neil Frampton leant forward, elbows on the desk, and gave Marks his complete attention. His eyes shone darkly and a healthier colour seemed to have flooded his face. 'Have you found her?' he asked.

Marks blanked the question, 'Can you explain your relationship to Miss Franks?'

'I don't have one.'

'Not currently, no, but I need to understand what it was and why you are clearly so keen to find her.'

Frampton pressed his lips together and the corners of his mouth formed a thin smile. 'I'm sure you know all the key details, detective. Do you want me to go through them all again so that you can pick me up on any discrepancies? Why does it matter whether my version is the same as my wife's, or the same as Melanie's for that matter?'

'Mr Frampton, you are not under caution, but I would appreciate your cooperation.'

'Because?'

'Because it's a murder investigation, because there are multiple strands, some of which involve your business and people connected to it. And because this particular line of enquiry involves you. I would have thought that it was in your interest to see us move on without too much upheaval.' Marks was patient, and he had enough experience to remain so indefinitely. He returned Frampton's smile with his own.

Frampton shook his head and the smugness vanished. 'I'm sorry.' He held up his hands in surrender. 'I didn't like Lorraine, but I do know what it's like to lose a relative to murder. The worst emotions dull but they never go.'

'Understood, Mr Frampton, but my questions are important.'

'So is what I need.'

'And what would that be?'

'To find Melanie.' His tone had calmed quickly but his eyes had lost none of their new-found intensity. 'I've spent years searching for her.'

'I see, so she's chosen to move away and remain untraceable. When did you last see her?'

'Eighth of July 1990. It was a Sunday.'

Marks waited.

'She was having our baby; mine and Carolyn's.' If Frampton expected

202

a reaction from Marks, he would be disappointed. Even if Marks hadn't already known this he was well practised at staying impassive. The silence pushed Frampton on. 'Carolyn couldn't conceive and she was desperate to become a mother.' He paused to consider the statement, 'I think she was insecure and it was her way of cementing our marriage. I'm not going to guess,' he waved the comment away with a flick of his hand, 'but, in my experience, if a woman wants a baby that's an unstoppable force. Some go down the route of throwing money and misery at it, but Carolyn's always been a pragmatist.' He stopped there as if that answered everything.

'So you entered a surrogacy arrangement?'

'We did.'

'And how was the arrangement with Melanie going to work? Were you paying her?'

'Expenses, nothing more.'

'Because that's the terminology that keeps it legal?'

'We didn't do anything wrong and we certainly didn't break the law.'

'And, during her pregnancy, she was to live with Lorraine Martin who, in turn, would eventually deliver the baby?'

'Her pregnancy wasn't secret. She would have gone to Addenbrooke's Hospital.'

'Unlike the other women in her care?'

Frampton stayed poker-faced but kept eye contact for far too long, 'I know nothing about that.'

'Who does then? Your wife?'

'I don't know, but not me.'

'And was Mrs Frampton happy with this surrogacy arrangement?'

'Of course; for one thing, it was her idea.'

'But biologically the child would have been yours and someone else's?'

'No different from an egg donor except that she would have skipped the getting fat part.'

'I think there's more to it than that for most women,' Marks told him dryly.

'You're absolutely right.' Frampton flashed a brief smile at Marks accompanied by an equally brief laugh. 'Those were Carolyn's words, not mine, and when she found out she was pregnant she cried for days.'

'She was facing the prospect of two new babies to care for. That's assuming you planned to keep Melanie's?'

'Of course we did. Back then, I didn't feel that the baby was Melanie's, it was ours.'

'And now? What is it that you're expecting after all these years?'

Frampton rested his forehead to his clasped hands. 'I've always had the feeling that Melanie had a son.' It wasn't spoken as a question but he waited for a reply.

'I can't comment.'

'So you know?'

'I can't comment.'

'I want contact with him. I've never given up looking.' He lifted his head and studied Marks for a moment. 'Do you have first-hand experience of losing a child?'

It was a question that Marks had been asked too many times in the past, one he hoped he wouldn't have to hear once he was retired. 'No, Mr Frampton, thankfully I don't.'

'It was quite a while after Melanie left when Theo died – eight months, to be precise. Melanie's baby had been on my mind but after we lost Theo . . .' He shook his head. 'My thoughts were constantly on nothing but Theo and the baby. Theo and the baby, Theo and the baby . . . going round and round.'

'What about Alex?'

'Carolyn struggled, emotionally I mean, she didn't want anyone near him. I felt detached from him and Carolyn for months, so I didn't bond with him until much later.'

'And hence the affair?'

He blinked a couple of times but apart from that showed no surprise that Marks knew. 'It was barely that and I didn't plan it but it helped me cope until Carolyn and I got ourselves straight again.'

Marks pursed his lips; the man was adept at playing the victim, the victim of crime, of circumstance and of other people's agendas. It would take longer to work out which of his statements were genuine. 'So your interest in finding Melanie is to connect with your child?'

'Of course.'

'When she was pregnant, did she tell you she wanted to keep her baby?'

'No.'

'How do you think you would have responded if she had?'

'Carolyn and I would have been disappointed.'

'Would you have threatened her?'

'Absolutely not.'

'So tell me why she was so terrified of you that she felt it necessary to change her identity? To cut ties with her family and start over?'

'I don't know,' he replied. It was the second time he'd said that and on both occasions he'd been lying.

Marks outranked him so Kincaide knew it made sense that Marks would choose to interview Mr Frampton rather than the wife but he didn't relish the prospect; she was one of those high-maintenance women who looked like she did spa days and probably had her own clothing budget. She looked at him with slight amusement and he couldn't decipher whether it was disdain or her attempt at being alluring.

He followed her through to the other office where her tattooed son was fiddling around with a floor plan. 'Alex?' She had a sharpness to her voice and he responded immediately. 'This is Detective Kincaide and I need to speak to him privately.'

'No problem,' he replied, and less than a minute later they were treated to the throb of the Suzuki Bandit. He revved the engine a couple of times before pulling out into the street. Kincaide and Mrs Frampton waited for the sound to die away before either of them spoke. 'Melanie Franks,' he began. 'You were shocked to hear her name.'

'A blast from the past, as they say. I always suspected she'd turn up eventually. If my husband's anything, he's persistent.'

'He didn't find her, though.'

'He'll have had a hand in it because he always does. I don't see what any of this has to do with Lorraine Martin.'

It already felt as though Mrs Frampton was in the driving seat and Kincaide didn't like it. He settled back in his chair and took a breath before speaking. 'We know about the surrogacy agreement with

Melanie Franks.' He'd had his brief, Marks had been clear about how he wanted this revelation handled and this wasn't it, but he'd said enough to make Mrs Frampton's confidence falter and that had to be a good thing. 'Think back to the time when you and your husband made that arrangement. What did you think that Ms Martin did for a living?'

'She was a midwife.'

'Ex-midwife.'

'She'd gone freelance.'

It was time for Kincaide to employ his own knowing smile. 'Freelance? Was that her word for it, or yours?'

'Hers, I guess. I don't remember.' Mrs Frampton had rallied already and there was a new steeliness in her expression.

'And what exactly do you think that was a euphemism for?' Kincaide didn't usually pay much attention to eyes but Mrs Frampton's were a vivid blue, a colour that looked almost unnatural against her tanned skin. He wondered whether both shades were fake.

'I think she meant that she delivered babies.' The blueness glinted. 'But you're the detective, what interpretation would you put on *freelance midwife*? If you want to ask me something specific, then go for it.'

'How did you first make contact with Lorraine Martin?'

'Nadine had been introduced via Moira, then Nadine came to me and told me about her friend. She suggested the surrogacy option.'

'We have a witness who says that Melanie agreed to go through with it to help herself out of financial difficulty and you paid for this via the . . .' he made quotes with his fingers, '"adoption agency", which turned out to be Lorraine Martin and her . . .' more quotes, '"freelance" business.'

'We paid Melanie's expenses, I was told what those were and handed over the money accordingly. As far as I knew she wasn't making a profit.'

'You thought she was doing it out of generosity then?'

'Why not?' Carolyn clearly didn't care whether or not he believed her.

He didn't. 'So, to clarify, you were aware that Melanie Franks was intending to make financial gain from the transaction?'

'I'm not surprised that she had money left over, the expenses we paid were generous, but I took the advice I was given and had no idea whether or not it was legitimate. Seems to me that Lorraine Martin was filling a niche.' She held out her hands palms upwards as if they were weighing scales, 'Too many babies on one side, not enough on the other. And of course I would have notified the authorities if I had any suspicion that things weren't above board. Please put that in your notes.'

She was lying, she made that clear in the way she said it, but words, not intonation, went into statements and this was even less formal than that.

'How do you feel about Melanie Franks now?'

A shrug. 'Nothing.'

Kincaide took a moment to study her. The detachment seemed genuine at first but then he noticed the way her hands were clasped together, fingers intertwined. He wouldn't want to be either of those hands being crushed by the other. The way to tackle this was all there in those manicured hands. 'I would have thought,' he began, picking his words carefully, 'you would have mixed feelings about being reunited with the person who could have been your child. You can't get away from the fact that your husband is still the father.'

Again with the shrug. 'It's in the past, detective, I dealt with my feelings a long time ago.'

'But it won't stay in the past now. This is the child your husband has spent years searching for. He has some catching up to do.' Kincaide spotted pinkness rising at the sides of her neck.

'Of course he wants contact.'

'Doesn't it bother you that you and your son will have to move over to make room for a complete stranger? Someone who's never had a father figure . . .'

'You're being ridiculous.'

'Am I? Why has he spent all that time and money on the search if it doesn't turn into something more?'

She opened her mouth to speak then hesitated, as if she wasn't sure what to say.

'That's his son and heir, his eldest living child.'

Her lips moved just enough to silently echo the new information. *A boy.*

'Are you ready for your life to change for him?' he asked.

There was a tiny shake of her head and it was all he needed.

'You have dreaded this day, haven't you?'

She looked at him, stricken-faced and wordless.

'Haven't you?' he pushed.

'Yes,' she whispered. Then again more clearly. 'Theo was everything to Neil and I needed to give him a child. Do you know the saying "second wife, second best"? Well, that was how I felt and that's how it would have stayed if we hadn't had a baby.'

Kincaide couldn't follow her logic; the idea of parenthood repulsed him slightly.

'If she'd just done what she was supposed to do then everything would be fine.'

'You had your baby, she had hers. I don't see the issue.'

'Because . . .' She pressed her lips into a hard line and glared at him.

'Because your husband wants his son and you can see your importance and your luxuries being shoved aside by his bastard child.'

This time she found her voice. 'That's not how it is,' she told him.

Kincaide shook his head; he didn't believe her, 'If Lorraine Martin suddenly discovered the whereabouts of Melanie Franks then you had a motive to kill her, didn't you?'

'No,' she snapped. 'And we're done here.' She rose to her feet and brought her face close to his. 'There's nothing more I'm prepared to add to what I've already said and I'd like you to leave now, detective.' She turned away, pulled the door wide and held it open for him.

'Detective Sergeant,' he corrected.

She didn't speak again until the door was closing behind him. 'By the way, detective, most married women have motive to kill, even your wife, but it doesn't mean we do.'

He glanced back long enough to see her tremulous expression and guessed that her bravado was an attempt to hide another lie.

CHAPTER 36

Most days since Amy's first meeting with Alex had involved a work-related email exchange followed by a flurry of short messages containing nothing but casual chat. Both of them had studiously avoided any mention of their parents or the fire. Until now.

Her inbox was open when the new email arrived, the message title simply said 'Please read'. Its contents weren't much longer, 'Who is Melanie Franks?'

'Why?'

'The police are here about Lorraine Martin. They said the name Melanie Franks and some kind of shit hit the fan.'

'Like what?'

'Don't know, I've just been chucked out of the office so I couldn't hear more. I'm coming over to the yard. Will you be there?'

Amy thought for a moment before replying, 'In a bit, I'm going to see my dad and find out who she is.'

Amy was parking up when she saw DC Goodhew entering her dad's house. In itself, the arrival of one junior detective probably didn't mean much, and if she hadn't had the emails from Alex then her senses wouldn't have felt jarred, but seeing Goodhew triggered a surge of unrest. Of anxiety even.

She didn't intend to sneak but found herself approaching the house quietly; she avoided touching the gate and turned the key gently in the lock. She wasn't expecting to burst in and discover any great revelation but she knew from the years when her mum had struggled with depression that the first moments through the door could be the most telling. Her father only had two rooms downstairs, the lounge and the kitchen-diner. Both were visible from the front door. The men sat on opposite sides of the kitchen table and they both looked across at her as she walked in. Her father's face lit up immediately, Goodhew's didn't. He held a thin envelope and, although he didn't seem to be paying any attention to it, he furled it loosely in his grip if to protect it from her. His gaze shifted from Amy to her dad. 'You may prefer this to be a private conversation.'

Her dad's smile faded slightly but he seemed unaware of the look of consternation that had just passed between herself and DC Goodhew. She guessed their concerns were for very different reasons; Goodhew was worried about the conversation he didn't want to have in front of her. Amy was worried that she was about to be excluded from it.

She made eye contact with her dad and held his gaze, 'What's private, Dad?'

'DC Goodhew hasn't got that far.'

'I thought there weren't any more secrets for me to worry about.'

He shook his head. 'There aren't.' The reply had been a reflex and it sounded defensive rather than genuine.

'Not convincing, Dad.' She turned and had every intention of walking away.

'Amy, don't.'

She hesitated, her back to him.

'Please, there's nothing you can't hear.'

She turned back to them. If anything, Goodhew seemed to have tightened his grip on the rolled envelope.

'So, I can stay? No matter what this is about?'

Her dad's reply was to pull back the chair next to him and beckon her towards it, 'No more secrets, Amy, I promise.'

Goodhew held an envelope in his hand and a backup plan in his pocket. Amy's arrival had the potential to complicate this meeting but Goodhew needed Robert Buckingham to tell him the truth and couldn't let Amy's presence jeopardise that. She had settled down next to her father and neither of them had any intention of asking her to move. He unfurled the envelope and laid it on the kitchen table making sure that the label displaying the sender's name was clearly in sight. Goodhew was pretty certain that Amy had no idea what was coming but Robert Buckingham was harder to gauge.

'Mr Buckingham, you knew both Theo Frampton and Nadine Kendall.'

'Of course.'

'Your previous relationship with Miss Kendall was investigated as a possible motivation for you setting fire to the house in Romsey Terrace.'

Buckingham shot an apologetic look at his daughter. 'Yes, it was. But I didn't start that fire.'

'Why was Nadine's baby never mentioned?'

Buckingham's surprise appeared genuine. 'What baby?'

'She was pregnant at the time of your affair and we have a witness that states that you put pressure on her to have a termination.'

Goodhew was conscious of Amy staring at him but he kept his attention firmly on her father.

'What witness? That's an absolute lie.'

'Which part?'

Amy interrupted, 'I know about your affair, Dad.'

After a short pause Buckingham replied. 'If she was pregnant, it wasn't mine.'

'And was she?'

As a liar his voice was convincing. He could have pulled it off in a telephone conversation but everything about Buckingham's body language was on the defensive. 'What do you want to pin on me this time?'

'Nothing. We just need some straight answers.'

'I don't have to listen to this shit. Or deal with your questions.'

Beyond Goodhew was the front door and Buckingham directed his gaze towards it. Perhaps he would have headed that way if Amy hadn't been here. Or refused to answer anything. He couldn't do that when he'd promised her no more secrets and Goodhew was suddenly pleased that she was in the room.

Amy reached across and placed her hand over her dad's. 'I think you should just tell him what he wants to know. If everything's in the open . . .'

'What? It will be for the best?'

'Dad, the police are with Neil and Carolyn right now.' Buckingham's attention shot towards his daughter, then to Goodhew.

'Is that true?' he asked.

'It is.'

Buckingham shook his head. 'I don't know who got Nadine pregnant and I regretted ever getting involved with her. I certainly didn't feel jealous of her relationship with Theo. Good luck to them, that's all I thought. I don't understand why all that matters now.'

'A baby's body was found at Lorraine Martin's property.'

'That's not . . .'

He stopped.

'Not what? Not yours? You knew about it then?'

Buckingham's hesitation had been more telling than if he had finished the sentence.

'Do you know if her baby was delivered safely?'

'If she'd had a baby then the autopsy would have shown it.'

'Except you know that their bodies were beyond any analysis like that.' Goodhew slid the envelope closer, 'Now tell me, what happened to Nadine's baby?'

'It's nothing to do with me.'

'Lorraine Martin has been murdered. This isn't about what's convenient for you to answer; we need every detail to try to identify her killer. You just told your daughter that there would be no more secrets so right now I need to know what happened to your baby.'

The bombshell took a moment to explode. Amy's eyes widened and she sagged back in her chair, her hand falling from her father's arm.

Buckingham glowered and hissed, 'It wasn't mine.'

There were plenty of people like this who would stick to their stories in the face of irrefutable evidence. Goodhew slipped his hand into the envelope and pulled out a section of broken bangle. 'This was an item of jewellery made by Lorraine Martin for Nadine. Do you recognise it?'

Buckingham barely glanced at it but shook his head.

'It is made from a form of acrylic and Lorraine Martin specialised in making pieces like this with small items embedded within them. In this case . . .' Goodhew held it out towards Buckingham, 'those small flecks. They are trimmings of baby hair.'

He let the words settle.

'Perfectly preserved.'

Amy's face had grown ashen. 'So there's DNA?' she whispered.

Goodhew tapped the envelope and saw her focus for the first time on the printed label and the words 'Forensic Laboratories'.

'Mr Buckingham, I have just been to pick up these results and I want to know what happened to your baby.'

Buckingham ran his fingers through his hair and stared at the envelope. 'Like I said, the kid wasn't mine.'

'And when you were facing a murder charge for killing Nadine Kendall it didn't occur to you to mention this other man? He would have been the perfect person to have cast doubt on your guilt.'

Buckingham took too long to find an answer. 'I didn't know his name.'

'That wouldn't have mattered, someone else would have done if he'd existed.' Goodhew rested his hand flat on the envelope, 'Do you know the odds on a DNA match coming up against the wrong person?'

Robert Buckingham brushed it off. 'You've fiddled with the results. Someone's trying to set me up for this just like they did with the fire.'

'Dad?' Then more urgently, 'Dad? Stop it.'

'Stop what, Amy? Standing up for myself?'

'You said there wouldn't be any more secrets.'

'There aren't.'

'That's your baby, though. It's bloody obvious. I'm not stupid, there's evidence right here.'

'I don't believe it, Amy.'

'Listen to yourself. They have a hair sample, actual hair from Nadine's baby that proves you are the father. But if you can't bring yourself to own up at least think about me. That child is my sibling.'

Buckingham glowered at the envelope, then replied, 'She had a girl and it died. That's all I know. I never even knew the baby's name.' He looked across at Amy then but she was already on her feet and heading for the door.

Robert Buckingham didn't call or chase after his daughter but he stood at the window and watched her until she'd disappeared from view. 'Are you pleased with what you've just done?'

'You could have asked her to leave,' Goodhew replied.

'You could have held back.'

'And what happened to "there's nothing you can't hear"? Or did you forget that you had another child?'

'I never wanted that baby. I gave her money to get rid of it but she decided not to. And when it died it felt like the best outcome.'

Robert Buckingham's expression was filled with a combination of distaste and indignation. To Goodhew it seemed childlike, only a breath away from shouting 'it's not fair'. 'Mr Buckingham, forget about what you'd prefer to whitewash from your past. Tell me about the baby.'

'For fuck's sake,' Buckingham muttered but, when he realised that Goodhew was planning to sit it out until he answered properly, he began to talk. 'Nadine was refusing to have an abortion, I don't know why because I'd finished the relationship and she knew we weren't going anywhere.'

'Perhaps she didn't agree with it.'

'I told her it would be less hassle in the long run.'

'And that didn't sway her?' Goodhew asked dryly.

'No. Everyone at Buckingham's knew.'

Goodhew silently corrected it to Frampton's.

'Moira and I were good friends and she told me about her sister. I knew Lorraine was a midwife but I didn't know about the adoptions until then. Moira spoke to Nadine and it seemed to be the answer to everything; we'd both be able to move on as if there'd never been a baby.'

'And you really believed that?'

'Why not? If she'd had an abortion it would have been the end of it. I didn't get a say in that and it was her choice alone to carry on with the pregnancy.'

'Therefore the baby was nothing to do with you?'

'Exactly.'

Buckingham was clearly convinced of his own logic and for several seconds Goodhew felt lost for words. 'So Neil and Carolyn Frampton knew about the baby and never spoke up at the trial?'

'They had their reasons.'

'The surrogacy?'

'You don't miss much. That, and the fact that they were busy distancing themselves from me. A criminal investigation doesn't do much for business. It was the fact that his son died that bought him some goodwill.'

'Did you know where the baby had been buried?'

'I didn't want to know but as soon as I heard about the grave in Lorraine's garden it was obvious.' A mocking smile played on Buckingham's lips. 'Don't expect me to feel any more than you people do.'

'Are you trying to bait me, Mr Buckingham?'

'Why would I do that?'

'I don't know but I doubt that Amy would think so much of you if she could hear you now.'

The amusement vanished. 'I missed out on Amy's childhood because of people like you. Yes, sometimes I can lack subtlety, but who wouldn't after losing all those years to the sodding prison system?' His scowl deepened and there was sincerity in his voice. 'And one thing about Amy; she's always loyal. She's annoyed right now but she's always going to be there for me. And for her mum. She can't help herself; it's the way she's wired.'

Goodhew nodded slowly. 'Mr Buckingham, do you know who killed Lorraine Martin?'

'No, but she pissed someone off, didn't she?'

'Like who?'

'Her problem was getting an idea into her head and never letting it drop. And alcohol made her mouthier. But even if I knew who'd done it I wouldn't tell you; I will never do anything that helps you do your job. You've done your damage and I'd like you to leave.'

'I'm afraid I'll be here until I've written this up and you've signed it off.'

* * *

215

Buckingham had scowled but hadn't argued. Goodhew called Marks and gave him the key points, then settled down to take Buckingham's statement. He had expected it to become prolonged by Buckingham's increasingly bad mood and him picking over every sentence, but in the end it went the other way and Buckingham had hurried through each point, keen to see Goodhew leave as soon as possible.

Despite this, it had still taken nearly two hours to complete and Buckingham's expression had been set to glower for the duration. Finally, Goodhew folded the signed statement and tucked it away.

'Will that become public?' Buckingham asked. 'I don't want the press turning up on my doorstep.'

Goodhew didn't reply at once. He picked up the section of bangle from the table as he stood to leave. 'Did you notice how the baby hairs were just tiny trimmings?'

'So?'

'From a new-born baby all that gives us is mitochondrial DNA. It was enough to make a familial connection to the mother but it wasn't enough to identify you as the father. Your confession did that.'

The words winded Buckingham. 'You're kidding?' he breathed.

Goodhew allowed himself a small smile, 'I appreciate your cooperation, Mr Buckingham.'

Goodhew drove the unmarked car away from Buckingham's house, turned the first corner and immediately saw Amy waiting ahead. She sat on a garden wall and moved slowly to her feet. It was now two hours since she'd left her father's house. He lowered the passenger side window and leant across to speak to her. 'How long were you planning to wait there?'

'As long as it took.' She folded her arms, 'That wasn't the way I should have found out that I had a sister.'

It hadn't been his first choice either. 'I know, and I'm sorry. It might be better than never knowing.'

'You think he would have kept it secret?'

Goodhew turned off the engine and left the car at the kerb. 'Yes, I do, but my opinion doesn't really matter.'

'Except it does. I've set out with this idea that I could find out something that would prove his innocence. He might not have started the fire but he's not innocent of much else. I've spent so many years imagining that I could make our family right again . . .' She began to walk and he fell into step alongside her. 'But you know what it's like to have your family screwed up by a crime. At what point do I let it go?'

'I haven't worked that out yet.' His natural instinct was to stop there but Amy was waiting for more and he was conscious of the link, however tenuous, between the cases and their situations. 'My grandfather's death affected me, still affects me, and I suppose I'm the same as you and think that I need answers before moving on.'

'What if the truth makes it worse?'

He liked her directness. 'It won't,' he assured her.

'And it's as simple as that?'

'I believe so.'

'So I just found out that, however briefly, I had a sister and that's fine because it's the truth? I just forgive my dad and it's all OK again? Good old dependable Amy.' Her eyes shone darkly, brimming with anger. 'He promised me that there were no more secrets . . .'

'In his eyes it's in the past and he never expected anyone to find out—' Goodhew had no idea why he was saying anything in the man's defence. Amy cut him off sharply.

'He had no right to keep it from me.'

'He might have been afraid to—'

'No. It wasn't fear, it was cowardice. He didn't tell me because it wasn't convenient for him and he's a fool if he thinks it'll all blow over. Not this time.'

CHAPTER 37

In the first minutes after walking out of her dad's house, Amy had felt a now familiar surge of anger. Most recently it had been directed at her mum but now it was her father's turn and she paced the pavement just out of sight of her dad's house as she worked to dispel it. Two hours had been enough to tame it and by the time she'd started speaking to Goodhew she knew there had been a shift in the way she saw her father; the trust had gone, the respect wrecked.

She'd refused Goodhew's offer of a lift and her anger dissipated as she walked back towards town. Maybe she was shocked because the calmness had come in waves and in between she'd seen her situation with clarity; this was what was meant by a pivotal moment and it couldn't be undone or denied. And, because of it, certain things had run their course.

She'd had a mile to go when she'd made a call to Alex. 'I'm sorry, I never asked my dad about Melanie.'

'It doesn't matter, I know the answer now.' A pause. 'What's wrong, you sound weird?'

'I had some news. Look, I'm walking back from my dad's, would you mind giving me a lift?'

'Of course.'

He'd ridden into view within ten minutes. He'd brought a spare crash helmet but removed his own before offering it to her. 'I don't know what's happened to you but, personally, I could do with someone to talk to; can we get a drink?'

Perhaps he'd meant alcohol but she agreed and asked to go to Clowns. And now they sat facing each other across the same table where she'd met with Goodhew. 'So,' she concluded, 'you're not the only one with an extra sibling. Only yours is alive. It's a shock.'

He blew into his tea and didn't reply immediately. In the end he put the mug back down onto the table without drinking from it. 'It's a parent's job to fuck us up but ours have really done a job of it. From birth in my case.'

'At least they're consistent.'

Neither of them smiled.

'Are you going to leave Frampton's?' he asked.

She shook her head. 'I don't know. My reasons for everything seem to be changing daily. If anyone's going to prove my dad's innocence it will be the police, not me. I not even sure if I care any more.'

'But you still need a job.'

'Of course.'

'Why move unless you have to?' He made it sound like a casual question but it didn't feel like it. Plenty of the clowns on the shelf behind him had eyes that followed her; usually she didn't mind.

'I like the work,' she admitted. 'And some of my colleagues.'

He grinned impishly. 'Am I on that list?'

'No, you're in File 13 with Stan.'

'Ouch.'

'Just kidding.' They smiled across at each other until Amy realised that the eye contact had continued for too long. She hadn't even had a date in the last year. She felt an unexpected jolt of emptiness. 'I'm sorry, Alex. I think I should go home.'

He looked disappointed but smiled. 'Sure.'

'If you speak to Stan, tell him I'll be there tomorrow and I'll work late to make up the hours.' She dropped some coins onto the table. 'Thanks, that's for the tea.'

She was already leaving by the time Alex was only half on his feet. 'There's no need . . .' was the last she heard before heading out onto King Street. She drew a deep breath of the outside air and hurried towards the Brew House pub, planning to take the shortcut behind it that led to her flat. She'd only walked a few yards when she felt a hand on her arm.

'Amy?' She stopped and he turned her gently towards him. 'Can I get you dinner? Or we could drive somewhere?'

She shook her head.

'A drink then?'

'No, I don't think so.' But his hand was still on her arm and she didn't step away. She hesitated then said, 'There are things I need to do right now.' She closed her eyes and leant her forehead into his shoulder. 'I like you, Alex . . .' He wrapped one arm around her.

His mouth was close to her ear, 'It's a bit soon for the I-like-you-but speech, isn't it?'

She shook her head, 'No, it was going to be "I like you a lot." Or "I like you despite this mess we're in." I just hadn't decided.'

'It's our families that are in a mess, not us.'

'We are our families aren't we? We're right in the thick of it and maybe I like you because we're kindred spirits right now and when all this passes . . .' She could feel his warmth through his shirt and the urge to slide her arms around him.

'You've been in my head since you walked into the office,' he said, 'and that was at least five minutes before I knew who you were. And that was when I thought my family was the same dysfunctional nightmare that it had always been. I'm attracted to you, Amy, but not because of the situation.' He ran his hand across her hair and cupped her face, his fingertips made her skin tingle and she felt his breath close to her face.

'I'm sorry but I do need to go to my mum's.' She slid her hands around his neck. 'It's not an excuse, though.'

He kissed her softly on the lips, 'I know,' he grinned. 'I'll come and find you tomorrow and we won't settle for the pavement outside a pub.'

'OK,' she kissed him. 'You choose.'

CHAPTER 38

Amy took the direct route to her mum's house and was within sight of Fair Street in less than five minutes. The Hopbine pub stood halfway along the short road. She didn't want a drink but needed a few minutes to gather her thoughts so ordered half a cider. Orchard Pig apparently. She guessed it would have tasted good if she was tasting anything at all. She felt detached from everything. What she needed were some opening words for her mum; 'Just because I'm here doesn't mean I've forgiven you' wasn't going to be the best start. Her mind remained blank.

She finished drinking with the glass close to half full and left it on the end of the bar. She still had no idea what she would say but decided that she would have to trust the words to find her when the moment arose.

It was 8.05 p.m.; too early for her mum to go to bed, but heading towards nine when her habit was to settle down in front of the latest crime drama on the television with a glass of red and both house phone and mobile set to mute or diverted to answerphone.

Amy knocked. The door opened and her mum didn't wait for her opening line. 'Amy, come in.' She managed the same watery smile that Amy had seen on her last visit. Her mum swung the door wide and then walked back into the heart of the house leaving Amy to close the door and follow her to the lounge.

The TV was already on and a half-drunk bottle of Malbec stood open on the coffee table. 'Would you like a glass of something, Amy?'

'Sure, thanks.'

'Same as me?'

'Yes, please.' She turned off the TV while her mum was out of the room and chose to sit at the other end of the settee; not too close but still within touching distance.

Geraldine filled Amy's glass but stopped pouring her own at the three-quarters mark. 'I'm ahead of you.'

Amy smiled politely but the right words still weren't coming.

Her mum found hers first. 'I've missed you.'

'I'm finding it hard to accept what you did, but I understand Dad more now too . . .'

'And we're both a disappointment?'

Amy thought about it. 'Maybe my expectations are unreasonable.'

The glass had been close to Geraldine's lips, but she placed it back on the table without taking a sip. By the time she looked back at Amy she was frowning. 'Your expectations are too low, Amy, not too high.' Amy opened her mouth to protest but Geraldine spoke first. 'That's not a criticism of you. Trying to put things right is in your nature. So is having broad shoulders. They are strengths but I haven't shown you how to draw the line. I drew that line with your dad but you wouldn't have seen it like that.'

'You should have told me what he was like.'

'By the time he was freed we had our own life. I didn't have a need to tell tales on him; I wanted you to form your own opinion.'

'I thought he'd been unfairly convicted. I couldn't see anything beyond that except an image of what our family could have been if he hadn't been in jail and you'd tried harder to love him.' She took a hefty swig of the wine. 'I think the reason I've never had a relationship that's lasted more than a few weeks is because of the way things were between you and Dad.'

Geraldine looked startled but didn't comment.

'When I was small, preschool age I suppose, I can remember how desperate you were for the divorce to come through and how many times you told me that we didn't need a man.'

'But I wasn't aiming to make you feel like that about your own relationships.'

'Each time I've had a boyfriend I've known that it's going nowhere. You've always said that all men are the same but I don't believe that any more.'

Geraldine slid an arm around Amy's shoulders and pulled her close. Amy nestled her head under her mother's cheek and listened to the words spoken softly in her ear. 'I thought I was protecting you by teaching you to be independent, teaching you that you don't need to be in a relationship to be happy.'

'I don't need one, but maybe I'd like one.'

Her mum straightened and studied Amy's face for a moment. 'Have you met someone?'

Yes, Neil Frampton's son.

'No,' Amy lied, 'not yet. But I want my life as straight as it can be first and that means dropping this obsession I've had with Dad's case.'

'Really?' Geraldine's face flashed with sudden optimism, 'What's brought this on?'

'The police. They were at Dad's today . . . don't look worried . . . they came to speak to him in connection with Lorraine Martin's death and I found out some things.'

'What things?'

She squeezed her mum's hand. 'It's OK, they didn't arrest him or anything.'

'Thank God, I wouldn't want to go through all that again . . .'

'Listen, I'll tell you, but the first thing you need to know is that as I walked out of Dad's I thought, I can't do this any more. He's lied to me too many times now. And it's not because I don't care, or because I'm disloyal or . . .' she shook her head and fished around for the rest of the sentence. 'I've just had enough, Mum. I won't stay long but I wanted you to know.'

'I'm really sorry about everything. About your dad and the way I behaved.' Geraldine exhaled slowly and reached forward to top up Amy's glass and refill her own. She drank half immediately. 'What else do you need from me, Amy?'

Amy smiled weakly. 'Peace? Sanity?'

'Have you eaten?'

Amy became serious again and shook her head, 'I am tired but I need to tell you the rest too.'

She didn't speak immediately and Geraldine must have sensed her apprehension because she too began to look worried. 'Go on.'

'I know about Nadine's baby.' Amy couldn't bring herself to say 'Dad's baby'. 'You should have told me . . .' The suggestion of blame hung in the air but she was beyond caring about that. 'I would rather have known.'

'I understand, but to tell you about her would have meant telling you about your father's affair. It would have been a mistake. Why should I dump all that on you when you were small? Why tell you when you're older?' she said when she finally spoke. 'She died.'

'I know, but it proves so much about Dad. And she should have had a funeral. Dad knew she'd died and he didn't care. Did you know she was buried in Lorraine Martin's garden?'

'Not then. When I saw the baby in the news, I guessed.'

'What if she'd lived, would anyone have told me then?'

'No. She would have been adopted. He was doing everything he could to deny anything about Nadine. He would never have wanted her to keep the baby.'

'I don't understand how you're so calm about it.'

'I'm not calm because I know that we're about to get dragged through the papers again, your dad will be in the frame for Lorraine's murder, and the story of baby and Nadine will be smeared across every tabloid.'

'They won't arrest him, will they? He wouldn't have killed her.'

'Give him an alibi if you're sure. Or refuse to because of everything else he's done. Exactly the same dilemma I faced and it's tough.'

'I see,' Amy said slowly. There had been no suggestion that her dad was under investigation for Lorraine Martin's murder and she wouldn't be prepared to lie for him even if he was. 'It would have been wrong for you to cover for him, wouldn't it?'

'I think so.'

'It makes sense now and I'm really sorry, Mum, I shouldn't have blamed you. Would you do something for me?'

'Of course.'

'Tell me the things you can remember, the small details; I need to put all of this in one clear picture and then I think I can deal with it and leave it behind.'

In reply Geraldine slipped her arms around her daughter and hugged her tightly. Amy leant against her mum and felt the wine and the effects of the day start to overtake her. She closed her eyes.

Geraldine picked up the two glasses and the empty bottle. 'We'll talk, I promise, but right now you need to get some sleep. The spare bed's already made.'

'Thanks, Mum.' Amy opened her eyes enough to watch her mum leave the room. She knew she needed to rouse herself before she fell asleep on the settee but it was only when she stood that she realised that her mum was in the hallway waiting. 'Mum?'

'It is just a small detail; her name was Abigail,' she whispered, then carried on towards the kitchen.

CHAPTER 39

When Goodhew returned to Parkside, Jack Worthington was alone in the office. 'Where is everyone?'

'Everyone? You make it sound like there's a decent number of us on this one. Kincaide went with Marks to see Moira Trent, the others have gone for the day. I'm just leaving, I've been in since seven.'

Goodhew checked his watch: the day had disappeared into evening and he hadn't noticed. 'I won't stay long either,' he said, but he was still going through paperwork when Marks and Kincaide returned an hour later. 'What happened with Moira Trent?' he asked.

Marks held up a sheet of copier paper. Goodhew was too far away to read the details but he could see the shape of the printed characters forming two columns that reached three quarters of the way down the page. 'She admitted that she knew about the babies but claimed that Lorraine had told her that it was cash-in-hand money for looking after the women.' Marks passed the page to him. 'Dates and amounts, it's the money that Lorraine gave to her to look after.'

The font size was small, eight point, no more. The entries were chronological, the first dated 27 May 1987 and the final entry 4 April 1996. Goodhew counted forty-two lines. 'One line per adopted child? Four or five per year – it's possible.'

Kincaide spoke next. 'Moira Trent wouldn't be drawn on that and tried to stick to the story that the fees were for accommodation.'

'Over £200,000? That's a lot now, it would've been a fortune back then.'

'She carried on denying knowledge of anything even though we knew that both Robert Buckingham and the Framptons claimed they'd met Lorraine through her and that she'd introduced her as a midwife.'

'And?'

'We heard back from the NHS. Lorraine had been sacked for drinking on duty in February 1985 and struck off the nursing register later that year on a charge of gross misconduct. She had no right to be practising. Moira knew about the drinking but nothing else so when we dropped that bombshell she became slightly more forthcoming,' Marks reached across to point to 1990, halfway down the sheet. 'She was told that Nadine's baby was stillborn. She claims that she didn't know that the baby was buried in the garden, that she never knew its name or sex.'

'So Frankie is Nadine's baby?'

'Yes.'

'That's forty-three babies.'

'And Lorraine started drinking again after Nadine lost her baby. From there on out it was a cycle of sobriety, relapse and a succession of breakdowns.' Marks tapped the sheet, 'and forty-two illegal adoptions. This will all belong to the Major Crimes Unit by tomorrow.'

'Lock, stock and barrel,' Kincaide smiled. 'You could call it in now?'

'In the morning, Michael. First thing, when I'm not too tired to think straight.'

Goodhew took a copy of the list and it was still in front of him an hour after the others had gone. Everything was too tightly interconnected, Major Crimes would take Lorraine Martin's case too, and his grandfather's. The mass of detail would belong to other officers and it would be for them to continue or drop the current leads, to pick up on elements Parkside had missed, and, worst of all, also miss the clues that the current team were missing too. And, in the case of his grandfather and the fire, the things that had been overlooked back then.

His gaze fell on the boxes of information from those previous cases. They'd been brought in and stacked by the wall. He wondered how many had been recently searched or if they had done what the next team might do and assume that there was nothing to find?

He wandered across the room and removed the lid from the first box. Lying on top was a note from DC Knight, 'Box 2. Cross-referenced everything in here and in boxes 1, 3, 4 and 5.' He lifted the lid on a couple of the other boxes and found a version of the same note in each. He wasn't surprised; she was incredibly thorough with documentation. But there'd been no mention of the sixth and final box. He squatted beside it and noted that it was still taped shut as it had been when it was moved up from the archives. He grabbed scissors from the nearest desk and slit it open. It contained nothing but a small box of DAT tapes and a few sheets cataloguing the contents of each. 'Only one way to find out,' he said in reply to his own silent question, then he picked up the box and left for home.

Goodhew owned a DAT player. If he'd visited his grandfather's storage unit, he probably could also have played back most audio formats from PlayTape and Microcassette onwards. He realised that his need for gadgets was yet another part of his personality he had probably inherited from Joe.

He took the DAT player and tapes to his grandfather's study and sorted them into chronological order. All interviewees bar one were names he recognised. The first tape was marked 'Steven Powell'. Goodhew read the accompanying notes then listened to the recording. Mr Powell had lived in the adjoining property and had been alerted by shouts, which he could hear through the party wall. 'I had the TV on and wasn't paying too much attention to them at first, but I suddenly realised that the tone of their voices was wrong. Panic-filled. So I turned down the volume and moved outside – out the front I mean, into the street. It wasn't shouts by then but screams and other people came out of their houses too and we could see smoke at the windows. "Call the fire brigade" I shouted and someone else grabbed a ladder and we propped it up at the front. We didn't get any further; we could hear the sirens but the screaming had stopped.' He seemed to say it all in a single breath and every subsequent question about anything suspicious he'd seen in the days preceding the attack drew a consistent and monotone negative response.

The next tape was Neil Frampton's. Goodhew scanned through the others; unsurprisingly about half of them were labelled as interviews with Robert Buckingham, their frequency increasing as they drew closer to charging him. But date order made the most sense and he lay back, closed his eyes and waited for the familiar voice of Neil Frampton to speak.

'I last saw Theo that afternoon.'

A male voice with a soft Scottish accent prompted him. DS Montgomery according to the notes.

'Sorry, I mean 30 March 1991.'

Goodhew's eyes drifted open again – it was hard to match this voice to the Neil Frampton he'd seen this week. The tone sounded familiar but he spoke more rapidly then with words that were clipped and more driven.

'I was in the Cow and Calf on Pound Hill with my business partner, Robert Buckingham Theo popped in, had a half and then left us to meet Nadine.' He'd hesitated as he spoke his son's name and the second syllable wobbled and for the rest of the sentence his voice shook.

'We barely spoke. He was quiet but we chatted to Robert for a few minutes. I asked Theo if he wanted another. He said no and that was the last time I saw him . . . until afterwards.' Frampton had identified Theo's body then.

'He seemed fine. In good spirits actually.'

Montgomery again, 'And between him and your partner?'

'That business between Robert and Nadine was a long time ago.'

'I'm sorry, what business?'

Goodhew listened as the first seeds of doubt were sown.

After that DS Montgomery seemed to look for links to Buckingham. He interviewed Geraldine Buckingham. He questioned her about Theo and why she'd failed to mention that he had visited her house.

'I forget. He came to see my husband who'd gone out.'

'Was it usual for Theo to visit your home?'

'The only time as far as I know.'

'Did he tell you what he wanted?'

'Just to speak to Robert.'

'Was he agitated?'

'No.'

'How did your husband react when he found out that Theo wanted to speak to him?'

'I don't remember.'

'Were you aware of any problems between your husband and Theo?'

'No, but I don't think he would have told me. My husband doesn't always share his thoughts.'

And then the interview with Carolyn Frampton. She'd been twenty-four then and still had a girlishness to her voice and vocabulary. She claimed that she'd last seen Theo at home the night before. 'He was keeping himself to himself. He'd just hang around sometimes, brooding over stuff.'

'How was your own relationship with him?'

'Fine. Yeah, it was pretty good. We hadn't worked together since I had the baby and that helped too.'

'So you and he had had issues?'

'Sometimes he'd get on my nerves. But Neil says that's how it is if you work and live with someone.'

'And you both worked for your husband's company?'

'Yes, that's right. Theo started a couple of months before I went on maternity leave.'

'Was the age gap between you and Theo ever an issue?'

'It was only five years.'

'But you're married to his father.'

'It wasn't a problem.'

'Fair enough. And how was he with the other employees? It was his father's business, were there any conflicts with management; with Robert Buckingham for example?'

'With Robert?' He thought he could hear a smile in her voice. 'It's hard to comment when they're never in the same room at the same time.'

And so it went on. Goodhew changed tapes again and waited for Stanley Mercer to be led down the same path.

'When was the last time you saw Theo Frampton?'

'On Friday,' he replied.

Before Goodhew could think his hand had shot forward and hit the stop button. He rewound and played it again. Goodhew listened and his blood ran cold.

CHAPTER 40

It was 4 a.m.

The only person he knew he could ring at that time was his grandmother. *Ellie*, he reminded himself. But Ellie was the one person who didn't need to know. Not yet anyway.

He called Sue instead. Ellie usually answered with a sharp comment and gave the impression that she'd already been wide awake. Sue grunted, 'What's happened?'

'I need to talk to someone.'

'And not over the phone?' Another grunt then the sound of a drawer being hauled open.

'At mine. I'm sorry.'

'It's fine, I'm not complaining. I sound like this when I talk in my sleep.'

'There will be a taxi outside yours in a couple of minutes.'

'You just assumed I'd come straight over?'

'I booked it online, confirmed it just then when I heard you getting dressed.'

'No one should be that alert at 4 a.m. You're abnormal.' She hung up and ten minutes later he met her at the front door. 'Normal people sleep, Gary.'

'Ellie does that.'

'What? Sleeps?'

'No, starts the conversation, hangs up, then walks in and carries on as if there hasn't been a fifteen-minute gap in the middle.' He meant it as a throwaway comment but, as he spoke, he knew that his voice sounded hollow.

Sue reached out and caught his arm, 'What's happened, Gary?'

He tipped his head towards the stairs and she followed him up to the second floor. She sat beside him on the settee and he placed the DAT tape player between them. 'I need to put this in context.'

'OK.'

'I've been playing the interview tapes from the Romsey Terrace case. It seemed to be the only box file that Sandra Knight hadn't been through. They had Robert Buckingham in their sights from the start and I was listening and trying to put myself back there, hearing it all for the first time so that I was in the shoes – in the mind-set – of the team back then.'

'OK,' she repeated.

'Then I heard this.' He pressed play. Montgomery asked the question and Goodhew felt his chest tighten in anticipation of the reply. He held his breath even though the audio had been repeated relentlessly and he knew every beat and breath in the detective's question and Stan Mercer's reply: 'On Friday.'

He pressed pause.

'He sounds different now, doesn't he?'

'From two words?'

He pressed play again and let her hear a few more seconds.

'Yes, he does.' She then agreed, 'Age, smoking and years of yelling at people I guess.'

Goodhew nodded. 'Stan Mercer is one of the people I heard when I hid in my grandfather's flat. I didn't recognise his voice when I met him, but from this,' he tapped the tape player, 'I have no doubt. He's either an accessory, a witness or the one who struck Joe.'

'Phone Marks.'

'No. As soon as I do that these tapes will be out of my hands. Last night, the Lorraine Martin murder just turned into the Lorraine Martin baby-selling scandal and Marks reckons Major Crimes will be taking it all from us tomorrow.

'Shit.'

'Marks will be in at seven at the earliest. Help me check these tapes. If there's anything else here, I need to find it.'

Sue stared at the pile. 'What are we looking for?'

'I have no idea.'

'Great. There's one tape player and a pile of DATs, it's not like we can take half each.'

'Sue?'

'What?'

'I'm glad you're here. I could go through the rest on my own, but I'd rather have company.' Her skin was pale with tiredness and her hair was untidier than usual. 'I'm sorry I dragged you out of bed.'

She supressed a smile. 'I don't mind. Not really, Gary. I just don't do well on three hours sleep.'

'Well, I'll nudge you if you doze off.'

'Don't you dare.'

Neither of them flagged but by quarter to seven all they had were notes and questions, and still no answers. 'I keep looking out for a link between Stan Mercer and the fire or even Lorraine Martin's murder.' Sue sat cross-legged on the floor. She moved her notes around on the floor to see if changing the order helped, 'It all looks different now we know that he was involved with Joe's death but I'm not seeing a way forward.'

Goodhew looked at his own notes. 'Yeah, I keep seeing bias against Robert Buckingham but who's to say that they weren't right when he was arrested the first time. He's unpleasant. And a liar; one of those who'll say whatever gets them off the hook.'

'Unpleasant isn't a crime, Gary, but I do wonder what he and Theo talked about in that pub. Could have been something that wound him up; Theo and Nadine were dead within hours.'

'I'll ask whether Buckingham can be re-interviewed.' Goodhew checked his watch. 'We need to get in soon and update Marks.' They gathered up their papers and he didn't speak again until they were ready to leave his flat, 'Sue, you know I don't want you to leave Cambridge, don't you?'

'And you know I've made up my mind.' She took a step closer to him and he took hold of her hand.

'I do but I need to say this anyway. Last year when I heard that an officer had been killed, all I cared about was that it wasn't you.' He squeezed her hand and neither of them looked away. 'At that moment I knew that it has been you all along. And when we kissed . . .'

'I know and at that moment we both felt the same.' She began to withdraw her hand again but he held onto it. 'Gary, it won't work out.'

'My grandfather said Ellie was a better reflection of himself. Suddenly I understood what he'd meant. For me, that's you.'

'Gary?'

'It's OK, I just wanted to make sure you knew, that's all now. But it shouldn't be your reason for leaving.'

Finally, she looked away. 'It isn't, not entirely.' She squeezed his hand this time and then let it go, turning away and taking her phone from her pocket. 'I'm going to call a taxi.'

'For 200 yards?'

'I don't want to get spotted coming out of here, it'll look like I'm doing the walk of shame. I'll get a cab home then come back in as soon as I've changed.' She placed the call then stood with her elbow resting on the jukebox and looked around the room. 'You were here when Joe told you to hide, and here when you played the recording. It's come full circle.'

CHAPTER 41

Abigail. The name conjured up a freckled face with brown eyes and long brown hair. The image was a child's drawing at first, cartoon-like and just the approximation of being human; the ears were level with the eyes and the nose and mouth were just two dots and a straight line. That was 3 a.m.; by six Abigail's image had become a Facebook profile photo, she was tanned, wearing a vest top and holding a piña colada with the straw to her mouth. Amy was glad she'd woken and pushed the pictures from her mind.

Abigail. Perhaps she would have been Abbie by now. Amy washed and dressed quickly while mulling over the name-shortening possibilities. Abbie or Abi or Abby. The dream had been mundane and had wedged itself into her short-term memory in an eerie impersonation of real life.

She brushed her teeth then splashed her face with cold water. 'Wake up, Amy.'

She'd asked her mum for the small details, the minor facts that no one would bother fabricating. She figured that they were the ones that hovered in the background and either validated or disproved the rest of any story. She awoke in the middle of the night and realised that she had some of those facts too. She checked her watch.

Over an hour before work and it was time to visit Moira Trent.

From Fair Street to Clarendon Street was a short walk. In June it was the route to Strawberry Fair from town, and back again. It would be packed with revellers, waves of them in each direction, painted and tawdry and loud in every way. Today, the road was grey and silent. Milk bottles were on the doorsteps of the houses that still took deliveries and a lone cat crossing between the parked cars was the only movement. Moira Trent lived in the same sash-windowed terrace that Amy remembered from visiting as a child. She rang the bell then stepped back to the roadside edge of the hop-scotch-paved footpath, and remembered her dad telling her that it was good manners not to crowd an entrance. She watched the half-circle of frosted glass above the door and straightened as soon as movement rippled the light seeping through it.

There was a pause and Amy guessed she was being observed through the spyhole. When the door opened, it was easy to see the weariness on the older woman's face.

'I'm sorry about Lorraine.'

Moira acknowledged the comment with a dip of her head but then moved straight on. 'Why are you here?'

'I need to speak to you. I'd like to come in.'

It wasn't a question and Moira obediently stepped back to allow Amy inside. Amy walked towards the kitchen at the back of the house where she'd often sat at the stripped pine table reading or doing her homework while Moira and her father discussed the accounts. The kitchen hadn't changed much. It had the same mushroom walls and red-tiled floor. The wooden units had been repainted cream. She'd hated sitting in here. Mushroom, she'd decided then, was the colour of boredom. Now its familiarity warmed her. She reached for the nearest chair. 'I hope you don't mind?'

Moira shook her head and pulled out a chair so that she could sit opposite Amy.

'I asked Neil for the job because I wanted to prove that my dad never started the fire.'

'I guessed that.'

'It hasn't exactly worked out the way I'd hoped and I might not have tried if I'd known everything in the first place, like about my dad and Nadine . . . Then I realised that, while those things are important to me, they might not mean so much to someone else . . .' Her words faltered. In her mind's eye coming here had been a good idea, but now she wasn't sure. She spread her hands flat on the table, took a breath and carried on staring down at them as she spoke. 'I want to tell you something in case it's important to you and ask you something else because that's important to me.'

'OK,' Moira replied gently.

'The police know but I started thinking about how I've been kept in the dark . . .'

'Go on.'

'Lorraine tried to contact me.' She didn't wait for Moira to respond. 'She posted a card through the door in the yard, said she wanted to speak to me but, by the time I saw it . . .' She hesitated and softened the words she was about to use. 'By then it was the following morning and she'd already been found.'

Moira stared at her, bewildered. 'Why would she?' she mouthed the words, more to herself than to Amy.

'I think she was going to tell me about my half-sister, about Abigail.' It was enough to startle Moira.

'You know?'

Amy nodded. 'The police confronted my dad yesterday; he didn't want to admit it but in the end he had to own up.'

'And he told you her name?'

'No, that was Mum.'

'I see,' Moira murmured. She gave Amy a sympathetic smile and reached across the table to squeeze her hand. 'Maybe Lorraine was going to tell you something else.'

'Like what?'

'I don't know.'

'Did Abigail die because Lorraine made a mistake?' Amy felt Moira's fingers stiffen. 'I'm sorry, that was tactless.'

'No, it's fine,' she replied, but Amy knew it wasn't; she could see a new hardness in Moira's expression. 'We won't know that, but I'm sure that burying the baby in the garden must have troubled her. Perhaps that was what she was going to tell you. The place where they found the baby was well tended, I really don't think she buried the baby to forget about her. You said you wanted information from me? About your dad?'

Amy hesitated. Moira's mood had shifted and she was conscious that she'd hit a nerve. 'You were there at the time, I just wondered if you'd tell me . . .'

'About your dad?'

'About any of it. You and he were friends.'

'And even after everything, you want someone to speak in his favour?'

'I want a balanced picture. I want to see my parents clearly.'

'OK, well I thought we were friends . . .'

'Just friends?'

'Yes. Absolutely. But maybe that's why I hadn't seen that other side of him. I thought I knew him pretty well until I saw the way he treated Nadine. She knew he was married and should have had her eyes open but she fell for him and he used her. She was his lunchtime shag, nothing more.'

Amy grimaced.

'Obviously that's not how we like to think of our parents but there you go. The pregnancy was her biggest mistake. He dumped her and she hung on. He really, truly despised her in the end. Wouldn't acknowledge that the child was his so I'm surprised he even knew her name.'

'No, I told you, Mum did. My dad didn't know it.' She paused to think. 'I don't know how she knew.'

Moira didn't respond.

'Well,' Moira said finally, flicking the comment away with her hand, 'I kept making excuses for Rob until his arrest. And then those rose-tinted glasses of mine fell and smashed. Of course he killed them; he hated Nadine. I made too many excuses for Lorraine too. Recurrent hypermetropia.'

Amy looked blank.

Moira leant forward and whispered, 'It means that I couldn't see what was right in front of me.' She smiled but her expression had become taut. 'I'm returning to work today. Will you be there?'

'Yes, in the yard.'

'Good.' Moira's intonation changed suddenly. 'Now I must get ready.' She left the room and returned with a makeup purse. She applied foundation in her compact mirror and began on her eyeshadow.

'I could give you a lift?' But her tone was brusque and the real question was 'Don't you think it's time you went?'

Either way the answer was the same. 'Thanks, but no.' Amy rose to her feet but waited, thinking that Moira might say something else. But Moira finished adding shadow to one eye and switched to the other without a word. For the first time, Amy saw that the hand holding the eyeshadow brush was shaking.

'What's wrong?'

Moira paused but didn't look at her. 'I need you to go now.'

'OK.' Amy took a step back. 'I didn't mean to upset you.'

'I just need you to go,' Moira snapped back, spelling out her reply syllable by syllable. She reached out to put the makeup on the table but fumbled and brushes and a lipstick rolled from the purse and clattered on the floor. 'Shit.' She reached down for the lipstick but it slipped from her fingers.

As Amy bent to pick it up Moira grabbed her arm.

'Don't you understand? My sister has been murdered and this is my first day back at work. That's big enough without you coming in here and swamping me with all this other stuff. Now go.'

Amy stood and began to apologise when Moira swept the rest of the makeup onto the floor. She grabbed Amy again, this time at the elbow, and manhandled her towards the hallway. 'Just get out,' she shouted until Amy had been propelled back onto the street. The door slammed behind her and, from the other side, she heard Moira sob.

Moira gathered the makeup items from the floor and lined them up on the kitchen table and then she cleansed her face and started again. Have I misunderstood? That was the question that mattered beyond all else. Her hands had stopped trembling and her breathing had settled but she wasn't ready to speak to anyone yet.

This time the foundation went on evenly, the eyeshadow subtler. She turned her head from left to right and checked it in the mirror from multiple angles. There was a tiny amount of puffiness left from crying. She paused to make eye contact with herself and tried to decide whether she was now looking at an intelligent woman or a foolish one. Neither, or both, she told herself, then reached for the phone.

The call was answered and she spoke without any preamble: 'Amy came to see me. She knew that Nadine's baby was called Abigail. Geraldine told her, but I don't know how she knows.' Moira had already gone through the potential explanations and, unless there was something she'd missed, had narrowed it down to a single possibility. She waited, imagining the same logic unfolding at the other end of the line and nodded to herself as the same inevitable conclusion was reached.

'What do you want me to do?' she asked.

The instruction was brief and clear. Hang up and wait.

CHAPTER 42

The box of DAT tapes sat on Marks's desk next to the player. Marks released the pause button. It was the third time that he'd listened to the same two words: 'On Friday.'

He stared at Goodhew. 'And that was enough?'

'Absolutely.'

'Without a shadow of a doubt?'

'None whatsoever.'

'But you didn't recognise his voice when you met him in person?'

Goodhew sighed. 'That's right, sir. He's forty-four now but sounds at least a decade older; he was only twenty-one on this tape. You can hear the difference, can't you?'

'Devil's advocate, Gary. I need to make sure this stands up. His accent is the same and there's bound to be an expert who'll swear that his patterns of speech haven't changed, but, in all honesty, I wouldn't have thought it was the same man.'

'Well then,' Goodhew replied.

'I need a statement from you formally identifying Mercer's voice. But without a confession, all we'll have is a witness statement with an identification based on two words heard twenty-two years ago. And the fact that you were just eleven at the time won't add anything to its credibility. I hope you can see the issue with that.'

'Of course, and it's a greater problem because I can't name the second man.'

'About that,' Marks tilted his head and looked at Goodhew over his glasses, 'I'm thinking that Stanley Mercer is more likely to be the second man . . .'

'To Neil Frampton's lead?'

'Exactly.' Marks agreed. 'Frampton had the motive to visit Joe . . .'

'Taking Mercer for support . . .'

'But we don't have a scrap of evidence.' Marks rewound the tape and played it one more time. He steepled his fingers as he weighed up the options. 'We'll bring in Mercer and simultaneously question Frampton – all we can do is keep him occupied so Mercer and he can't collude. We'll put pressure on Mercer and hope that he places both of them at the scene.' Marks removed the tape and handed it to Goodhew. 'Get that copied and then filed. And as a witness you won't be involved with interviewing either of them. We do have another bonus.' Marks tapped a sheet of paper too far from Goodhew for him to read. 'A local resident, Stuart Whitt, puts Mercer in Argyle Street with Lorraine Martin shortly before her estimated time of death.'

'And he's just come forward?'

'He was leaving for the airport when he saw them. He's back now and just caught up with the local papers.'

'How reliable is he?'

'Solid. And very precise with the timings.'

Marks had arrived in Argyle Street, his unmarked car chasing the tail of the leading response car; their arrival wasn't intended to be subtle. The gates to Frampton's yard had been open and a Transit pickup stood just inside the entrance. PCs Thompson and Marsden had waited at the gate while Marks and Worthington approached the Portakabin. Walking alongside Worthington felt similar to turning up in the company of a pit bull. Their whole entrance had been rather on the showy side for Marks's liking but then he'd seen Mercer glance out through the window. If a single expression could have been captured and put forward as evidence, then they would have been able to charge Stanley Mercer on the spot.

They'd read him his rights and had him back at Parkside and in an interview room within fifteen minutes.

Now Mercer's initial shock had subsided and he sat glowering at Marks from the other side of the table. 'Your solicitor is on his way,' Marks told him.

'This is bollocks. You can't bring me in on some random charge.'

Marks levelled a cold stare in his direction. 'There's nothing random, Mr Mercer, we have two witnesses that connect you with two separate crimes. One who connects you to Lorraine Martin's murder. And the other who puts you at Joseph Goodhew's house at the time of his attack.'

'I have nothing to do with Lorraine's death. Who's said that I do?'

'Mr Mercer, if you want to start the interview immediately then that's possible, but if you want to wait for your brief then I'm not having this conversation now.'

'I'll wait, but it's all bollocks. I never touched her'

'Interesting,' Marks mused. 'Two denials over Lorraine's death and no mention of Joseph Goodhew.'

'Because there's no point; Detective Goodhew is a relative and you all look after your own.'

'You'd be better off wondering who's not looking after you.'

'Meaning what?'

'The witness claims he was in Joseph Goodhew's flat with you on the day Goodhew died.'

'Who?' Stan Mercer's complexion had been darkened by the years he'd spent working in the open air, but that couldn't hide the way the colour drained from his face. His glare barely wavered but if Marks hung around he guessed he'd start to see him sweat. 'What witness?'

Marks gathered up his notes; some people were easy to read and Mercer was the kind of man who liked an audience, liked to be heard as long as it was at no one's convenience. Hand him a microphone and he'd be as good as mute. He didn't like Marks breaking eye contact and made a predictable grab for attention before Marks reached the door. 'You're bluffing, otherwise you'd tell me.'

Marks opened the door then turned back and gave Mercer a deliberately pitying smile. 'If I were bluffing, how would I know that you were in Joseph Goodhew's flat? That there were just the two of you and the victim. The witness isn't the dead man, is it now?'

Marks stepped out of the room and closed the door behind him; he'd leave Mercer to sweat and then see what that shook loose. The moment of optimism was short-lived. Gully hurried into the corridor and he immediately saw her worried expression.

'What's wrong?'

'They arrived at Neil Frampton's house to bring him in but he'd taken off already.'

'When?'

'Obviously before Kincaide arrived at his house, before anyone at the yard could have tipped him off that we were coming. But I don't know more than that. His car's gone and there's no trace of it so far on traffic cams.'

'So where's Kincaide now?'

'Back at his desk.'

'And he sent you to find me? Why the hell aren't I having this conversation with him?' He hurried down the corridor, heading for Kincaide. 'That was rhetorical by the way,' he grunted as an afterthought.

'I guessed,' she replied.

He pushed open the door and shouted across the office, 'Michael, get Carolyn Frampton on the phone. Now.'

CHAPTER 43

Geraldine Buckingham had slept later than she intended. She planned to be out of bed by the time that Amy was waking up, envisaging the kind of sit-at-a-sunny-table-style breakfast that only seemed to exist in American TV shows. Obviously without the pancakes and maple syrup; who ate desserts at 7 a.m.?

But when she'd first heard Amy stir it had been much earlier and after a few minutes of moving around she had heard Amy open and close the front door and then listened to the sound of her daughter's footsteps gradually fading as she walked away. She'd cancelled her alarm then and drifted off again.

Now she stirred enough to follow the sounds that travelled up the stairs and across the landing: Amy had returned and she was boiling the kettle, making toast, washing her hair. Geraldine lifted herself onto one elbow and discovered that her head throbbed each time she moved. 'Amy,' she called. 'Amy?'

'Coming.'

Amy nudged the door open a few moments later. Her hair was damp and hung over her shoulder leaving a damp patch on her T-shirt, 'OK, Mum?'

'Headache.'

'I'm not surprised. What do you need?'

'Paracetamol and codeine from my bag. I'm sorry, love.'

Amy came back with the tablets and a glass of water, and sat on the edge of the bed until Geraldine had taken them. 'Are you still up for breakfast?'

Geraldine winced at the idea of food. 'Where did you go?'

'I popped round to see Moira; I'm going in at ten. What do you fancy, fried eggs, greasy bacon?' Amy raised an eyebrow. 'Or toast?'

'Toast. Now let me get dressed, I'm coming down.'

Amy closed the door and a few seconds later Geraldine heard her in the kitchen again. She sat on the edge of the bed and cradled her head in her hands. She tried to remember how much of the wine she'd drunk. Probably most of it. And it had been much stronger than her usual Pinot Noir. She doubted she would have drunk it all if Amy hadn't come home and, conversely, she wouldn't have drunk at all if she'd known that she'd have company.

She screwed up her eyes and focused on their conversation. The details began rushing back to her then. Amy's disgust with her father and Geraldine's own relief at having her daughter back in the fold. Amy claiming to want to leave the past and her dogged determination to pick over the details. She'd always been like that; picking at the minutiae, returning to a subject, chewing it over, then asking for more.

And there had been something more. Geraldine pushed her memory . . . something she'd said to Amy, hoping to impress her perhaps. Her eyes snapped open and brightness of the room made her cringe.

Abigail.

'No, no.' she gasped. Why had she said anything? 'Amy?' she called out to her daughter just as the doorbell rang. She scrambled to her feet as a wave of nausea hit her. 'Amy,' she shouted. 'Come up here, don't open the door.'

Amy's light-heartedness vanished as she headed back downstairs. She was glad she'd patched things up with her mum, and now that she'd begun to understand the depths of unhappiness that had existed in her parents' marriage she could see that Geraldine had done an excellent job of shielding her from it. Amy hadn't grown up witnessing endless rounds of fights and recriminations or been dragged through the trauma of prison visits.

She made herself tea, well brewed but with plenty of milk. The way she'd always liked it. From where she stood she could see into her mum's tiny walled garden; it had been her favourite spot when she'd lived here. *This* had been her childhood; a tranquil home and just the two of them.

She opened the back door and stood on the threshold. Weak sunlight was coming over the back wall and the pale brickwork and dense shrubbery vied for attention. It wasn't spectacular but she found it beautiful.

She smiled to herself then. What she was searching for wasn't spectacular either, just a version of her family story, one that she could accept as fact and know that it wouldn't change. Then she'd be able to confine it to the past and let it go.

She could feel that point was close and it didn't scare her. She tried to remember the exact conversation she'd had with DC Goodhew about truth. Just then she heard her mum calling her and the train of thought was lost. 'Hang on.'

She'd made it as far as the foot of the stairs when she saw the outline of a person through the frosted glass door. The bell rang as she reached across to open it. She'd twisted the catch by the time she registered her mum's voice.

Don't open the door.

But it was already flying towards her, the back of it simultaneously smacking her in the face and the side. Her right arm was flung wide and glanced off the banister, her ankle twisted over and she crumpled to the floor. The back of her head seemed to bounce on the tiled floor and she found herself staring in the direction of the landing. Sound separated itself from image. There was shouting. Her mum's legs on the stairs. And the taste of rust in her mouth.

CHAPTER 44

Marks stood next to Kincaide's desk and was using that desk phone to call. Carolyn Frampton picked up on the first ring. 'Mrs Frampton, this is Detective Inspector Marks, we need to speak to your husband urgently.'

The office had stilled and he didn't need to check the room to know that everyone was listening to him make the call. They could only hear his end of the conversation and not her replies.

'He's not here.'

'Can you tell us where to find him?'

'I don't know where he's gone. He had a phone call on his mobile but I didn't hear any of it,' she said. 'The next thing I knew he'd gone.'

'We've attempted to contact him on that number but his phone isn't responding.' Marks did his best to sound patient. 'I need to go over it again with you. Did you actually hear him leave the house?'

She sighed. 'I heard the car start, he over-revved it and reversed out onto the street too quickly. I heard the exhaust scrape the ground.' She sounded as though she wanted to add yada, yada, yada to the end of the sentence.

'Is that how he usually drives?'

'No, not these days, and never in that car.'

On the edge of his field of vision Marks could see the doorway. Goodhew entered the room now and stopped just a few feet from Gully. She moved to his side and whispered to him.

'What were his plans for the morning? Did he intend to go out?'

'No. He was supposed to be here, in meetings. And you're not letting me phone out so everyone from customers to planning officers are going to turn up and find us closed. My son's a no-show, our accountant's a no-show and the yard is calling and I can't pick up.'

'Alex and Moira?' He said it clearly and gestured to Kincaide to follow it up. Marks quickly covered the mouthpiece, 'Locate them both.' Kincaide immediately began directing the officers at the nearest desks.

'Yes,' Carolyn Frampton continued, 'Alex and Moira, Amy and Stan for all I know.' Without warning her tone had changed from frustration to weariness. 'Now please tell me what's going on.'

Marks nodded. It was time to give her something. 'We're following a lead we've had in relation to a separate murder investigation. Does the name Joseph Goodhew mean anything to you?'

She sounded cautious. 'I remember the case.'

'We have a reliable witness who can identify at least one of the two men present.'

'Oh.'

There was a long pause. Marks glanced towards the door. Goodhew had gone.

'Mrs Frampton?'

'Are you planning to arrest him?'

Marks hedged. 'I'm sorry, I can't comment. But I would like your help.'

This time the pause lasted longer. 'OK, but I need to speak to you in person.'

CHAPTER 45

'Alex and Moira.'

When Marks spoke the names and the room broke into activity. Goodhew stood for a moment amid the sudden flurry of activity and weighed it up.

Alex had been a toddler when Joe had died. He might be with his father or know where he might be but Moira was the better bet. And she lived closest. He made his decision and ran.

He left the rear of Parkside and took the route through the smaller streets before cutting down the footpath at the rear of Elm Street. He guessed it was a quarter of a mile and he was in Clarendon Road before he'd heard any siren. Moira's house came into view just as she stepped outside. The door slammed behind her and she hurried across the pavement, pressing the remote to unlock her car. She had the driver's door open before he reached her. 'Ms Trent?'

'I need to go out,' she mumbled. 'I'm supposed to be at work.'

'No. We need to speak to you.'

All colour had faded from her face and she'd clearly been crying. She stared into the interior of the car as though she was still contemplating driving somewhere. 'I don't understand what's happening.'

'Where's Neil Frampton?'

'I don't know.' She looked along the street and then back towards Goodhew; her focus had drifted off into a thousand-yard stare.

'Moira? I need to find him.' Goodhew pushed, 'You know him well; where would you look?'

She didn't seem to have an answer.

It was no great leap of logic to work out that she'd been the one who had phoned Neil Frampton. 'You called him this morning.' Goodhew didn't wait for confirmation. 'What did you say?'

'I didn't know how he'd react.'

'Moira, what did you say?'

Moira rubbed her forehead with the side of her hand and gathered herself enough so that she could concentrate. 'Amy came to see me. She knew that Nadine's baby was called Abigail.'

'So?'

'When Nadine came back to Cambridge she never mentioned her baby. Not to anyone apart from Theo; it was a closed subject. She wanted to blank it out.' Moira snorted at the irony. 'She was too young to realise the naivety of that idea. But it worked for a while. After the fire we each had our own reasons not to mention it. Neil just folded in on himself.'

The first response car had arrived in the street, the officers held back but the seconds were ticking away. 'Moira?'

'Neil and I never really talked until my sister died and suddenly we've been talking like we used to. That's when I found out the baby's name. And, in all those years, no one else knew. Not even Carolyn.'

'And Amy?'

'She said her mother told her. I didn't think that Geraldine ever knew about Robert's baby back then, but she must have done because the only people who could have told her the name were Nadine and Theo.'

Realisation hit him; the clue had been on the very first interview tapes and everyone had missed it. Theo hadn't been to the Buckingham's house to visit Robert, he'd gone to see Geraldine. Geraldine's refusal to provide Robert with a fake alibi had been her masterstroke.

And now Neil Frampton knew the truth.

Moira's expression reflected his own. 'I didn't think he'd do anything,' she gasped.

Goodhew grabbed her by both shoulders, 'Where does Geraldine Buckingham live?'

Moira glanced over her shoulder. 'Fair Street.'

'Number?'

'Fifteen.'

Goodhew took her keys and tossed them at the nearest constable. 'Ms Trent is a witness.' He turned away, shouting into his radio as he ran, 'Fifteen Fair Street. Assistance required.'

Clarendon Street to Fair Street was a two-hundred-yard sprint but this time a police car arrived at the head of the street as Goodhew came in via a footpath at the other end. Kincaide jumped from the first vehicle as Goodhew reached the front gate. Goodhew banged on the door with his fist.

'They've gone,' Kincaide told him, then shouted over his shoulder at Holden, 'Quick as you can.'

Holden swung the Enforcer out of the vehicle and strode towards the door, holding it in both gloved hands.

'We've found Frampton's Jag,' Kincaide told Goodhew as Holden reached the door. 'He's swapped it for one of their own Transits. We're searching for it now.'

Holden lined the Enforcer up to the lock, swung it back then into the door with full force and on the second strike the frame split. He pushed the door wider with the flat of his hand.

The hallway was dark and narrow. Even with the light from the open door the blood streaks on the floor were barely visible against the dark red tiles. A mirror that had hung from a hook on the wall now lay smashed at the foot of the stairs with shards of its glass scattered the length of the hallway. Here the blood stood out against the bright fragments.

They moved quickly through the house disturbing as little as possible as they checked from room to room. Each stood empty and the only signs of disturbance were at the entrance.

Kincaide decided to state the obvious, 'So they came and left this way and at least one of them was injured in the process.'

'Nothing reported by the neighbours?' Goodhew glanced along the short street and realised that there were only a few properties within sight.

Kincaide did the same. 'I'm leaving you here to secure this place,

Gary, and I'll send you a couple of uniforms and a SOCO.' He turned the car keys over in his hand. 'Keep me posted.'

Holden was staring at the damaged door and pretending not to listen.

'No chance,' Goodhew replied and ran back the way he'd come.

Stanley Mercer had demanded a solicitor with a smug expression. Perhaps he thought that he'd bought himself time with a get-out-of-jail card waiting at the end. The reality was different; sometimes 'I want a solicitor' worked better for the police than no solicitor at all; the seemingly endless wait made the suspect sweat and it took a strong mind to deal with the boredom of four walls and no view.

Marks opened the door and Mercer's relief was palpable, he'd had too long to think and no longer cared enough to wait. Marks cut him short. 'In the last couple of minutes, I've been informed of a significant development and I need a fast decision from you.' Marks had received confirmation that Robert Buckingham was safe but the whereabouts of his ex-wife and daughter remained unknown. He could see he'd hooked Mercer's interest but knew he needed to tread carefully. He decided to start the conversation at a less direct angle. 'Carolyn Frampton's about to make a statement. You can pre-empt her or not . . .'

'She's your witness?' Mercer stood with his hands folded and his back straight; attempting and failing to make himself appear bigger. 'She doesn't know anything.'

'Well, I mentioned Joseph Goodhew and she volunteered to come in.'

The corners of Mercer's mouth curled downwards. 'You're bluffing.'

'You like the idea that I might be bluffing, don't you? She's had enough of the lies and she's ready to make a statement. We have a witness who places you in Joseph Goodhew's house at the time of his attack. That's two people against you.' Marks hoped that Mercer would still picture Neil Frampton as the second. 'This is not the time for misplaced loyalty.'

'It's not misplaced,' Mercer replied.

'No one is protecting you now.'

The two men stood toe to toe for several seconds.

'Fuck,' Mercer growled and drew a heavy breath, tipped his head back and stared up at the ceiling. 'It was a single punch.' He exhaled slowly, shaping his mouth into an 'O' and blowing loudly. 'The old man was an accident, but it wasn't me. Neil lost his temper and hit him.'

'Neil killed him?'

'Yes.'

'And now I have the situation where Neil Frampton is at large and considered a risk to two members of the public.'

'Wait. Neil's not the witness?' Stan did a double take as he realised he'd been misled. 'You bastard.'

Marks continued, unfazed, 'You're an accessory, it's a serious charge. You have the chance to help us.'

'With what?'

'I need to find him before anyone gets hurt. I want you to cooperate with us, but it needs to be right now.'

Mercer's eyes narrowed. Part of him wanted to deflect whatever Marks had to say but his focus drifted off to his left before returning to Marks, 'Who's in danger?' A moment later he put his hands out, making the stop gesture. 'No, forget it. Robert Buckingham is the only person that Neil has ever wanted to hurt and I wouldn't interfere with that.'

'Robert Buckingham isn't in danger but two women are.' Marks drew closer to Mercer. 'You've just admitted that he's a killer. What's he going to do next, Stan?'

'Nothing.' Mercer shook his head. 'Why would he?'

'What if he thought that Robert Buckingham was no longer the answer?'

Mercer looked mystified. 'Then who?'

'Stan, what would he do if he thought he had found the person who set the fire and it turned out to be someone he knows well, someone who's been above suspicion for all these years? Someone he's supported even? He's going to want revenge, isn't he?'

'No, he'll want justice.' Stan shook his head. 'And I'll tell you what he won't do.'

'What's that?'

'He won't leave it to you.'

CHAPTER 46

As far as Amy knew, the journey had been brief and silent and dark. She was aware of them moving, of tilting in directions she couldn't predict. She lay on some kind of plastic sheeting, a crumpled pile of it that rucked uncomfortably under her back. It was dusty and she was aware of trying to cough but only achieving something between a gag and a spit. She felt a hand on her arm, a soft squeeze and it felt like her mum

They stopped moving and she began to hear again. Her mum repeating her name, telling her she needed to wake up.

She opened her eyes and found that it was possible to see a few details in the gloom. A small amount of light was seeping through from the driver's cab and she could make out the wood boarding on the walls of the van, pieces of equipment and the silhouette of her mum leaning over her.

'I'm so sorry,' her mum whispered.

The side panel door opened, rattling against the van's bodywork. Amy expected light to flood in but outside was only slightly brighter. Neil Frampton stood in the doorway. His skin shone with sweat and his expression had become blank and disconnected. He shone a torch into her face. 'You're awake, now sit up.'

She began to raise her head, then dropped it again as she was hit by a wave of nausea. 'I feel sick.'

He grabbed her upper arm and pulled her upright. When he released his hold she began to sag backwards. 'No,' he growled and dragged her straight again. His fingers left her arm throbbing.

'Neil, you're hurting her.' Her mother's voice was a mixture of desperation and fear.

He shone the torch on to Geraldine. Her mother looked terrified and, for the first time, Amy felt it too. 'Mum, what's happened?'

Geraldine's hand found Amy's and squeezed it tightly. She was shaking. Her entire body trembled, her mouth quivered as she tried to speak.

'Tell your daughter what you did.'

Geraldine started to cry, heavy sobs wracking her body.

Neil stepped back then slammed his boot against the side panel of the van, 'Tell her. Fuck you.' He kicked the van again and again, 'Fuck you,' screaming the words and kicking the metal with each syllable. 'Tell her what you did.'

Geraldine started shouting through her sobs. Just distorted and unintelligible words at first. Spit flying from her mouth.

Amy managed to decipher, 'It was Robert. He pushed me and pushed me.'

'Mum, tell me, talk to me.'

'I couldn't stand living with him.'

Neil reached towards Geraldine but Amy cut in. 'Do you want her to talk?'

Neil lashed out with the flat of his hand and caught Amy across the side of her head. 'Then talk, Gerri, or I swear I'll hurt her.'

This time it was Amy gripping her mother's arm. 'Take a breath, Mum. Talk to me.'

Her mum continued to pant heavily as she spoke. 'I wasn't going to leave him. We would have lost too much; I would have lost too much of you to him. And why should we have been punished for the things he'd done?'

'It's what happens in divorce, Mum.'

Suddenly Geraldine's expression changed. The fear was still there but mingled with a new steeliness. 'Amy, I wanted him to die. I took money from the business, made it look as though he'd used it. I researched different methods . . .'

'You *hated* him that much?'

'You have no idea. And then Theo came to see me . . .'

Neil hadn't stood still but had remained agitated and restless. He stiffened at the sound of his son's name.

'He told me about the baby. Abigail. I never knew about the pregnancy until that moment. He wanted me to know that Nadine was sorry.' She pursed her lips. 'Your dad stopped having sex with me when he was shagging her, even though he knew I wanted another child. She got pregnant and I didn't. So Nadine's sorry and, what, everything gets erased? Reset? Forgotten?' She shook her head. 'How could I kill Robert when I suddenly had a visible motive? I had no intention of living the rest of my life with that man.'

Staying silent finally defeated Frampton. 'Tell her, Geraldine.'

Geraldine looked at Amy and smiled. It was a calm expression, proud even. 'I set fire to that house and your father went to prison.'

Neil began to shout but Amy couldn't keep the nausea at bay any longer. She closed her eyes. Covered her ears and sank slowly to the floor.

Sue Gully stopped beside Jack Worthington's desk. Worthington could be abrupt and was usually taciturn but he always answered her. 'Have the ANPR cameras picked up the van?'

'Not yet.'

'I was thinking, swapping the car for the van didn't make Frampton anonymous because we had the registration number straight away.'

'It bought him time and he's moving people; it's discreet.'

'He's only gone a short distance or the cameras would have picked him up. And it cost him time to swap vehicles . . .'

Worthington frowned. 'What exactly are you thinking?'

'That there's a reason it needs to be a van? Or there's something a van can do that a car can't?' She shrugged. 'I thought I had something for a second.'

Worthington stared at her, his frown deepening. He picked up the phone and she saw him dial the number for the custody suite. 'Is anyone in with Mercer?' Worthington checked his computer screen, 'Ask him about Ford Transit Hotel-Golf-5-7 . . .' He finished reading out the rest of the registration number. 'Is there anything about it that makes it different to the other vehicles that were on site? Maybe the spec or what it's carrying?'

Worthington waited.

He listened to the reply and was on his feet before he'd finished replacing the receiver. 'We need to speak to Marks. It's the only one that carries welding gear. It's loaded with gas canisters.'

Amy lay still and just listened. She felt no panic or fear at that moment, just the sensation of feeling detached from everything around her. Was this, she wondered, how survivors of massacres felt when they played dead?

Without warning Neil Frampton lunged at Amy, grabbing her hair. He pulled her head straight and slapped her hard across the face with the palm of his hand. She inhaled with a shuddering breath.

Geraldine, wide-eyed, shook her head and mouthed 'I'm sorry.'

He gripped Amy's hair at the scalp and began to drag her upwards. Amy yelped.

'Neil,' her mum breathed, 'let her go, please.'

'I need you to confess properly, Gerri.'

'I will,' she told him, 'I promise.' But in her mum's face was a look that she hadn't seen for many years. She flashed back to the days she'd walked home from senior school. She'd been fourteen before her mum had stopped meeting her at the gate and she'd been teased for that too. But once she'd started walking home alone she hurried every step, worried about the trouble she'd be in if she arrived home late. Worried that a couple of minutes talking to another kid would be seen as a slight by her mum.

Her heart would beat harder when she crossed the threshold.

'Why, Mum?'

'Look at him,' Geraldine pointed to Neil. 'He's beyond seeing reason and it's my fault. That's how I was when I found out about the baby; out of my mind.'

'Don't compare us,' Neil snapped, then without warning his voice dropped to a harsh whisper. 'You killed my son and then you came to his funeral. You sat in court with us. You apologised for Robert and then let him go to jail. And for all those years I helped you.'

'Out of guilt,' Amy said softly. This was the only thing she had worked out. 'You saw us as victims of my dad, just as you and Theo had been.'

He just stared back at her but she knew she was correct. 'What did any of us do to you?' he asked her mother.

Geraldine shook her head. 'It wasn't about you, Neil. When Theo told me about the baby I snapped. I reached the edge and went over. I don't have a word for the way I hated Nadine then, I would have taken my bare hands and twisted her neck.' Geraldine's hands briefly formed claws before she clenched them into fists.

'At any point you could have confessed.'

'Robert was going down and Amy needed me.'

'Amy needed you?' Neil stepped back from the van. 'I killed Joseph Goodhew because of you. I hit him and he died. I wouldn't have been so desperate to find my other child if Theo had been alive. I wouldn't have even been in Goodhew's house. So that's on you too.' Neil glanced at his watch and then shook his head. 'Every fucking thing I've done wrong is down to you, right up to today. But this one will be all mine.'

He slammed the door. It was followed by the muted peep of the doors locking and then they were in darkness again.

They both listened for a moment before Geraldine began to bang on the sides. 'Neil. Neil.'

'Mum, stop,' Amy said, then continued in a low voice. 'There must be a way to open this from the inside.' She shuffled across to the side door and felt for the catch, 'Check at the back.' The edge of the door was in complete darkness and she used her fingertips to feel along it. She found the location of the catch in seconds, she moved closer, attempting to see any part of it. 'It's broken,' she whispered.

A boot slammed against the metal on the other side, 'Of course it's broken,' Neil shouted. He yanked open the door just wide enough to come face to face with Amy. 'That's why you're not tied up. No one can hear you either. Now shut the fuck up while I get this ready.'

CHAPTER 47

Gully was the first person Goodhew saw when he pushed open the doors at Parkside. 'Have they located them yet?'

'No. But the Transit he's taken carries gas canisters. Worthington's with Mercer and he's listing every location Frampton might use.'

'Good. Where's Marks?'

'With Carolyn Frampton, Room 2. And Sandra's with Moira Trent in Room 3. They're all asking the same thing . . .' Gully broke off to look over his shoulder and they both turned as Sergeant Norris opened the door between them and the front desk.

'I've got an Alex Frampton out here, asking for DI Marks.'

'Thanks, I'll deal with him,' Goodhew replied. He and Gully followed Norris into the waiting area.

Alex stood holding his crash helmet in one hand and his leather jacket in the other and his feet firmly planted on the tiled floor. When he spoke his voice was calm but firm. 'What's going on? No one's telling me anything and, to be honest, I'm worried about Amy.'

Goodhew pursed his lips, made a fast assessment and decided that breaching confidentiality was the least of the risks. 'We believe that she and her mother are with your father. We're concerned for their safety.'

For a moment Alex appeared bewildered and studied Goodhew's expression for a sign that he'd misunderstood. His puzzlement rapidly became consternation. 'What the hell has triggered it?'

'You're not surprised?'

'Yes and no. He's complicated. Volatile.'

'He believes Geraldine Buckingham killed your brother and Nadine Kendall.'

Alex drew straighter, 'How accurate is that?'

'He may be right,' Goodhew conceded. 'He's picked a Transit van containing gas bottles and we're pretty sure he's somewhere in town. We haven't heard from him and at least one of the women is injured.'

'Which one?'

'We don't know. Can you think of anywhere we might find him?'

Alex's face drained of colour. 'Somewhere they can burn.'

Holden followed Kincaide back into the building. 'Let it drop, Michael.' If he said it one more time Kincaide swore he'd swing at the man. 'The man's a suspect in the Joseph Goodhew murder, you couldn't leave Gary on the doorstep.'

Kincaide stopped in his tracks, spun around and jabbed his finger into Holden's body armour, 'Back off, Kev.'

They carried on up to the office in single file, Holden saying nothing until they were at the door. 'Now let it drop,' he told Kincaide and pushed through the door in front of him.

Kincaide darted through after him but was immediately sidetracked by Worthington who was standing at Kincaide's desk and pointing to the phone in his hand. 'I've got DS Jerram on the line. Frampton switched on his phone.'

Everyone else in the room looked around too.

'Where is he?'

'He switched it on, sent a single text then switched it off again. They've triangulated it to within 500 metres of the north-east end of the Cambridge Retail Park.'

Kincaide reached across and took the phone from Worthington. 'We need to narrow it down more than that.'

The voice at the other end was male and droning and his reasoning involved multiple acronyms. 'So if it is switched on again and for longer we will have more data.'

'Can't you recalculate what you have?'

'No.'

'What was in this text?'

'We know that it went to a mobile registered to his wife. He sent a single message and, judging by the packet size, I would be happy to speculate that it contained data other than text.'

'A picture?'

'Possibly.'

'Can you retrieve it?'

'No.'

He shoved the phone back at Worthington. 'That's as good as useless. I need to speak to Marks.'

'I'm here.' Marks had just entered the room, urgently pressing buttons on his phone as he did so. He then held up a sheet of paper. 'This is a copy of the picture that Mrs Frampton just received on her phone. I was with her at the time and she is not able to shed any light on her husband's location. The picture is of a handwritten note which I have just forwarded to all members of this team.' Around the room several phones were already pinging and buzzing. He paused for a moment to give everyone the chance to look. 'We now have a narrowed search area; we have vehicles on the way and you are all to make finding Neil Frampton your absolute priority. This may be the only opportunity we have to find him.'

They'd just moved into a side room conveniently furnished with three chairs and one badly defaced table when a text arrived at both phones simultaneously. Gully glanced at hers first. 'From Marks,' she said as she opened it.

'Same,' Goodhew echoed.

Opening it must have also been in unison because Goodhew tensed at the same moment she realised what she was seeing. The photograph was of a sheet of ruled paper, from an exercise book, she guessed, judging by the size of the letters compared to the gap between the lines. It was being held between a man's finger and thumb with just a thin strip of dark background visible on each of the four sides. The penmanship was messy after the first couple of lines, produced by someone whose hand was hurrying faster than they were able to form words. In several places words had been crossed through and rewritten in an attempt to make them more legible.

Carolyn.

Hand this over afterwards. I was never going to be arrested for killing Goodhew without killing Robert first but it was never him.

Geraldine Buckingham killed Theo and she will be punished.

He didn't sign off and Goodhew guessed he'd just given up.

He finished reading but continued to study the photograph. Gully looked across and met Alex's eye. 'It's from your father to your mum.'

Goodhew looked at her sharply. 'Hold on, Sue.'

She shook her head. 'This one's my call,' she said and turned the phone to face Alex. 'Is it his handwriting?'

Alex winced as he read, 'It's erratic but yes, it is.'

'He was somewhere near Cambridge Retail Park when he sent this,' she explained. 'Does the company own any property near there? Are any projects located there?'

Alex began to shake his head then stopped and rose to his feet. 'Oh shit. Behind the retail park is the railway line and behind that is a road of old industrial units – warehousing and workshops. He'll be down there.'

He was talking about Coldham's Road, a half-mile stretch with both current businesses and the shells of long-forgotten ones.

'Where exactly?'

'Halfway down, further maybe. It's an old vehicle-repair shop, block walls, sheet roof. It's empty; Dad's been trying to buy it for years.'

Goodhew grabbed Alex's arm and propelled him towards the door. 'Is your bike outside?'

'Yes.'

'Spare helmet?'

'And with a full tank.'

'Then show me the building.' Goodhew turned for one second and looked back at Sue. 'I'll use my earpiece. Keep me posted and tell Marks what I've done.'

She hurried to find their DI, pushing aside the phrase Kincaide had used, the one that was trying to play on repeat inside her head. *He will crash and burn.*

Crash and burn.

* * *

Goodhew shouldn't have allowed Alex Frampton to leave the building. Shouldn't have allowed him to ride a bike either. But here they were; riding from East Road onto Newmarket Road in less time than it would have taken him to unlock any of the cars.

They had just over a mile to go but Sue would be directing the officers that were already in the vicinity towards the workshop. He prayed they were there already. That it was the right location. That is wasn't too late.

And behind them he could just make out the sound of more sirens too. He glanced back and saw a couple of response cars keeping pace.

Alex and he were just the backup plan and he expected to hear an update via his earpiece at any moment. They swung into Coldham's Lane, as usual clogged with vehicles. Alex slalomed between the cars, narrowing the gap between them and the turning they needed. A police helicopter hovered ahead of them near the junction of Coldham's Lane and Coldham's Road. That had to be a good sign but still nothing came through the headset.

As they crossed the railway line Goodhew glanced down from the bridge and saw Coldham's Road running in a thin line parallel to the train tracks. The furthest section visible was dotted with blue lights and strewn with vehicles and men. The road usually appeared bleak but today it looked desperate.

CHAPTER 48

Both Amy and her mother had stayed still and quiet since Neil had shouted. They listened instead and for the first few minutes only whispered when one or the other thought they'd heard something.

'He'll come back eventually.' Amy noticed that her voice had stopped shaking even though her heart continued to thud. 'We need to decide what we're going to do.'

'I can answer that; nothing. We're locked in and he knows what he wants.'

'I can talk to him. Or try to. I'm not going to give up. You should tell him you're sorry.' Amy paused to think about her statement. 'Are you sorry?'

'Does it make any difference? At the moment I did those things I didn't have a choice. You know what it's like to have compulsions, Amy, with your fact collecting and constant poking at the past. Same thing. That's how it starts and it takes over.' She looked pensive then cocked her head to one side a little. 'I killed Lorraine Martin.'

Amy clapped her hand to her mouth but managed a muffled 'Why?'

'She banged on my door. Kept saying that she knew.'

'Knew what?'

'About Nadine. She said that she was going to tell you. I was too slow and I let her go. I thought she was going to tell you about the baby but, when her words sank in, I realised that she might have meant that she'd worked out that I'd set that fire. I couldn't risk it, could I? I knew I had to find her. So I drove to your flat.' Geraldine's hands formed the fists again. 'Then I realised that she didn't know where you lived and was maybe looking for you somewhere else. I drove to her house and back again but when I saw Stan driving out of Argyle Street, I guessed where she might be.' Geraldine's eyes shone, proud of her deduction.

Amy thought of Alex and under her breath mouthed the words, 'I don't want to die.'

In the silence that followed, she could hear the distant throb of helicopter blades cutting the air. Slow and rhythmic.

Amy jumped when the central locking was released. The driver's door rattled open. 'Neil, please talk to us,' she shouted. 'You don't have to do this. You can let us go.'

Neil Frampton had considered letting one of them live. Like the pied piper who'd left a crippled child to tell the tale. There were two options and each depended on how much Geraldine loved her.

He thought about releasing Amy but remembered how many times he had wished he could have taken Theo's place. He couldn't risk Geraldine dying with a half-smile on her lips and the knowledge that her child was safe. And releasing Geraldine only worked if she truly loved Amy and the pain of losing her was absolute. It seemed to him that Geraldine loved Geraldine more than she loved her daughter; some people didn't love their children as much as they ought.

In the last few minutes he'd found a happy compromise.

He felt a pang of guilt then. He had obsessed over Melanie's baby, the child he'd never met, the one who, in his mind's eye, might have become Theo's replacement. It had been a nonsense, a fantasy. And he hadn't loved Alex as much as he should because that fire had burnt out his own ability to feel anything but the gap Theo had left. It had taken him a long time to understand that Melanie's baby couldn't have filled it. And neither could Alex; he'd never given him the chance.

He unlocked the van and took a bottle of vodka and a can of diesel from the foot well on the passenger side. He placed both on the ground near the side door and then opened the van.

The kick hit him from nowhere and sent him sprawling on the

grease-soaked floor. Geraldine scrambled from the van and he saw Amy stagger to her feet too. Clutching the doorway.

Neil scrambled upright and went for the mother, grabbing her and bringing her down before she'd made it halfway across the concrete. She fell hard and grunted as the air was knocked from her lungs. He punched her full in the face and fought back the urge to choke the life from her.

'Mum!' Amy shouted.

He dropped Geraldine's lifeless arm and leapt across to grab Amy. He pressed a hand across her mouth, bundled her back into the van and listened. The police were out there somewhere but if they'd been close the commotion would have been their signal to burst in. The helicopter wasn't overhead yet and the sirens sounded still too distant. He spoke into her ear. 'I'm calling it a *happy compromise*,' he told her. He dragged her back down onto the floor of the van and used his free hand to grab the vodka and then his teeth to break the seal. 'You won't know much, I can live with that. Or not.' He climbed on top of her prone body and used his weight to pin her arms. There wasn't much fight in her but she still gagged and tried to spit out the alcohol. It became easier after the first couple of involuntary swallows though and her movements quickly lost their coordination.

He dragged Geraldine back to the Transit and hauled her inside. She was semi-conscious and limp. Her listless eyes followed him as he pulled the gas canisters from the van and slid them underneath. He was pleased to see her eyes widen very slightly; she needed to know. 'Think of a cooker. Then think of Theo's last minutes.' He closed the door and swigged from the vodka himself. Then he grabbed a thick pile of yellowed newspapers from one corner of the workshop floor and piled them a few inches from the diesel and the gas canisters.

The helicopter was closer now. Blue lights flickered through a Perspex panel situated a few feet above the full-length doors. An amplified voice spoke to him through the wall, 'Neil Frampton, this is the police.'

'If you open the door I'll kill them,' he shouted. 'I need to speak to DI Marks.'

Timing was everything. He lit the papers and watched the lazy flame take hold before he climbed in with the women. He stood his torch on the floor with the beam pointing up at the roof. He swigged more from the bottle and watched Geraldine's face as she realised she would be paying for what she'd done.

The other response cars and the fire engine pulled in next to Alex and Goodhew. Already there were four cars at the scene, all uniformed officers and only Ted Moorey who knew anything of their investigation. 'He wants Marks,' Moorey shouted as Goodhew removed his helmet.

Kincaide stepped from the nearest vehicle. 'I'm in charge until Marks arrives.'

Goodhew checked his earpiece and tried speaking to Sue. 'What happened? I couldn't hear you.'

'I'd have told you if it was over. I stayed silent because you just needed to get there. I'm connecting you to Marks right now.'

Marks's voice took over seamlessly, 'I'm two minutes away. What can you see?'

'An old-style repair shop, large doors, solid walls.' Pretty much what Alex described. 'It's locked and we can't see in. Frampton is confirmed as being inside. He has issued threats if we try to enter and he's asked for you.'

'Keep him talking,' Marks told him and cut the connection.

Goodhew grabbed Alex's arm, 'Come on,' he said and moved closer to the unit's door. 'Mr Frampton,' he shouted, 'your son is here.'

He nudged Alex. 'Get his attention.'

'OK,' he replied, then turned to face the door and shouted. 'Dad, it's Alex. You need to listen to me. I need you to let Amy go . . .'

'This is DS Kincaide.' Kincaide was a few feet away with a megaphone and his voice swamped the end of Alex's words. Kincaide stared resolutely at the closed door but Goodhew's attention immediately switched to a sudden movement from the fire crew.

Their commander banged his hand on the appliance door to get police attention, 'We have a heat source in there. He's started some kind of fire.'

Kincaide lowered the megaphone. 'How much time do we have?'

'None. It's a fire.' He swore under his breath. He instructed his crew and they swarmed past Kincaide and the other officers to reach the door. 'And everyone else get back, we need a safe perimeter. You,' he shouted at Kincaide, 'sort it out.'

Beyond the fire engine another siren died and a door slammed. 'Kelday, what have we got?' DI Marks ran across to the crew commander.

He showed Marks the screen of their thermal imaging camera. 'The fire is beside the vehicle, it's not huge yet but there are three people in the vehicle and the engine is running. It's belt and braces: if the fumes don't get them the fire will.' He pointed to the small door in the nearest wall. 'That's the quickest way in. We need a hose in there right now before the canisters blow.'

Two firefighters swung a battering ram between them. After the third attempt it hadn't budged. 'It's reinforced,' they shouted.

'Shit.' Kelday raised his hand. 'Check the building for any other points where we can force entry,' he instructed and moved forward to examine the lock.

Goodhew's gaze scanned the building too. 'That's the only door,' Alex told him.

Goodhew pointed up to an off-white rectangle above the entrance. 'What's that?'

'It's for light. They're on the roof as well.'

Goodhew took a breath, 'OK,' he replied and grabbed the crash helmet from Alex. 'I'll try.'

CHAPTER 49

The roof had a low gradient and was lower at the rear of the building. Goodhew moved Moorey's patrol car to the back of the building; he wasn't bad at shinning drainpipes but starting from the roof of the Ford Focus made it a whole lot easier. He threw a tyre iron up first then followed with the crash helmet hooked to his belt.

There were half a dozen panels in the roof. He guessed they'd once been clear but were now opaque with age. He plumped for the most central of the three in the lowest section of roof. He struck it with the metal bar. The second attempt broke through and the sun-damaged Perspex split into brittle lines. He kicked at the rest and found himself directly above the ground and about eight feet behind the van.

The opening in the roof drew the fire upwards, it's burble beginning to roar.

He put on the crash helmet and closed the visor before lowering himself through the gap. He waited until his arms were fully extended then he dropped. He landed on his feet but hit the ground hard, pain from an old injury jolting the length of his spine. The air was thick with exhaust fumes and smoke but he reckoned the crash helmet contained one good clean breath; he drew it in and held it then ran for the cab.

He jumped into the driver's seat and rammed it into gear. Black smoke billowed past the passenger side window as he swung the van in a tight semi-circle away from the fire and towards the entrance. He sounded the horn and accelerated, smashing the van against the large metal door. It bent but held.

He released his breath and coughed as the thick air hit him.

He checked his mirrors. Small blue flames had begun to dance on the floor and the burning pile of newspaper was slowly crumbling towards the fuel can. He reversed towards it and then straight into first gear to hit the door again. He butted the van up to it and powered against the panelling but it wouldn't give.

He looked back. The flames had reached the canisters now. He saw the newspapers hit the fuel can, there could only be seconds now. He slammed the van into reverse and drove backwards in an arc, stopping at the back wall. The fire burnt between him and the door. The floor was alight now and the canisters smouldered. He revved the engine and hit the accelerator. He cut a path straight through it all. The fuel can exploded behind him and the first canister erupted as he hit the door. This time it gave way and the burning van careered into the light and crashed into the yard's perimeter fence.

Foam hit it first. Then Goodhew pushed open his door and was pulled clear. An oxygen mask was held to his mouth and his eyes stung from the smoke as he fought to keep them open. He saw the Transit doors open and firefighters pull the three people out one by one.

He was carried away from the fire and put on a stretcher. 'I'm fine,' he insisted but was strapped to the trolley and loaded into the ambulance in any case. He lay still and listened to the voices outside trying to work out what had happened to Amy, Geraldine and Neil. 'Are they OK?' he asked.

The paramedic checked his blood pressure. 'No one's dead. I hear that's a bit of a result.'

The van doors opened and Amy was hit by daylight and foam, acrid air and confusion. She only had to turn her head to see Neil or her mother but she couldn't bring herself to look at either of them. She kept her eyes on the space above the doorway where she could glimpse a patch of sky until she felt someone lift her clear.

They inserted a drip and began cleaning her wounds. A paramedic leant over her and shone a torch into her eyes, 'What did he give you?' he asked.

She managed the word. 'Vodka.'

'Anything else?'

She replied, 'Nothing,' but could hear him talking to his colleague. Weighing it all up. They could pump her stomach; she didn't care. She reached out and managed to tap his arm. 'I need to call someone.'

'You'll have to hang on for that, Amy.' His expression was calm and reassuring. 'You have a few bumps and bruises to deal with first. Hang on.' He disappeared from view for a few seconds and almost instantly she felt herself begin to doze. Then she felt his fingers tapping on the back of her hand, 'Amy? Amy love? Stay awake. Alex is here, he wants to sit with you. Is that OK?'

She nodded.

Alex stood beside her and held both her hands in his.

'We have shitloads of baggage between us, don't we?' she whispered.

'I'm not my father,' he told her.

'And I'm not my mum.'

'Well then, we're sorted,' he joked gently. One side of her mouth managed to smile. 'Our families are really screwed up, Alex.'

He kissed her softly on the lips. 'And we can't undo any of it.'

'That's depressing,' she murmured as she kissed him again.

'Absolutely,' he replied. 'Or it's the best thing for us.'

'Maybe it is,' she murmured and began to drift off, sure that he'd be there when she awoke.

Marks watched the third ambulance pull away and surveyed the mess left in Goodhew's wake. Four fire engines were still at the unit, although there was nothing to save and the risk of it spreading seemed to have passed. The remains of the Transit had been loaded onto a recovery vehicle and his officers were finally leaving the scene. The last ambulance was Goodhew's. 'I'll go back with you, Michael,' Marks told Kincaide. 'Let me speak to Goodhew first.'

He climbed the steep step into the back of the vehicle. 'What the hell was that, Gary?'

Goodhew squinted at him. 'I don't know. Spontaneity? How's Amy?'

'All three of them have gone to hospital. They're all in a bad way but not life-threatening. And you'll have your day in court with Frampton.'

'His airbags don't work.'

'You're a mess, Gary. And I may as well tell you that my final report will be damning: your behaviour, bad attitude, reckless endangerment of the public. Oh, and driving skills. The list goes on.' He placed his hand on Goodhew's shoulder. 'But Joe would be proud.'

'Thank you, sir.'

'Don't miss my retirement drinks either. If you're not there I won't believe that I'm finally rid of you.'

He stepped back out into the smoky afternoon and into Kincaide's car.

'I think you're psychic, Michael.'

'Really, sir?'

'Was that the kind of crash and burn you had in mind for Gary? You see, I have spoken to Sue. Do you really think I hold with the view that colleagues have to stay quiet in the face of unacceptable conduct from their superiors?'

Kincaide didn't reply.

'That's not a rhetorical question,' Marks added.

Kincaide reddened. 'No, sir.' Then added, 'Goodhew constantly undermines me, sir.'

'Goodhew constantly undermines me, but do you hear me whining or crying "he started it"? I have few regrets but seeing you promoted has become one of them. You have the makings of a decent DS but you choose to throw it away at every opportunity.'

Kincaide stared at him.

'My replacement will be fully briefed but, until then, grow some balls, Michael.'

EPILOGUE

Three days later.

The doors stood open on the unit in Hope Street Yard as Goodhew and Ellie watched the furniture being loaded into the removals lorry.

'You're sure about this?' he asked.

'If it feels like the right thing for you, then I am delighted.'

The second-floor room had always been his grandfather's no matter where Goodhew positioned the jukebox or how he painted the walls, and he planned to put the desk and bookcases back the way he remembered them. 'I'm going to move my furniture out of the attic and have everything together on the first floor.' He took the piece of broken bangle from his pocket. 'And this will go back where it belongs.'

Neil Frampton had been charged with his grandfather's murder, Stan Mercer as an accessory. 'How are you feeling?' he asked her.

She knew exactly what he meant. 'Lighter. And I've been thinking of Joe a lot more, remembering things about him. We had thirty excellent years, plenty of people aren't that lucky. And I don't mean that in an I'm-calling-it-a-day way. Doors open, Gary, and Joe encouraged me to go through them. I always loved that about your grandfather.'

Goodhew's own memories had been stirred by the recent events. 'By the way, I've been thinking and I understand why you kept Joe's murder from me; you tried to protect our childhood. In fact, the more

I look at it, you and Joe made our childhood. All the best memories I have are in that house.'

'Really?' She tried to sound casual but couldn't hide her pleasure at the thought. 'We both loved you and your sister so much.'

'I know.'

He nodded towards the entrance. 'Happy to walk?'

'I'd prefer to; I've heard your driving's poor, especially exiting garages.'

'It's abysmal. But I don't think they'll sack me this time.'

'Never on DI Marks's watch, Gary.' She smiled. 'But it doesn't mean you have to stay. You could do what Sue's doing and relocate.' She squeezed his arm. 'With Marks, Sheen and Sue all leaving . . . it won't be the same.'

'You're too smart. You already know I've made up my mind, don't you?'

'I guessed, although I thought Kincaide might make you stay.'

The junction with Parker's Piece lay ahead and soon he'd be within sight of the station. 'I knew I was at a crossroads; I could feel it. The reasons that drove me to join in the first place didn't exist any more. The way I worked was wrong. My ambitions for promotion were non-existent. But I couldn't imagine not being part of Parkside either.'

'So?'

'So I resigned anyway. For good this time. I want to move on.'

She didn't seem surprised and he wondered if this outcome had looked obvious to her all along, the way so many decisions did from the outside looking in. 'And Parkside?' she asked.

'I reckon I'll visit when I need to.'

'Like Joe and I used to do?'

'Something like that,' he replied. 'I just need someone I can trust on the inside.'

'Have you told Sue yet?'

'No, we haven't talked so much recently, but we will. I thought I'd tell her tonight.'

'Sometimes there isn't a right time; you need to make it.'

He didn't comment and they walked the rest of the way in silence. As they passed the Reality Checkpoint he looked across to his house and saw Bryn sitting halfway up the flight of steps to his front door.

Ellie followed his gaze. 'Coffee at Savino's for me I think. I'll see you this evening though.'

'At Marks's leaving drinks?'

'He tells me it's my round.' She grinned. 'Besides, I wouldn't dream of missing it.'

'Are you happy sitting there?' he asked Bryn. He was wearing jeans and a shirt and looked relaxed.

'Always a good view from here,' he grinned. Goodhew followed his gaze to the group of young women crossing Parker's Piece.

'I have furniture coming from Hope Street Yard. I'm hoping you'll help me move my jukebox again.'

'How many flights of stairs this time?'

'Just one.'

'Up or down?'

'Down.'

Bryn pretended to weigh it up. 'OK, but please tell me what the deal is with the music on that thing? Every time I look at it I think that it can't all belong to one person. Was it full of crap when you bought it?'

'No, I've filled it with the records that I like and the songs that remind me of people.'

'Really? Like what?'

'"Come On Eileen" reminds me of you.'

'How does that work? I don't even like the song.'

'Me neither, I hear it, I think of you and it disturbs me actually.' Goodhew grinned. 'I'll tell you some other time – definitely after you've moved it.'

'Great.'

'And by the way, I've decided to get a lodger. I'm moving down to the first and the top floor will be available. I need someone I can rely on.'

Bryn raised an eyebrow, 'Reliability isn't my middle name and being sociable isn't yours.'

276

'We've both improved, haven't we?'

'No, we're both pretty shit but yes, I'd love to.'

At the end of the afternoon Marks called everyone into the office for their final briefing. 'Drinks in the Grain and Hop Store tonight,' he reminded them. 'And well done to you all, the last couple of weeks have been difficult, but what a result.'

Holden used his football-terrace cheer.

Goodhew was standing near the back of the room when Sue approached him. She looked serious.

'Are you OK?' he asked.

She stepped to one side and pulled him with her. She turned her face away to shield herself from the rest of the room and kept her hand on his arm to keep him close. 'Marks called me in this morning; he wanted to wish me luck.'

'And?'

'We talked for a while. He thinks the world of you, by the way.'

He waited, knowing that wasn't all she had to say. 'He gave me some advice and I have thought it over, and he's right.'

'What advice?'

'There's something I should have told you before, Gary.' She looked worried. 'And now you'll find out along with everyone else. But not because I didn't want you to know.' Usually she blushed but this time the colour faded from her face.

'You can tell me.'

'I know that, but there isn't time.' She looked across the room and acknowledged Marks. 'He's letting me do this and it has to be right now.' She crossed the room and stood by their DI's side. 'I realised that this might be the only opportunity I have to speak to you all. Initially I wanted to announce my transfer to the Met, to tell you all at one time and DI Marks kindly agreed that I could do it now.' She paused and swallowed. 'That was the plan until this morning.' The room was still. 'He pointed out another way, and how many times do we deal with cases when those involved could have taken a different path?'

She made eye contact with Goodhew.

'Marks told me that the best way to tackle bullying was straight on and this is my response.' She paused and took a deep breath. 'I am the biological daughter of the man who raped my mother.' She looked away from him then and allowed her gaze to drift around the room, 'I am not going to leave here because of that fact, and I am going to support the police in any way possible to ensure that he is eventually apprehended.' Her gaze stopped on Kincaide. 'I'm not interested in attacking anyone who has put pressure on me to leave but it stops now.' She took another breath then exhaled. 'And on that note I would like to thank DI Marks for all the help and encouragement he has given me.' She turned to him and they hugged, 'Thank you so much,' she whispered.

'Be fearless,' he replied.

Then she looked back towards Goodhew, read his lips and smiled.

ACKNOWLEDGEMENTS

At this point, it is great to be able to look back over seven books and thank the people who have been there throughout. Top of the list are Krystyna Green and Broo Doherty, who have championed the Goodhew series all the way from *Cambridge Blue* to *Cambridge Black*. Equally important is the support I've received at home from Jacen, Lana and Dean, as well as my lovely step-daughter, Natalie, and my amazing sister, Stella.

During the writing of this book, the following people were generous with their time or expertise and often both. Thank you to: Dr William Holstein, Alison Hilborne, Richard Reynolds, Genevieve Pease, Lisa Sanford, Jane Martin, Kelly Kelday, Ian who prefers to remain anonymous, the members of the Newmarket Reading Round and fellow writers Lynn, Tracey, Jenna, Charlotte and James. Thank you to Rebecca Sheppard, Amanda Keats, Howard Watson and the very talented Poppy Stimpson at Little, Brown. Thank you to James Linsell-Clark for a cold but successful photoshoot – I love the front cover. And, as always, thanks to Christine Bartram and Claire Tombs.

Thank you to the Royal Literary Fund for your support and for the privilege of inviting me to return as an RLF Fellow.

This book contains several characters who have been named thanks to generous donations in aid of CLIC Sargent children's cancer charity. Thank you to Gary and Sue Franks, Alex Frampton and Tony Jeevar for supporting this good cause.

Finally, I'd like to thank all the readers who have followed Goodhew and have contacted me at various times over the years. It has been an absolute pleasure to release each book and to have the conversations that have followed at events and on social media. I hope you enjoy *Cambridge Black* and my future books.

THE SOUNDTRACK FOR
CAMBRIDGE BLACK

For each book in the series, I have listed the twelve songs that were played the most while I was writing. Each book is different, and so each playlist is different, too. When I think of Goodhew's jukebox, these eighty-four songs are all there.

'Baby, Please Don't Go' – Billy Lee Riley
'Dance For Evermore' – Si Cranstoun
'Don't' – Elvis Presley
'Forever's Much Too Long' – Go Cat Go
'Haunted Skies' – Lana Bruce
'(I Just Wanna Make You) Mine' – Nik Lowe
'Let's Fall In Love' – The Five Stars
'Mother Of Lies' – JD McPherson
'Oh What A Night For Love' – Roy Tyson
'Panic Cord' – Lana
'Pin-Up Girl' – Jacen Bruce
'You Don't Love Me' – The Go Getters

For more information please visit www.alisonbruce.com or find me on Twitter @alison_bruce.

Out in hardback in January 2018 and in paperback in July 2018:

**A chilling standalone psychological thriller from
Alison Bruce, author of the critically acclaimed
DC Gary Goodhew series set in Cambridge**

'From the first time I saw them together I knew it felt wrong. I
didn't like the way he touched her or the self-conscious way he
played with Molly and Luke. Joanne saw none of it, of course.
So I did it to prove to her that she was wrong. I did it for us.'

Emily's instincts tell her that best friend Joanne's new boyfriend
is bad news. Emily fears for Joanne. Fears for Joanne's children. But Joanne won't listen because she's in love. So Emily
watches, and waits . . . and then she makes a choice to act.

But Emily has a past, and secrets, too. And is she really as
good a friend to Joanne as she claims to be?